Patrick's Promise

Book Three in the Cloverleaf Series
Tales from Birch Valley

By Gloria Herrmann

Patrick's Promise

Limitless Publishing, LLC
Kailua, HI 96734
www.limitlesspublishing.com

Formatting: Limitless Publishing

ISBN-13: 978-1-68058-565-0
ISBN-10: 1-68058-565-7

Dedications

This book was written during the time when two terrible, senseless acts of violence occurred: one was in my old hometown, the other in one of the most romantic cities in the world. My heart hurt deeply for those whose lives were cut short, and for the people left behind to deal with their grief, their lives forever changed.

This is for all those who have loved and lost, and found the strength to love again.

Chapter One

Patrick

"Patrick...promise me. Just please promise."

His eyes shot open. Sticky perspiration covered his body. Another nightmare. God, it felt so real. Why was he dreaming about her again?

He'd seen her there in that hospital bed, the constant beeping sounds of machines echoing off the sterile walls. Her blonde hair was matted and stained a bitter rust color from the dried blood. Her beautiful face was bruised, covered in lacerations. Beth, his wife, his best friend and soul mate. The mother of their twin boys, who were neatly tucked away in the NICU fighting for their own lives, was beyond broken.

Their car had been a twisted and crumpled mess, completely destroyed. It'd already been hauled away. Beth had been heading home when a drunk driver swerved hard into her. They were not prepared for something like this to happen; this hadn't been part of the plan.

As he sat next to his wife, holding her hand and weeping, his brain was unable to comprehend that this wasn't a nightmare; it was an awful reality. The doctors had already explained the extent of her injuries, and that they had been lucky to deliver their babies, but Beth would not likely survive the night.

The rest of the family had been in the waiting room, pacing the halls, sipping on lukewarm coffee, completely devastated and shocked. Mary sat and prayed, her tears caught up in a wrinkled, damp tissue that she had clutched tightly in her palm. His brothers, Liam and Daniel, were the ones pacing, angry at the driver who had done this. His sister, Maggie, was over in Seattle but kept calling to check for any updates. Patrick's father and grandfather had their heads hung and were silently asking God for his mercy. It had become a waiting game—waiting for Beth to die.

Patrick rubbed his face, silently begging for the images in his mind to disappear. It had been almost four years. His twins, Finn and Connor, were turning four next week. Each year they grew older was another year that Beth had been gone. He tried readjusting his pillow. After he flipped it over to the cool side, he closed his eyes, but he could hear her voice. There was no point in struggling; he knew that he wouldn't be able to fall back asleep. When the nightmares came, they lingered, holding onto him, tormenting every possible crevice of his brain.

It took him years to get the smell of the hospital out of his nose, and the images of Beth in that room would always be permanently scarred into his memory. Even if he could get past the horror of her being gone, and thoughts of the pain she must have experienced, whenever he saw his curly, blonde-haired boys, with her crystal blue eyes, he was pulled right back into remembering.

Patrick's body grew agitated as he tried to lay there, silently begging for sleep to find him. His ears picked up on the distinctive sound of the ceiling fan above his bed. The comforter partially twisted around his legs was far too heavy for this time of the year. With summer quickly invading Birch Valley, he needed to start using a lighter blanket. He swung his legs over the side of the bed. Patrick knew very well there would be no going back to sleep. No point in begging anymore. *Coffee, now that should help,* he thought as he removed himself from his bedroom and trudged toward his kitchen. The house was still dark, and the only illumination came from a singular hallway nightlight, and the digital clock on the microwave lit his path. He flipped the switch of the bright overhead kitchen light on, which was harsh and blinding. Moving slowly, Patrick prepared a pot of coffee, and it wasn't long before the rich aroma filled the air. He inhaled sharply. Yes, coffee would definitely help.

Patrick grabbed his mug, went over to a small stack of unsorted mail on the granite counter that had piled up from the week, and picked it up. He headed to the table in his dining room, which was a large square of lightly stained wood surrounded by four comfortable chairs. The room itself neighbored the kitchen; it was fairly large, and sand-colored tile covered the floors. The walls were a glossy, stark white, and decorated with various photographs that Beth had taken, which were mainly images of barns in open fields or the surrounding hills and mountains, drenched in trees and wildflowers. The prints were incredible. Though it had only been a hobby, she had had an eye for capturing Birch Valley's raw, untouched beauty. Patrick hadn't changed anything in the house after Beth had died. It was too painful, and he felt like he would lose her forever if he did.

He savored the quiet and the warmth of his drink as he perused through the assortment of bills and junk mail. The anxiety from his earlier nightmare had dissipated, and he was grateful for that. There had been many days where he wasn't quite so lucky.

Patrick heard the boys' scampering little feet before he even saw them; they were closing in fast. Patrick could see one springy mop of blonde curls bounce into view as Finn outraced his brother, Connor, into the dining room. The energy the almost four-year-old twins contained simply astounded Patrick, who took another swallow of his coffee to ready himself for dealing with his sons.

"Daddy, Finn cheated." Connor's blue eyes were already forming tears as his bottom lip jutted out. He wrapped his tiny arms around Patrick's waist.

"No, I didn't cheated, Connor." Finn stomped his chubby bare foot against the beige tile floor.

Patrick eyed his boys—they looked identical, but

their personalities couldn't be any more opposite. Finn, who was the firstborn, was the fighter, the leader. Connor was more sensitive, sweet, and undeniably most like Beth.

"Hey, boys, it's early, no tattling until Daddy has finished his coffee. What do you guys want for breakfast?" Patrick asked as he patted Connor's crown of wiry curls.

"Can we have pancakes?" Finn pleaded as he moved to the opposite side of his brother. Patrick wrapped his arms around them both.

"I think pancakes sound great." Patrick pulled himself up and out of their embrace. "You guys want to help?"

Both boys happily nodded in agreement.

"Well, let's go make some pancakes." Patrick led them to the open kitchen. He fished around in an oak cupboard until he found a skillet. He retrieved all the fixings for making pancakes. Finn situated himself on one of the barstools by the breakfast bar, which fanned out, away from the electric range that sat on the light-colored granite countertop. Connor tried to pull himself up and whined as he struggled. Patrick went over and lifted him up and then placed a large mixing bowl in front of the boys.

"You guys can start stirring," Patrick instructed after he poured the mix.

"I want to stir it," Connor cried as he tried to pry the large wooden spoon from Finn's chubby little hand.

"No, I had it first."

Patrick rolled his eyes as he flicked a pad of butter to melt in the warm skillet. Lately, his sons had been fighting more and were always in a constant state of competition. "Finn and Connor, you guys, come on."

"But, Daddy, I want my turn." Connor pouted.

Finn released his grasp on the spoon and hopped down from the barstool. He skipped over to the drawer and pulled out another large spoon. He climbed up the stool quickly and handed it to his brother. "Here, you can use this one."

Patrick watched as Connor's blue eyes grew bright. He wasn't shocked by what Finn had just done; he was a take-charge and all-about-action type of kid. Patrick could almost describe himself the same way. He was the oldest of his siblings, and he had taken over the O'Brien family construction business. He knew what it meant to lead and to make sure things got handled.

"Okay, Daddy, we got it all mixed up," Finn announced proudly, with little pieces of batter on his face and arm. Patrick grabbed a dishtowel that was near him and gingerly wiped it away.

"Thanks, kiddos." Patrick maneuvered back in front of the range and poured a small amount of the batter onto the warm pan, which made a sizzling sound, and the instant aroma made his stomach growl.

Connor and Finn scurried down from their stools and ran down the hall to the living room. He assumed they were going to watch one of their favorite cartoons while they waited for breakfast to be made. He watched the batter bubble and then carefully flipped it over, revealing a perfect shade of golden brown. He had mastered the fine art of making pancakes. Patrick wasn't all that terrible in the kitchen, but he had had to learn. Luckily, his mother was there to coach him along the way, though he did try and sneak over to her house for dinner in order to avoid cooking. Who could blame him? Mary O'Brien was well known in town for being a fabulous cook and baker. Besides, she was constantly offering for him to stay for dinner. How could he refuse his mother?

After piling a large plate high with fluffy pancakes, Patrick brought it and a bottle of maple syrup to the table. He went back to the kitchen and found the twins' favorite plates, which were in the dish strainer—one was covered in dinosaurs, and the other had colorful trains. He wasn't quite sure why the boys always wanted their meals on these particular plates, but today he wasn't up for any kind of battle. Without question, he put pancakes on each plastic, obnoxiously colored plate.

"Okay, boys, breakfast is ready," Patrick called out as he finished pouring milk in a small cup for each child.

Finn pulled himself into his seat without a problem, but Connor wrestled with gravity as he tried to pull his body up. Patrick lifted him up and then placed a kiss on top of his blonde head.

"I didn't want 'nanas, Daddy," Finn complained as he poked at the fruit.

Patrick let out a huff. "Oh, Finn, just eat them. They're good for you."

Finn pushed the bananas around the plastic plate defiantly. Patrick had to swallow back his irritation. It was going to be a long day, and he could tell it was time for another cup of coffee.

***

After getting Finn and Connor cleaned up and dressed after breakfast, Patrick decided the best course of action would be to get them all out of the house. The weather was nice enough with summer settling in. It was actually a little too warm, almost on the brink of hot. He sat on his porch swing, watching the boys play on their swing set in the backyard, when his phone rang.

"Hello?"

"Hey, Patrick." It was his brother, Liam.

"How's it going?" Patrick asked, moving off his seat. He fumbled with his phone and positioned it in the crook of his neck as he went to help Connor get on one of the swings.

"Rachel and I were wondering if you wanted to bring the boys by. Going to barbeque and thought we could get the kids together. The weather's perfect for it."

Liam was right, the weather couldn't be better, and he had a beautiful lake on his property that might be fun to splash around in. Liam then mentioned that their sister, Maggie, might also be headed over there. Patrick was tempted to make up an excuse so he didn't have to accept the invitation. A couple of weeks ago, Maggie had decided to stick her nose where it didn't belong and had signed him up for online dating. She hadn't asked his permission, but the hard part was he knew, deep down, her heart had been in the right place; he just had no intention of telling her that. After that, they hadn't spoken much at work, since he'd given her the silent treatment. She hadn't been one bit happy with him.

"Look, Patrick, it'll be fine. Maggie and Rachel are planning on working on some wedding stuff. So I figure we can grill and just let the kids play," Liam assured him.

"I just don't know. We aren't really talking right now, so it might be a little awkward."

"Don't make it like that. Eventually, you two need to sort this out," Liam said firmly.

Patrick rolled his eyes. He wasn't the one who had started this battle; it was all his sister's doing. Why should he be the one to have to play nice?

"Come on, Patrick," Liam pestered.

"Fine. What can we bring?"

"Um, you know, how about some of that root beer?" Liam suggested. The thought of the sweet beer made Patrick's mouth water.

"Sounds good. I guess we'll be by in the next hour or so."

"Great. And, man, just be cool with Mags, okay?" Liam pleaded.

"I can't guarantee anything, but I won't start any trouble."

Liam laughed. "Well, that's all I ask."

Patrick huffed as they hung up and then called out, "Finn, Connor! Hey, guys, we're going to Uncle Liam's."

The boys cheered in unison as they bounded toward the house.

***

Patrick leaned back in the canvas chair as he relished the taste of the sugary beer in his mouth and savored the enjoyment of being outside. His brothers and brother in-law were seated next to him, all of their long legs stretched out, absorbing the sun's warmth. They all had a fantastic view of the lake's shimmering water and the tall grasses along the shore, which protected the croaking frogs. The angry sounds of quacking ducks echoed off the small, surrounding hills. The water fowl were clearly irritated at the several children splashing loudly in the water.

"Those ducks sure are pissed," Daniel commented as he took a swig out of his bottle.

Liam and Patrick both laughed as Michael shook his head. The air was warm and the scent of lilacs and pine hovered around them.

"They sure look like they are having fun though. I'm half tempted to join them," Liam said as he wiped a bead of sweat off his forehead.

Michael cleared his throat, which snagged Patrick's attention. "You planning on talking to Maggie today?"

Why ruin a perfectly good day? Patrick could feel his body tense at the mention of his sister's name. He had done pretty well avoiding her once he arrived at Liam's cabin. It wasn't as though he was never going to speak to her again. Granted, this was the longest they had ever gone without speaking.

"Michael's right. You need to talk to her." Liam looked at Patrick, his matching emerald green

O'Brien eyes peering into his.

Patrick swallowed another mouthful of the sweet beer as he tried to drown his building irritation. He threw his gaze to a neighboring hill covered in lavender flowers and then toward the lake where the children continued to play, creating muddy castles along the shore, dirt streaking their happy faces.

"Guys, there's really not a whole lot to say," Patrick muttered as he avoided eye contact.

"Oh, come on, you guys just give each other nasty looks all day at work. Sure makes for a pleasant work environment for me, thanks," said Daniel sarcastically.

"I'm not responsible for how she acts. I keep things professional at work, Daniel."

"No, you don't. You both are guilty. You can't use me as the go-between just because you refuse to talk to her," Daniel rebutted in a firm tone.

Liam put his hand on Patrick's shoulder and said, "Look, there's only one way to fix this. You know what has to be done."

"Nope, I'm not apologizing." Patrick shrugged Liam's hand off. There was absolutely no way he would even consider telling Maggie he was sorry. She was the one who went behind his back and invaded his privacy.

"She already said she was sorry," Michael chimed in, taking a swig of his beer as he looked straight ahead at the lake.

Patrick huffed. "Yeah, I know." He paused as he sorted out the words he wanted to say. "I don't know, it just really rubbed me the wrong way, guys. I don't hate her or anything. I wish she hadn't stuck her nose in my business like that."

"Her heart was in the right place, and besides, she isn't the only one that's guilty of being involved," Michael replied. Patrick internally rolled his eyes at his attorney brother-in-law; he always had to act like he was in a courtroom. Michael continued, "Rachel had her part, and honestly so did your mother. So cut Maggie some slack, okay?" His tone turned authoritative as he stared at Patrick.

He was about to respond when he heard the distant sound of Rachel calling out to them.

"Must be time to eat," said Liam as he removed himself a little too quickly from his chair. Daniel hopped up eagerly and followed Liam toward the cabin. He, by far, had the best appetite of all the O'Brien men. Patrick knew that neither of his brothers liked confrontation; they were laid back and easy going, and they always had been.

Patrick and Michael remained seated, an awkward silence hovering between them as both waited for the other to make the first move.

"Look, I'm in sort of an impossible position here. She's my wife, but she's your sister. Can't you guys just make up and move on?" Michael asked as he turned again to face Patrick.

"You know what I hate?" Patrick paused for a brief moment, as Michael looked curiously back at him. "I hate knowing that I'm in the right, and everyone wants to me to be the one to apologize and pretend that it didn't matter what Maggie did. That I should look the other way when people get in my business and do something behind my back."

"No one is asking you to do that. We are just

asking for you guys to get over this thing and to act normal again." Michael frowned slightly.

Patrick shook his head as he heard footsteps approaching behind them. Turning around and sheltering his eyes from the blinding rays of the sun, he saw Maggie and Rachel moving in cautiously.

"Hey, guys, the food is ready. We were headed down to get the kids," Rachel announced with a wide smile. Maggie stood next to her, noticeably quiet. Patrick could feel Maggie's eyes on him, until she leaned down to her husband and gave him a kiss on his cheek.

Avoiding any kind of eye contact, Patrick got up from his seat without a word and started toward the shore. He couldn't explain why he felt so utterly uncomfortable around Maggie. It wasn't as though this was the first time the two of them had ever fought, and it certainly wouldn't be the last. Maybe the invasion of privacy and the fact that everyone was siding with her was what had him feeling all angry and irritated. Did they not realize that of course he wanted things to go back to normal, and that he didn't want to feel like he had to distance himself from his only sister? Working with her had only complicated matters more, because when he avoided her there, she would run off and tell their mother or anyone else who would listen, making him appear to be the bad guy.

Why couldn't she have just left well enough alone? But deep down Patrick knew that all was not well; he was coping, but things were not good. Why did life have to go and mess up all of his plans, especially his and Beth's? Thoughts tumbled inside

Patrick's mind as he neared the edge of the water. His two precious boys were covered in mud, which was thickly caked on their skin and in their hair, making them look like feral, wild creatures. They had wide smiles, and their eyes emitted a happy glow as they noticed him approach.

"Daddy, wanna build a sand castle?" Connor asked sweetly as he reached for Patrick's hand.

Finn was crouched down, his chubby hands working the soft mixture of soil and mud, his fluorescent green life jacket bobbing with each movement. "Yeah, Daddy, you should play with us."

How could he deny his boys? Before Patrick realized it, he was down in the dirt, his shorts wet from the slapping waves that pelted against the shore. The sun was warm on his back. He was half tempted to rid himself of the polo shirt he was wearing, and the water tempted him to go in further. It was barely June, and he knew that the water only looked inviting. If he dared to actually venture out for a swim, he would get to feel how icy and chilly the calm waters actually were.

His niece waded over to him as she carried a pastel pink bucket. "Uncle Patrick, I got some dry dirt to help make the castles." She dumped the contents of the bucket, which half landed on the mound of squishy muck the boys were playing in, and the other half fell on his bare legs.

"Well, that's a good idea, Melanie," Patrick said as he brushed some of the dirt off.

Melanie gave him a cheery grin. Her cheeks were a tad too pink, and her bobbed, rust-colored hair shimmered in the afternoon sunlight. "I should go get my dad to come play too. I wonder if Uncle Liam and Uncle Daniel would want to play. Do you grown-ups like making sand castles?"

"I think it's almost time to go eat, sweetheart, but yes, us grown-ups love making sand castles, especially with a bunch of wonderful kids like you guys," Patrick said as Finn and Connor toppled onto him.

"Kids, time to come inside," Patrick could hear Rachel call.

He peeled the boys off him. "Okay, you guys hungry?" Finn and Connor nodded in unison.

After gathering some of their toys, the children followed Patrick up the slightly steep hill, as he led them to a deck off the side of the cabin. Rachel and Maggie stood there waiting with large colorful beach towels in their arms.

"You guys look like you had a lot of fun, but I'm thinking maybe you need to hop in the shower." Rachel laughed as she ushered the children inside.

Maggie remained planted and glared at Patrick. "So just how long are you going to keep this nonsense up?" she hissed once the children were out of earshot.

Patrick released a long sigh and looked up toward the sky—not a single cloud was present. He inhaled deeply, taking in the rich, pine-scented air, hoping it would calm him.

"Seriously, Patrick, this has gone on long enough." Maggie's voice was laced with irritation as she moved in closer, her gaze burning into his.

"I guess you don't see why I'm upset."

"I already apologized. I mean come on, this is ridiculous," she said, her hands on her hips.

Patrick grunted. There was no point in trying to sort this out with her, especially now at Liam's house. Maybe eventually they could sit and talk it out, but right at that moment he wanted nothing more than to put a little distance between them. "You know, I think I'll go check on the boys and see if Rachel needs help with them."

"You can't just keep walking away. How are we ever going to get over this, Patrick?" Maggie demanded.

"We will eventually, just not right now." Patrick moved past her, leaving her with her mouth slightly gaped open. He knew he was probably taking this argument further than it needed to be, but he wanted to ensure that such a thing never happened again.

***

Patrick carried a sleeping Finn in his arms, and Liam had an exhausted Connor draped over his shoulder. They worked silently, putting the kids in their car seats. After buckling them in and closing the door, Patrick could tell Liam wanted to talk. He wasn't really in the mood and wanted nothing more than to go home.

"Whatever it is you have to say, just get it out," Patrick said as he leaned against his SUV.

"Oh man, I hate seeing you guys fight like this. Dinner was uncomfortable and weird."

When dinner had been served, Patrick had sat as far away from Maggie as possible. During most of the dinner he would feel her glare at him, tears peeking behind her green eyes. He felt a little stab of guilt—he wasn't a monster, and sure as hell didn't want to see his sister cry. It didn't help the situation that she was also pregnant, and that seemed to gain her some sympathy votes from the rest of the group.

Several months ago, long before Maggie pulled her stunt, she had come home from Seattle, leaving Michael behind. Patrick didn't utter a single word about her problems, he didn't invade her privacy, and he had only offered her a job. He quietly watched as she shed tears over her shattered little world, but he didn't stick his nose in her business. Now that everything was all rosy between Maggie and Michael, she somehow felt that she could go on and try to fix his love life and repair the hole in his heart. It would have been one thing if she had come to him and asked. He probably would have told her no, but at least they wouldn't be in the sore place they were now.

"All I can say is sorry that you feel that way. I'm not trying to make things awkward," Patrick said as he moved around to the driver's side of his car. "I better get these kids home. Thanks for having us." He got inside and started the engine. As he pulled away slowly, he watched in the rearview mirror as Liam shook his head and walked back to the cabin.

He wished everyone could see his side. He wanted them to understand how violated he'd felt by Maggie's intrusion and that he wasn't quite ready to move on yet. Patrick looked back again in the rearview mirror and saw his two sleeping sons, their small heads tilted to the side, lips slightly puckered, in a deep slumber. He envied them for a moment, as he felt his heart squeeze tightly in his chest with the strong urge to protect them. Patrick loved Finn and Connor with every fiber of his being, and the intensity of his feelings sometimes frightened him. It was a love that was incredibly deep, which only grew as the minutes ticked by. He'd loved Beth the same way, and still did.

Chapter Two

"Look at those precious grandchildren of mine," Mary O'Brien exclaimed, as she carried a tray of cupcakes to an outdoor table which was stacked high with an assortment of gifts. Patrick moved a couple of gift bags out of her way as she set them down. "Thanks, dear."

"They're having a lot of fun. These look amazing, Mom," Patrick said as he examined the chocolate cupcakes, which had cream cheese frosting, thick with sprinkles.

Mary smiled at the compliment, but he saw the sadness behind her eyes. Without exchanging words, she hugged him tightly and left to return to the kitchen. As he stood there, he appreciated that she didn't try to use any words to soothe the ache he'd been feeling all day. Her simple gesture was enough.

Patrick looked at the backyard, which had been overly decorated with colorful balloons and streamers that hung off several of the smaller trees and the overhang of his deck. The weather was perfect, a tad warmer than normal, as the O'Brien family celebrated Finn and Connor's fourth birthday. Beth's parents had arrived earlier that day to celebrate with the boys. Patrick tried to include them in various family get-togethers and special occasions. The couple lived in town, as did Beth's younger brother, Nick. He knew how the loss of Beth had crippled her family. Her parents loved the twins and spent a good deal of time with them, which helped them hold onto their last remaining pieces of Beth.

Everyone was sprawled out, the older men of the family seated in camp chairs or plastic patio chairs as they watched the children run around the yard. Several of the ladies were in the kitchen putting last-minute touches on the food and catching up on gossip.

Patrick was seated next to Liam and Daniel under the shade of a large maple tree. It felt at least ten degrees cooler under it, which was a huge relief. June was proving to be warmer than usual, which meant they were in for a hot summer.

There was an obvious sadness that seemed to hover over everyone. While Finn and Connor were happy, the joy of the occasion was tainted for everyone else because Beth wasn't there. Patrick had tried to keep any of his emotions hidden. It was bad enough that everyone still expressed their condolences, but he understood that they were still grieving too. It didn't change the fact that he had been up since around three that morning, and that his mind had replayed awful images that were tucked away in his brain, or that his pillow was damp from the tears he shed from missing Beth. No one could possibly understand how difficult it had been to crawl out of bed and put on a smiling face and a good show for his birthday boys. But he had done it.

"When are we doing cake and presents?" Daniel asked. Patrick had been so lost inside his mind he almost hadn't heard his brother.

"Oh yeah, we probably should start soon."

He watched as Finn and Connor raced around the yard with Melanie; he could hear their joyous squeals of utter delight. His emotions were a tangled web: he was thankful that his children weren't weighed down with sorrow, but he was a bit jealous that they could carry on, not knowing that their birthday was also the day their mother died. Again, he was far too consumed with his thoughts that he didn't notice that Maggie was now standing next to him.

"Patrick, you doing okay?"

"Yeah."

Maggie sighed loudly as she cradled her growing belly. "Are you sure? I know today has to be hard."

"It is, but it's also the day my boys were born."

He could hear the sadness in her voice as she said, "Look, I don't want to fight with you anymore. I just want us to get along. Life's too short, Patrick."

No kidding. Maybe it was how vulnerable he felt at that particular moment, but he didn't want to argue with her anymore either. She was his sister after all, and he knew she wasn't trying to hurt him. Without saying anything, Patrick pulled Maggie to him and wrapped his arms around her. He could feel her grow tense at first with confusion, then soften against him with relief. It felt good to hug her and to let his guard down, even if it was temporary.

***

The evening sky was a blended mix of purple and orange as the sun started to set. Patrick carried the large black trash bag with him as he scooped up forgotten plastic cups and paper plates, which still had various remnants of food on them. His family had all gone home, and his sons were inside, already tucked into bed. The day had completely worn them out, and Patrick himself was feeling beyond exhausted. Now that he was finally alone and able to process his thoughts, Patrick was thankful that he was somehow able to survive the day for another year. He wondered if it would ever get easier; would that hole in his heart ever heal? He started to tear down the streamers with a tad more force than necessary, enjoying the feeling of the paper ripping from the branches and trunks of the trees that lined the backyard.

He surveyed the now tidy yard and deck, a full garbage bag next to him as he took a seat in a patio chair, absorbing the sweet remaining warmth of the day. Evenings were quiet in Birch Valley, and he remembered all the nights that he and Beth would sit outside; the glasses of wine they shared as they stared at the blanket of stars as they planned their future; the nights when they sat on that deck; the countless tears of frustration that streamed down Beth's cheeks as she learned of yet another failed attempt at getting pregnant; the time they held each other when they learned that they were finally going to be parents, and to twins no less. They had shared a lot of talks about their fears, hopes, and dreams out there on that deck. But four years ago he never could have imagined just how precious that time was, and how those conversations would replay in his mind.

Patrick released a deep sigh. People had constantly told him that God had done this for a reason, or that she was in a better place, and so many other irritating, uncomfortable condolences. What if it had nothing to do with God? How could He be this cruel, to rob him and their two sons of their mother? No, there wasn't some divine reason. Though she may be in a better place, Patrick knew that Beth would have chosen to be here with them, to finally be a mother. He wasn't buying into the idea that this was all part of God's plan. Any sensation of relaxation he had felt was now gone. Patrick wanted nothing more than for the day to end, and he hoped he wasn't plagued with nightmares once his head finally hit his pillow.

***

Monday was the dreaded start of the work week, and Patrick just wasn't in the mood. Most Mondays were manageable. No one really cared for them, but something about the day irritated him more than usual as he walked into the large metal building with the great sign with bold lettering that said, *'O'Brien Construction.'* He saw Maggie hunched over her keyboard, typing away at a rapid speed.

"Good morning, Patrick," she said without looking up.

"Morning." He still hadn't had any coffee yet.

Daniel poked out from his office. "Hey, Patrick, how's it going?" His voice matched the overly cheery expression on his face. Daniel was always jovial, regardless of what time of the day it was. Right now, it was far too early for Patrick to deal with Daniel's abundant glee.

Patrick walked into his office and closed his door. He had a couple of minutes before they needed to set out for a bid on a new job. A moment later, he heard a soft knock on his door. Maggie let herself in and closed the door behind her.

"I just wanted to make sure you were okay. Are you mad at me again?" Maggie's eyes were filled with worry as she nervously twirled her long, chestnut hair around her finger.

He shook his head. "No, I'm not upset with you."

Maggie released a sigh of relief. "So, what's going on?" She planted herself down in a chair on the opposite side of his desk.

"I don't know. I didn't sleep so great and haven't had my coffee yet." He rattled his empty coffee cup in the air.

"Did you want me to go get you some?"

"Oh, I didn't mean it like that, Maggie. Just stating a fact. Plus, the boys were a little difficult this morning when I dropped them off at Mom's." Patrick had felt like pulling his hair out when his sons refused to get dressed, then fought with each

24

other in the car. The constant whining and crying this morning had set the tone for the day. It didn't help that Patrick had hardly slept; he tossed and turned most of the night. He started to feel the beginnings of a headache.

Maggie rose up from her seat. "Here, let me go and get you some." Her voice was calm and soothing as she grabbed the cup from him and left the office.

Patrick was staring at the wall in front of him when Maggie appeared minutes later, cup in hand. She set it down in front of him and smiled. "Now, hopefully this will help. You and Daniel need to be at that site in less than an hour. We can't afford you being grumpy and not getting the job."

He couldn't help but laugh. She was right. He appreciated his sister and was glad that they had somewhat resolved their issue at the birthday party. Patrick just hoped that she would now mind her own business when it came to his love life, or, well, lack there of.

She left his office, leaving him alone with his thoughts and some invoices to sort out. A half an hour had passed when Patrick glanced up at the clock mounted on the wall when another knock interrupted Patrick's thoughts. "Come in," he said.

"Hey, man, you about ready to go?" Daniel said as he peeked in.

Downing the last sip of coffee, Patrick grabbed his keys and followed Daniel to the work truck. He waved to Maggie as he passed her desk. The coffee had helped once again. Thank God for those little magical beans.

***

Patrick walked to the driver's side of the large truck and went to open it, but the handle was hot to the touch. He rubbed his two fingers after burning them. "Damn."

Daniel hopped inside the truck. "Come on, quit being a baby. Get in, we need to go."

The drive to the site was a quiet one, the radio on low, a country song playing softly in the cab of the truck. Every now and again Daniel would sing along, and when it seemed like he forgot the lyrics, he would hum. As their truck rounded the stop and they found themselves down Main Street, they couldn't help but notice how alive the town appeared. People were out and about; they lined both of the sides of the street.

"Boy, town's hopping. No surprise, though, look at how nice it is outside," Daniel commented as he looked out the window.

"School will be out next week, I think."

"Yeah, I think Liam was telling me that. We sure are going to be having a busy summer, with him getting married and all."

"So, what do you think about that?" Patrick took his eyes off the road briefly and looked at Daniel.

"You know, I like her. Rachel's really nice to him. Plus, they kind of don't have a lot of choice in the matter, expecting a baby and all."

"Two babies," Patrick said as he gripped the steering wheel a little tighter. "God, can you imagine, barely dating some girl, then finding out she's pregnant, then to find out it's twins?"

Daniel frowned and shook his head "Nah, but Liam loves her, Patrick. I kind of think he loved her from the moment he saw her."

"Maybe, but I still worry it's a little soon. I mean, Daniel, in less than a month they are getting married."

"Hey, at least it's not you or me. So, I'm good with it. He seems happier, and honestly isn't that what it's all about?"

Patrick considered this for a moment; Daniel was right: happiness was what it was all about. It was how Beth had made him feel. He should want Liam to feel that way, but something inside him shuddered at the thought of his brother getting married and having a family. He was jealous, simply put.

Of course, he wanted his brother to get married and have children, but Patrick wanted that for himself again. The hard part was that he'd had it once, until it was taken from him.

***

The sky was still rather light when Patrick locked up the shop at the end of the day. They had landed the job, which wasn't a huge surprise; he'd had a good feeling about it when they arrived at the site. They were honest and offered a fair price to do the work. He got into his SUV and drove toward his family's home. Patrick was hopeful that his sons were either fully exhausted or in fantastic moods, neither of which they had been earlier that morning.

As he parked along the curb, Patrick noticed

Maggie and Rachel's cars—both sleek, sporty, and very expensive, and quite out of place in Birch Valley. He walked past them, his fingers itching to touch them; the glint of the evening sun bouncing off the flawless paint teased him. He looked back at his own car, which was a somewhat modern SUV. It had a lot of the bells and whistles, and Beth had insisted they purchase a nice family vehicle, so they had settled on the forest green mid-sized four-wheel drive SUV. But there was something about a racy sports car that intrigued Patrick.

"Oh, Patrick, sweetheart," Mary cried out as she poked her head out from the kitchen, her favorite room in the house.

"Hi, Mom." Patrick hurried down the hall to her, planting a gentle kiss on her soft, weathered cheek.

Mary wore her favorite floral apron. She wrapped her arms around him. "How was your day? Did you want to stay for dinner? I made pot pies."

How could he refuse? "Sure, that's sounds great." After he hugged her, he moved to the dining table, where Maggie and Rachel greeted him with happy smiles. "Hey, what are you gals up to?"

"Wedding planning." Rachel rolled her blue eyes toward the ceiling and let out a long sigh.

Maggie laughed. "You and Liam insisted that you guys wanted to have your wedding on the Fourth of July."

"Well, I didn't have a whole lot to say in the matter, now did I?" Rachel rubbed her stomach, which wasn't nearly as protruding as Maggie's.

Patrick shook his head and pivoted his body toward the kitchen. "Mom, how were the boys today?"

"Good, as always." Her smile beamed from across the kitchen as she was checking on several pot pies that were in the oven. With perfect timing as usual, the two young boys ran into the kitchen and made a beeline for Patrick.

"Daddy!" they shouted in unison.

"Hey, my lil guys." Patrick scooped them up and squeezed them tightly.

Finn giggled as Connor announced. "Grams is making pop pies."

"I heard. That's nice of Grams to make pot pies for dinner," Patrick corrected.

Rachel covered her mouth to stifle a laugh. "Oh, I just can't wait. They are so adorable."

"They have their moments," Patrick said as released Finn and Connor, who took off running to go play in the backyard.

"How is it? I mean, having twins," Rachel asked carefully.

Patrick shrugged. "I don't know. It's been my only experience so far."

"You have a point there. I'm just so scared. Like, if one needs to be fed and the other changed, how do you manage?" Rachel looked up at him, her eyes nervous. He knew why.

"You guys will manage." That was the only answer he could think to say. He didn't feel like going into any further detail.

Rachel bowed her head. "I suppose you're right."

Instantly he felt terrible and mentally kicked himself for not being more sensitive. She hadn't meant anything by her questions. "Trust me, you guys are going to do great. You will be a good mom, Rachel." Patrick offered her a smile, which she promptly returned.

Mary came over to the table with a stack of plates. "Do you mind setting the table?"

Patrick nodded. "No problem, Mom. Is Liam coming over? What about Michael and Melanie? I didn't see her running around."

"Mel's with Michael. She's hanging out with him at his office," Maggie replied as she rose from her seat to grab the silverware her mother was now bringing to the table.

"Yeah, when is he planning on opening?"

"Well, hard to say, he's really taking his time setting up the new practice. He worked so much back in Seattle, I think he kind of enjoys just doing nothing." Maggie started to set the table.

The table was quickly set, and Mary brought over the steaming pot pies from the oven. "I think it's just lovely that Michael is spending so much quality time with Melanie. It will be even nicer for her when school lets out," Mary added after she placed all the flaky, golden pies on each plate. "I'm going to let Dad and Grandpa Paddy know that dinner is ready," she said as she left the kitchen.

Patrick started to head for the back door. "I'll go get the boys and have them wash up."

"Yeah, I'd better get out of here. I need to go make dinner for my family," Maggie said regretfully. She bent down to give Rachel a hug and then walked over to Patrick, hugging him briefly before departing.

Patrick called out to Finn and Connor to come

inside as he waited by the door for the boys.

They ran at full speed, again racing to see who could get to the door first. It surprised Patrick to see Connor outrun his brother. The confused look that Finn wore on his little face was priceless.

"Daddy, did you see that? I beated Finn. I'm the fastest." Connor smiled widely as he passed Patrick to go wash up.

Finn looked almost teary eyed at having lost. Patrick reached out and grabbed Finn's shoulder. "You can't always win, son. You guys are both pretty fast. Now go wash up." He watched as Finn sulked away.

"There's my little lads." Patrick could hear his grandfather's thick brogue as he entered the kitchen, the twins brushing past him. "Patrick, how's your day been?"

"Good, Grandpa Paddy," he replied as he followed the older man to the table.

"Everything fine at the shop then?"

Patrick made it a point to keep his grandfather in the loop about the business. When there were any new contracts or ideas, he went to his father and grandfather. They trusted Patrick to run it, but he knew that they appreciated that he came to them for advice and included them in some of the decisions. "Just landed a new job, went for the bid today."

Grandpa Paddy nodded and took his place at one end of the table. "Well done, son."

Mary entered shortly after with the twins. "Now go have a seat, my little loves," she said as she ushered them toward the table.

"Everything looks great, dear." Patrick's father,

Pat had joined them. He stopped to give Mary a peck on the cheek, and she blushed instantly. Patrick couldn't help but smile at the simple exchange of affection.

"Everyone help yourselves. Go on, now." Mary fanned her hands at them encouragingly.

Moments later, Daniel and Liam arrived. "Smells amazing in here," Daniel announced loudly as he found his place at the table.

"Grams made pop pies. They are so yummy, Uncle Daniel," Finn said as he tried to fork a rogue potato from his dish.

"Well, they do look yummy." Daniel ruffled Finn's springy mop of blonde curls and mussed Connor's as well before sitting down next to the boys.

Liam bent to kiss Rachel before taking his seat. "Mom, everything looks great. Thanks."

"Good, now go on and eat. Everything is bound to get cold if you don't dig in soon," Mary said. She took her place near Pat.

Patrick surveyed the table. His family looked content as they ate and chatted. He glanced over at Liam and Rachel, but they were unaware of his gaze, lost in their own little love-infused bubble. His own parents' love could be seen radiating from them as they ate; theirs was that solid kind of love, the foundation upon which their entire family had been built, strong and everlasting. Patrick could feel eyes on him, and he looked to see Grandpa Paddy, the older man's green eyes speaking volumes to Patrick. He clearly understood what Patrick was feeling; he knew loss. It was as though Patrick was looking in a mirror at a reflection of his future self—the same eyes, the same dark Irish features, even the same name. Even with the family gathered around, he could see how alone his grandfather was, and he sensed their shared sadness. With that, his grandfather gave him a curt nod of sympathy, which Patrick returned with a tight-lipped smile.

Chapter Three

Amber

"Damn." Amber heard the loud pop sound and felt the car shudder and swerve. She gripped the steering wheel tighter as she eased her foot on the brake.

"Mom, what was that?" Dylan removed his headphones and looked over at her. His messy, overgrown, sandy brown hair hung in his eyes. He swatted it away, revealing his sea green eyes, which were the same color as her own. But he looked just like his father, and it made her heart squeeze tighter in her chest. It had been almost two years—two long, miserable years.

She pulled over to the shoulder of the road, the gravel crunching under the tires. She undid her seat belt. "You stay inside. I'm going to see what's going on."

"You want me to go with you?" She could see the hurt behind Dylan's eyes.

"No, sweetie, it's fine." Amber watched as he

shrugged and then placed his headphones back over his ears. He was twelve, almost thirteen years old, and in a rush to leave childhood behind.

She unplugged her cellphone from the car charger. She figured she could try and call for help. Once outside the small car, Amber saw she didn't have much of a signal on her phone. She looked up and down the desolate road. Not a sound. It was eerily quiet. Why did she have to take this old country road? She should have just stayed on the main one, which would have led her straight into Birch Valley. Amber thought she remembered her way around the rural little town. She was born and raised there, after all.

Amber lifted her phone toward the sky in hopes of getting a better signal. She looked down and noticed the frayed pieces of rubber strewn across the pale asphalt road. *Well, crap, that sure doesn't look good.* She caught sight of the shredded tire on the trailer, which was carrying all of their belongings—what was left from leaving Portland behind. But they were needed in Birch Valley; her parents needed her. Amber bent down to get a closer look at the tire. Anxiety started to burn through her as she realized she was in a little over her head. She had no idea how to change a tire. She looked at her phone again, and when she saw that there was still no signal, panic started to fill her. Amber rose from her crouched position and considered several things as she mounted her hands on her jean-clad hips. She could always try to ride her trusty bicycle to town to get help. Back in Portland, she pedaled her way just about everywhere. The city was incredibly bicycle friendly, and she'd loved it. She loved a lot about Portland, but the last two years had been rough; some of the most trying times in her life, in fact. She was thankful, even relieved, almost, that her parents had asked for her to come back home to help out at their diner. Her son, Dylan, wasn't thrilled about leaving all of his friends, and basically everything he had ever known, to come to some town in the middle of nowhere. It wasn't as though they hadn't visited Birch Valley over the course of the nearly fifteen years she had been gone, but it was one thing to visit, another thing altogether to move there. Lost in her thoughts and focused on her dire situation, Amber almost didn't see the dark green SUV slowing down on the opposite side of the road.

She couldn't deny the relief that flooded through her. She was completely out of her league dealing with the blown tire. Maybe the driver of the SUV would be able to help her. She raised her hand slightly, and as the driver rolled down his window she was met with the most incredible emerald eyes staring back at her. They were eyes she remembered a little too well; all of the girls in Birch Valley had fallen in love with those eyes; they belonged to none other than Patrick O'Brien.

***

Patrick

He could see something coming up in the road

and started to reduce his speed. He'd wanted to go for a drive. He wasn't headed anywhere in particular, he just wanted to clear his mind. People hardly traveled on this old country road, and as he pulled up he noticed that a car with a small trailer had its hazard lights on. A woman was standing by the side of it, one arm extended high toward the sky, not to flag him down, but by the looks of it trying to get a signal for her cell phone. *Well, good luck with that.*

Rolling his window down, he cautiously asked, "Excuse me, do you need any help?"

What Patrick wasn't prepared for was the most incredible eyes that stared back at him; they were a deep, sea green, and they appeared helpless and lost. Her face held a hint of something familiar, but he couldn't place it. Her long black hair hung down to the middle of her back, several strands flying wildly with the swift breeze.

"Hi, thanks so much for stopping. We blew a tire on that trailer." She pointed at the small rental trailer that was connected to the car.

"Do you mind if I take a look?" Patrick offered.

"I'd be very grateful."

He maneuvered his own vehicle off the road and parked behind the trailer. Patrick hopped out and met her by the shredded tire; bits and chunks of rubber were scattered nearby. He knelt down to see if there was a spare. Luckily there was.

"I can change this and get you back on the road," he said as he assessed the situation. "I'm Patrick O'Brien, by the way." He extended his hand to her after wiping it on the back of his jeans.

Her mouth opened wide into a pleasant and grateful smile. "I thought that was you. I'm Amber Mills," she said but then shook her head as Patrick gave her a confused look. "I mean, I was Amber Herrick. My parents own the diner in town. You and I went to school together."

That's where I know her from. I knew she had looked familiar. Patrick was floored with how gorgeous Amber was. He didn't remember her looking like that in school; he would've remembered her for sure.

She stood a lot shorter than him, her curvy figure hugged in dark wash jeans and a soft red cotton shirt. Patrick couldn't explain the sudden attraction he felt toward her as he tried desperately to pull himself together. This wasn't like him at all, easily stirred up by a woman.

"So, what brings you back to Birch Valley?"

Amber bit her lip. Patrick tried hard to resist staring at her full mouth as she said, "Well, I'm moving back."

Damn.

Patrick swallowed, his eyes trained on the fullness of her pink lips. "R-really?" he stammered as he fought to focus on anything else than the movement of her mouth.

Amber lowered her gaze to the weathered asphalt road. "Yeah, my parents need my help at the diner."

Patrick furrowed his brow as confusion started to set in. "Everything okay there?"

"Not really, no," he heard her say as they started to walk back to his car. He lifted up the back hatch of his SUV to grab the tools for the job. Patrick wasn't quite sure what to say next; he wasn't one for prying into others' lives. He decided to wait until she elaborated a bit more.

Amber let out a heavy sigh. "My dad's health isn't so great. To be honest, the last couple years haven't been so great either."

Patrick heard a door shut and saw a figure shuffling its feet, headed in their direction. He noticed pale brown, shaggy hair. The kid, not quite a teenager, was in need of a haircut. The boy was dressed in slightly baggy jeans and an oversized, fluorescent blue t-shirt. As he reached them, he moved protectively closer to Amber.

"Oh, hey, Dylan. This is Patrick O'Brien. I went to school with him." Amber's smile sent an unexpected jolt through Patrick as he extended his hand to Dylan.

"Nice to meet you, Dylan."

There was a resilient stance to the kid, who stood noticeably shorter than Patrick, but nearly as tall as Amber. She was a small thing herself but curvy in all the right places, and he couldn't keep himself from noticing.

Dylan gave Patrick a solid handshake, but the gleam in his eyes, which were the same color as Amber's, were telling. They said a great deal— there was a spark of interest, of irritation and warning, but something frailer. "Nice to meet you as well, Mr. O'Brien."

The kid had manners, which really impressed Patrick. He looked over at Amber, who as anyone would expect, was beaming with pride.

"Would you mind helping me put on the spare?"

Patrick couldn't stop the words coming from his mouth. He wasn't sure why he had just invited this kid to help him, but he could tell by the pleased look on Amber's beautiful face he had made the right call.

Dylan proved to be fairly decent at assisting Patrick with the changing of the tire. The boy wasn't too familiar with the tools needed, but he seemed eager to help and that was enough for Patrick. The small bit of chit-chat and general getting-to-know-one-another made the task go by quickly. Amber stood by waiting, but more importantly watching. When they were done, she thanked Patrick and hugged Dylan close to her side; he could see that the motherly affection embarrassed Dylan.

Patrick couldn't explain the deep ache he felt as he watched her get back into the small, blue sedan, giving him a friendly wave as she pulled out carefully and slowly onto the desolate road. No woman had ever caused this kind of reaction, at least not since Beth died. The thought of Beth was sobering as he got into his SUV and started to trail Amber's car.

***

Amber

"I think he seemed pretty cool, Mom," said Dylan as he looked out the window. They headed toward town.

Amber looked in her mirror and could see

Patrick's SUV behind them. She couldn't explain the sudden nervous knots she had felt when she had said goodbye to him. She found herself staring at the gorgeous Mr. Patrick O'Brien as he effortlessly changed the tire and allowed her son to help. So not only was this man beyond good looking, but seeing his patience with Dylan had sparked something inside her, a little, wicked, yearning flame that had been quiet for a very long time. Amber thought she would never feel this way again. Maybe moving back to Birch Valley would prove to be far more interesting than she had originally thought.

Amber pulled into the large parking lot. It was nearing dinner time, and she could see the diner was hopping. The restaurant was one of Birch Valley's favorite places to eat, so the bustle was no surprise. The small town didn't have a ton of eateries, and Amber had been spoiled by the ample venues in Portland. In the last couple years, she had relied on dining on take-out quite a bit. She hadn't felt like cooking, which had been a passion of hers for years. Hopefully being back in the restaurant and being forced to cook would inspire her love for it again.

She looked over at Dylan, a mixture of emotions present on his face. "It's going to be okay, Dylan," Amber attempted to reassure him as she patted his leg.

"I just wish we were back home."

"I know you do, sweetheart, but your grandparents need us right now."

Dylan huffed and stared back at Amber. "All my friends are back in Portland. This place is so…tiny."

Amber forced herself to smile. "You'll make

friends here. There's only a couple weeks left of school, so that will give you time to meet some kids. Trust me, summers are awesome here. There are tons of things to do." Amber caught herself sounding overly animated, as though she needed to convince herself that Birch Valley was more exciting than it really was. She had been so quick to leave after she graduated from high school, and winding up in Portland had not been part of her plan. But having her husband die hadn't been part of her plan either. "Let's go in and let them know we're here."

"Okay, Mom." Dylan gave her a weak smile. He was a good kid, but he'd been through a lot over the last couple years, and it killed her having to take him away from all that he really knew. Portland was home; it was where all his memories had been made, where his friends were, and where his father was buried.

The little bell on the weathered and tattered string still chimed as Amber opened the door. *Some things never change.* Instantly, she was hit with an array of delicious scents that hung in the air, and her stomach growled. The diner was almost full; there were customers seated along the long counter, the booths were all packed, and only a couple of empty tables remained in the center of the dining area.

"There they are!" A high-pitched squeal of delight came from a short woman, who had the same shade of dark hair as Amber's.

"Mom." Amber was pulled into a tight embrace. She inhaled her mother's light floral perfume, which made her always smell like gardenias.

"Ah, my precious grandson. Oh my, you're getting so tall." Dylan was almost past her mother's height, but that wasn't saying a whole lot. The women in Amber's family all had been on the shorter side, and a little plump.

"Is Dad here?" Amber craned her neck to see if her father was back in the kitchen.

"No, he's at home resting." Her mother's eyes, which were a soft brown, turned wet. Amber reached for her and gave her another hug. She could see the exhaustion etched onto her mother's face, despite the feeble attempt at giving Amber and Dylan a smile of over-exaggerated happiness. "You guys are probably starving. Let me feed you."

"Well, I can help," Amber said as they were ushered to an open spot at the counter. Dylan mounted the bar stool excitedly. She knew he was thrilled with the prospect of eating, since that was all he ever did these days. The saying couldn't ring any truer about boys eating you out of house and home, at least in Amber's case.

"No, you guys had a long day. That's quite a drive from Portland. You will be helping me soon enough anyhow." Her mother winked at her before she turned to grab two glasses for them.

"So, you're going to cook and stuff here, Mom?" Dylan asked once his grandmother was out of earshot.

"That's the plan." Amber had grabbed a laminated menu and started to scan it, knowing full well what was already listed on it. "What do you feel like eating?"

A happy, boyish grin appeared on his face,

making him look less like a soon-to-be-teenager. He eagerly looked at the menu. "It all looks good."

"Well, how about a cheeseburger and fries?" His grandmother suggested as she returned with two glasses filled with water. "Maybe a chocolate shake for dessert?" she offered, and Dylan nodded excitedly.

"Mom, are you sure you don't want me to help?" Amber felt guilty being waited on as she surveyed the busy diner.

"Hon, trust me, your ol' ma has everything under control."

Amber didn't doubt that for a minute and smiled as she watched her mother head down the counter, coffee pot in hand, to check on a customer. Lynn Herrick had been waiting on these people since they'd bought the diner so many years ago. Amber's father, Dean Herrick, had turned this failing business around and created it into something of a landmark in town. People were constantly gathered here, the food was great, the service was out of this world, and you were sure to run into someone you knew. Amber remembered growing up in the diner, where she'd helped clear tables and wash dishes. She had spent so many hours beside her father by the grill, assisting him with more meals than she could count. All good memories filled her mind, but then they turned ugly as she recalled her sudden desire to leave Birch Valley and her father's disappointment. Most of her friends had left for college, which wasn't something her family could afford, though they offered to help with the costs if she truly wanted to go. She didn't.

Amber didn't quite know what she wanted. She knew only a couple things: that almost all of her friends had left Birch Valley, and that she didn't want to work at the diner for the rest of her life.

"Here you guys go," Lynn Herrick announced as she balanced two plates, both of them covered with golden French fries piled high next to enormous and juicy cheeseburgers.

"Thanks," Dylan and Amber replied in unison, which made them to look at each other and grin.

***

Patrick

He had followed Amber's car until they had reached Herrick's diner. He was relieved that the spare tire was working out just fine for now. As he drove the couple of blocks to his childhood home, where his mother had been watching the twins for the day, he couldn't help but feel out of sorts. The small interaction with Amber and her son had thrown him for an unexpected loop. He had just been looking for a little quiet time—a sliver of solitude just to clear his mind of the all the thoughts that had been pestering him over the last week. Patrick loved going on drives on that old, deserted country road, which was lined with trees and fields that seem to go on forever. It was one of his favorites. Just being alone, away from everyone, seemed to set things right. He found himself wondering when he would see Amber again. He wanted to look into her penetrating eyes, and worse, he wanted to kiss her soft pink, rosebud lips. What had gotten into him?

Lost in his thoughts, Patrick arrived at his parents' house. He tried to shake away the images of a voluptuous Amber, which were dominating his mind: the way her legs looked in those snug jeans, or her soft, red cotton shirt that clung tightly around her full chest. Patrick had towered over her compact frame, and he couldn't help but wonder how she would feel next to him...under him even. He swallowed back the unexpected wash of desire. Guilt had found a way to creep in, causing a sudden battle of conflicted emotions.

"Daddy!" Connor shouted. He ran toward Patrick when he entered the house. As he spotted Connor's blonde hair and blue eyes, he saw Beth, and his guilt cut him a little more deeply.

"Hey, buddy." Patrick scooped him up and carried him toward the kitchen, in search of Finn and Mary.

"We're in here," Mary called out from the dining room. Patrick came in to see Finn and Mary seated at the table. Finn munched on some graham crackers, and seated next to him was Mary sipping tea. "Just finishing up a little snack, aren't we?" Mary looked over at Finn as a giant, crumb-covered smile appeared on the little boy's face. Mary turned back to Patrick, who was still carrying Connor, but the little boy was now resting his small head on Patrick's shoulder. She had a serious look in her eyes that told him that she needed to speak with him later, when the children weren't around.

"Well, I will go load this guy into the car. Finn,

you almost done, buddy?"

"Yes, Daddy." Finn hopped off his chair and sped toward Patrick.

Mary followed them out to the car and waited patiently as Patrick secured each child in their large booster seats. Closing the door, he turned to her. "What's up, Mom? Everything okay?"

"Well, son, today was kind of an interesting one. The boys were asking questions about their mother," Mary said softly. Patrick felt as though he had been punched in the gut. It wasn't as though he had kept Beth's death a secret, but the boys hadn't been able to fully understand or miss something they had never known.

"What happened?" he asked, leaning against his SUV. His gaze searched his mother's, and there was sadness behind her eyes.

She offered him a tight-lipped smile before speaking. "Well, we had been having a really lovely day, as usual. I noticed that Finn seemed a little down, though, so I asked him if anything was the matter. He asked why he didn't have a mommy." Mary's voice grew weak as emotion started to choke her.

"Oh, Mom," Patrick said as he took her in his arms.

Pulling back, Mary looked up at him. "It makes sense that they would wonder. Rachel and Maggie had stopped by earlier, and I'm sure the boys are hearing them talk about babies all the time now. I know that Mel is excited and probably talks about it with them."

"These are the cards we were dealt. There isn't a

whole lot we can do," Patrick muttered.

"I just feel bad for those little boys. Beth really would've enjoyed them, and they are the highlight of my day." Mary's eyes were red as she wiped away the tears that streaked her cheeks.

"I'd better get them home. Thanks again, Mom." He hugged her once more before getting into his car. It bothered him to see his mother hurting, but he was used to the pain; it was with him every day.

Patrick started the engine and headed home. He lived only a few blocks away. When they arrived, he let the boys out of their seats and trudged into his home. Immediately, he was bombarded by how much this house was filled with Beth's essence. Everything from the decor to where things belonged, he hadn't changed a thing. Of course, when the boys came home from the NICU, Beth had already set up where all their baby stuff was to go. As they grew older, Patrick figured out where to put things and had tried to organize their lives as closely to how Beth would have wanted it. But the home was still hers—exactly how she had left it. Patrick still had her clothes hanging in the closet, though they no longer held her scent. But he didn't have the heart to donate or throw them out. How was he ever going to be able to move on? Sneaking thoughts of Amber crept in, and he couldn't erase the guilt he felt. Patrick remembered the promise he had made, as Beth lay dying. Of course during that moment he would have agreed to anything she had requested, but he just didn't know how to go about living up to the promise he swore to her.

Chapter Four

Rachel

"It's okay, baby." Liam held Rachel as she surfed another wave of pregnancy-induced emotions.

"No, it's not. I hate the way she acts."

"It'll all work out, I promise." His voice was soothing, his long arms cradling her as they lay in bed. She had just gotten off the phone with her mother, Evelyn Montgomery, who was not very happy with Rachel at the moment.

Rachel looked up at Liam and stared into his gorgeous eyes. Rachel asked, "How do you figure, Liam? She's so pissed that we won't push the wedding back."

"Well, that's too bad. It's not her wedding, it's ours." Liam planted a kiss on top of her head.

Life during the past couple of weeks had been wild, as if things hadn't been hectic enough with finding out that she was pregnant, planning a wedding, and wrapping up the end of the school year. But to make matters worse, her mother was hellbent on driving her crazy.

When Liam had proposed to Rachel, he told her to choose the wedding date. She had decided, after careful consideration, that the Fourth of July seemed like the perfect date. Not only would Rachel not look noticeably pregnant, but everyone had promised that the weather would be amazing. Liam was the man who had completely changed her opinion about love, and it seemed fitting for their ceremony to have fireworks bursting brightly over the lake they resided by. She had consulted with Maggie and Mary about the details for her and Liam's nuptials, and they had had some fantastic ideas. Rachel couldn't help but feel excited. After plans had been made, she contacted her mother and told her the game plan for the wedding. That's where the problems started. She could understand some of her mother's concerns. After all, her parents hadn't even met Liam yet. But with the wedding quickly approaching, Rachel didn't want to bicker with her mother.

"What about your dad? What did he say? Does the Fourth work okay for him?" Liam asked as he began feathering soft kisses along her brow. "Don't be so stressed out."

Rachel sighed. "How can I not be? My mother is trying to make it seem like I'm the one being unreasonable."

"And your dad?"

Rachel rolled her eyes. Did she dare go there? Saying that her father was pretty upset with her was a complete understatement. He had not been thrilled when Rachel left Newport Beach to accept a position as principal at a school in the rural community of Birch Valley, sight unseen. When he learned that she had wound up pregnant, he had been livid, and they were barely speaking. She called and asked if he could come up to walk her down the aisle, and he'd said he would need to check his schedule. As a plastic surgeon for some of the most elite people in southern California, Robert Montgomery had always placed his family low on his list of priorities, which was partially why her parents were no longer married.

"He's going to get back to me on if he can make it up."

"Get back to you?" She could hear Liam's tone turn angry, and he looked at her with shock. "So you mean to tell me he needs to see if he can pencil in his only daughter's wedding? Oh, geez."

"Are you all that surprised after everything I have told you about my family?" Rachel faced Liam again.

He cupped her face delicately, his mouth meeting hers as he kissed her softly. "It just makes me a little sad, that's all," he said after releasing her lips.

This was why she was marrying Liam; love and tenderness came easily to him. He never hesitated to show her affection, to comfort her, and she didn't understand how she had gotten so lucky.

***

Liam

He hated seeing Rachel upset. He felt a responsibility for her, and Liam wanted to do everything in his power to protect her, even if that meant protecting her from her family. He knew that the circumstances weren't ideal. He tried to imagine how upset Rachel's family must feel, but she was still their daughter. Liam just wanted to hold her, to cradle her in his arms for the remainder of the day.

"We probably should get up," Rachel interrupted his thoughts, her blue eyes still sad, but she looked at him with longing. "As fun as it would be to lay in bed with you all day, we need to go over to your parents' place for lunch."

It was Sunday, and the following weekend would be Father's Day. They would be married two weeks after that; the thought had settled well into his mind. Liam wasn't the least bit nervous and had never been surer about anything in his entire life. Granted, the wedding was still over three weeks away. With the added stress from Rachel's family factored in, he might be more of wreck, but knowing that he would get to grow old with the beautiful woman next to him, well, that made it all worth it.

As Rachel attempted to slip out of their bed, he pulled her down toward him. They still had a little time, and he knew exactly how he wanted to spend it.

***

Maggie

Maggie brought out a large glass bowl of potato salad to the table that been set up in the backyard. The family was gathered outside. No one could resist the temptation of the warm weather. It just beckoned them to the massive deck right outside the O'Brien kitchen. After setting the dish down, she gazed out at the lush yard, which was a remarkable shade of green. Melanie and the twins were playing, their screams of happiness a little louder than Maggie would have liked, but they were kids. She felt a sudden, hard kick in her belly.

"You okay?" Michael came up behind her and asked.

"Yes, just getting beaten up by your child." Maggie and Michael both laughed as he placed his hands on her growing belly.

Dropping his head a little lower to her waist, he whispered, "You be nice to your mother." His words were met with another powerful kick, causing them to both laugh again.

Maggie was finally starting to enjoy the pregnancy. The start had been anything but perfect; she had been overcome by wicked morning sickness, her marriage had been on shaky ground, and she had left Seattle. Now life was moving along smoothly, as was the pregnancy. These were the good months, the second trimester, when she felt like an actual human again. She was almost six months along and starting to show. Maggie looked over at Rachel, who was a little over four months along. Rachel and Liam were seated in patio chairs and appeared to be lost in their own world. She couldn't believe that Liam and Rachel were getting married in three weeks; there was still so much to be done. Maggie couldn't have asked for a better future sister-in-law and was thrilled they were also pregnant together, and it seemed to cement their already strong bond.

Maggie saw her other brothers, Daniel and Patrick, who were also seated out near the yard, looking completely relaxed as they chatted loudly with their father and Grandpa Paddy. Their animated expressions were met with laughter as Daniel told one of his tales. Her brother was always exaggerating everyday occurrences and was the teller of many legends. You never could quite tell if the stories he was telling were true or not, but if nothing else, they were always entertaining.

"You probably should go sit for a while," Michael said, his hand perched on the lower curve of her back.

"I'm fine, I need to go help my mom in the kitchen. Don't worry about me so much." She reached up on the tips of her toes and placed a kiss on his cheek. Maggie was met with rich, mocha-colored eyes that were filled with concern.

"Sorry, I can't help it." He moved his head down, his lips brushing against hers as his arms pulled her closer to him.

Maggie was thankful that their life was on the right path. They had been so close to losing their deep connection and love, they almost hadn't made it. But now, they were enjoying their new home, which Michael had insisted they purchase, and they were decorating a nursery with muted neutral tones since they wanted the gender of the baby to be a surprise, just as it had been with Melanie. Michael still hadn't really opened his practice in town; he had taken on a couple of clients here and there, but overall he spent the majority of his time with his family. He was able to finally relax. He'd discovered he truly loved fishing and spending time with her brothers. Maggie thanked God daily for saving her marriage, and she couldn't wait for them to add more children to their family.

***

Michael

He watched Maggie walked back inside the house, and he turned to join the rest of the men that were seated outside. Michael was growing comfortable in their new life and wondered often why he had ever resisted the idea of moving to Birch Valley. It had been the best thing for their family. Melanie was happy and thriving, Maggie was glowing, and their marriage felt stronger than ever. When they lived in Seattle, the thought of being surrounded by her family had scared him a little. Maybe it was because his family was hardly like hers, and the constant feeling of togetherness at first seemed odd to Michael. Now he wanted his own family to feel the same way.

Michael plopped down into an empty chair. He inhaled the sweet scent of lilacs that filled the air. Beautiful trees were lined up against the fence in the back yard, their delicate flowers withered and dying. The unusually warm weather was the culprit. Michael had chatted with some associates back in Seattle. It was hot and borderline miserable. If weather was the only thing to complain about, that suited him just fine. He relished his new life; no more insanely long hours at the office, missing everyday moments, and having Maggie upset with him. He learned that simple was sometimes best, and he was getting used to the much slower pace of life in Birch Valley, but he was happy. The one thing he still missed about Seattle was coffee. He still hadn't found anything that compared to some of his favorite coffee shops.

"It's a little warm today," Michael commented as he took a long, leisurely sip of his canned soda.

"It's a wee warm, I agree. But better than rain," Grandpa Paddy replied, raising his own drink.

"Can't argue with you there, Grandpa Paddy." Michael lifted his can slightly.

One thing Michael had discovered about living in the eastern side of Washington state was that the weather was temperamental. He thought Seattle had a funny weather pattern, but that was nothing compared to Birch Valley. The sun could be shining brightly one moment, pouring down buckets of rain the next, possibly even hail, and then go right back to be down right warm and balmy. So far with the beginning of summer of approaching it had mainly been warm, far hotter than Seattle, and Michael was trying to acclimate.

"Everyone ready to eat?" Mary called out from the deck. The entire family, children included, hurried toward the long table, where a platter of fried chicken sat in the middle, along with large dishes filled with several cold salads, and a basket of homemade biscuits. That was another thing Michael was grateful for; they hardly had to eat take-out now. Maggie was learning how to cook like her mother, and then with all the shared family meals, Michael was starting to consider joining the small gym in town.

***

Patrick

Patrick carried Finn out of the SUV and planted him on one of the couches in the living room, and he quickly went back outside to retrieve a sleeping Connor. Sundays always wore the kids out; all the playing and eating just tuckered them out. The boys were usually fast asleep before they left the driveway of his parents' home. Patrick went back to his car to bring in some leftovers his mother insisted that he take home, like every Sunday. He wasn't sure why he even bothered trying to argue with her. She had been giving him leftovers every Sunday since he had moved out. But he was thankful, because it usually meant he didn't have to cook for a day or two, and it made the start of his work week a lot smoother.

After tucking away the various plastic containers filled with chicken and cold salads in the fridge, Patrick grabbed a beer and went out to his back deck. He sat down on the porch swing and absorbed the quiet. The sky was a pale tint of violet as night and a few twinkling stars began to emerge. He glanced at his watch and noticed the time was nearing nine. This was one of the great things about summer; it got dark late. He raised the bottle to his mouth and took a long leisurely sip and noticed a deer silently walking into his yard. It stopped to look at him briefly, before gnawing away at the grass, unconcerned with his presence. The area was full of wildlife that made themselves quite at home in everyone's yards. He had seen deer use the crosswalk in town, and the thought made him laugh. Only in a place like Birch Valley would you see something like that. As Patrick swung slowly on the swing, he felt himself being lulled to sleep. He felt relaxed, almost content, which wasn't a feeling he got to experience often. His mind was tame, and that's when visions of Amber decided to appear. He could see her sea-green eyes, which were like small lagoons, clear and bright but filled with mystery. Patrick had a hard time believing that he never really noticed her before, that they'd gone to the same school. Granted, she was in Liam's class, and hadn't run in the same social circle as Beth and Patrick. But how could he not have noticed such a beautiful girl? Because he had been madly in love with Beth, the blonde goddess of Birch Valley.

Thoughts of Beth pushed any of Amber aside. He remembered how much everyone loved his wife. She was kind and outgoing, and calling her pretty had been an understatement, with her classic girl-next-door looks. She was the center of attention, studious, outrageously popular, and head-over-heels in love with Patrick. In high school he only had eyes for her. Though many of the girls did anything they could to get his attention, he only wanted Beth. They were voted the cutest couple multiple times, and everyone knew that they were meant to be together.

They both graduated and went to the same college in the lower, eastern part of Washington, where their relationship continued to flourish. They both knew what kind of life they wanted, and that it would be back in Birch Valley. Patrick understood that it was his job to take over the family business eventually, even Beth helped at the shop, where she used her accounting skills. They both wanted what their parents each had—a loving and strong marriage. They wanted children and a simple life. Beth and Patrick just wanted to be happy and be together. He didn't feel that they had asked for much.

After returning to Birch Valley, they married and immediately set out to make their dreams of starting a family a reality. Months turned into years, which then turned into visits to the doctor, then to a specialist, all of which were met with frustration and tears. The strain of not having children put their marriage to the test. They'd had to answer questions about why they didn't have kids yet, which only made matters worse. Beth blamed herself, and finally, one day, it happened. It was as though all their prayers that had gone ignored for so long had finally been answered. When they found out about their pregnancy, they were back on track to have the life that they were planned for, the life they were meant for. But fate decided to step in again and rearrange and alter their plans. There would be no getting back on track; their plans were permanently derailed.

Patrick downed the last of the contents in his bottle, the feelings of relaxation gone. He took this as a sign of punishment for even thinking about Amber. He didn't even know her. What kind of person was she? He knew nothing about the dark-haired woman, other than she was sexy as hell, and had sprouted feelings of desire and need in him that had long been dormant. He knew the moment she had said she was moving to Birch Valley he was in trouble, big trouble, and he wasn't sure he minded it all that much. Maybe it was the beer or sheer exhaustion that clouded his reasoning, but he wondered. What would it be like to be with someone else? He hadn't asked himself that question before.

Chapter Five

Amber

Putting the apron on and standing in front of the grill, Amber was overcome with various emotions. She never thought she would be cooking at Herrick's diner again, but this was important. After only having arrived a little more than two days ago, she had learned just how needed she really was here. She couldn't help the stinging tears that threatened to spill as her thoughts traveled back to the first day she arrived. She had been told that her father wasn't feeling well, but the details had been left out, and now she knew why. Her father had cancer.

Letting out a heavy sigh, Amber was thankful for the distraction of cooking, even if her heart wasn't in it. She had always loved cooking; food brought so much comfort and joy to people. That's why, when her husband died and the joy was drained from her, she had no desire to cook anything, at least from scratch. Everything was either take-out, in a cardboard box, or frozen. Dylan had quit asking her to make his favorite dishes, as her answer had always been the same. Amber would make an excuse, find some sort of reason for not being able to provide whatever desired dish he'd asked for. The truth was she could barely manage to survive menial tasks. Getting through the day was hard enough. She was thankful that she was able to work from home; she had been a blogger and did freelance writing. Amber was able to crawl out of her grief and work through her muddy mixture of emotions through journaling. Writing was what had saved her.

But now there she stood, in front of a grill, its stainless steel exterior shiny and hot. She almost didn't know where to begin.

"Looks like an order for breakfast, hon," her mother called out as she pasted a bright yellow paper ticket on the spinning, metal carousel that held orders. Amber snatched a glance at the order: pancakes and scrambled eggs. Simple enough. It was now or never. Her body went into auto-pilot as she poured the batter onto the griddle. The bubbling mixture let out a sweet fragrance. The yellow, gooey blend of eggs sizzled as she scraped it on the hot steel. She could do this.

More orders poured in, and her mother gave her encouraging smiles throughout the day. Amber realized how much she had missed cooking, dominating a kitchen, and creating food that people enjoyed. She found herself smiling a couple of times. She would remember all the times she had spent in that very kitchen, in tight corners with her father, where they used to talk about everything under the sun as they worked together to quickly cook up orders. She had a lot of good memories at the diner and now was questioning her reasons for leaving. But if she had stayed, she never would have met Peter Mills, the man she missed every single day for almost two years.

As she scrubbed the steel surface of the grill, using her anger to clean the burnt remnants of food from the day of cooking, she tried to expel the thick feelings of frustration with each motion she made. Her mind lost in thought, she recalled the day she had learned her husband had been killed.

She had been washing dishes, Dylan engrossed in his homework, sitting at the dining room table in their small home in Portland, when the doorbell rang. When she had opened the door and saw two policemen standing there in the light drizzle, sympathetic looks hanging on their faces, she knew the truth before they even had to utter a word. Peter was gone. He had been on the Portland P.D. before he had even met her. He came from a family of men that were all in law enforcement, and it'd only seemed natural that he would follow in their footsteps. Amber had met Peter at a local bar, when she had been there with a small group of friends she had made from work. Their eyes connected, and he had approached her. After laughing for hours and finding they had nothing in common, they never spent another day apart, until that moment when his buddies stood in her doorway. Their lives had been robbed.

"You almost ready to head home, dear?" her

mother, Lynn, called from a distance, bringing Amber back to reality.

"Yeah, Mom."

They locked up the diner, got inside Lynn's pick-up truck, and headed home, which was only a couple of blocks away. Amber planned on riding her bike to work. She needed to, as it had been part of her routine back in Portland, and it was one of the ways she tried to exercise. It was actually the only form of exercise that she didn't mind. Sit-ups, no thanks; jogging, not likely. But riding offered more than toned legs; it gave her a sense of freedom and peace.

"Dylan seemed happy when he came into the diner today."

To Amber, he seemed anything but happy. He had started his first day at the junior high in Birch Valley, and he'd walked to the diner after school, where his grandmother spoiled him with an enormous strawberry shake. Amber chatted with him during a brief lull but had to get back to work, and only learned from Dylan that he wasn't thrilled about his new school or not having any friends. She hoped to learn more about how his day went, and she wanted to reassure him that school would only be in session for two more weeks. He could survive this.

"So, Mom, do you know of any homes for rent?" Amber asked as they turned onto their street.

"Why? Are you in rush to be in your own place?"

"Well, I just think it might help Dylan adjust better, and now that we are going to be here…"

"I think you guys should stay with us for a little while. You just got here," her mother said firmly.

"I know we did, but I just want to get settled," Amber responded. She looked out her window and saw their home coming up. The small Craftsman-style home was similar to all the others on the tree-lined street. It was painted a dark slate color and had black shutters. There was a decent-sized porch, and a beautiful deck in the small backyard that her father had built. But the home was far from large, and living here too long would make Dylan and Amber feel cramped and that they were in the way.

"Amber, I hate asking you to stay. Your father and I are so grateful you have come home to help us out." Lynn's voice grew wobbly. "I don't know what to expect with your father, and it's just nice for us all to be together right now."

She had a point. Amber couldn't argue that her parents would be relying on her now more than ever and that spending any time that they could with her father was important. Her husband had lost his father to cancer, and Amber remembered how difficult that had been for the family. She sort of knew what to expect and hoped that the outcome would be different for her father. Imagining him going through the treatments, the pain, and suffering was more than Amber's heart could bear.

"Well, there's no rush finding a place, Mom." Amber could see relief wash over her mother's face.

Once inside, Amber found Dylan on the couch. A laptop reflected a blue light on his face, and headphones covered his ears as he zoned out.

"Hey, Dylan, what are you up to?" she asked as

she plopped down next to him.

He lifted one side of the headphones and gave her a half-smile. "Nothing much. Just playing a game on here."

Amber nestled up closer to him as she rested her head on his shoulder. "So, how was school? I know we talked a little at the diner."

"It was fine."

"Come on, Dylan. I know it's hard, honey."

Dylan sighed and trained his eyes on the glowing screen of the laptop. He was trying his hardest to tune her out.

"Dylan…" Amber nudged him softly.

"Mom, it was fine." There was no point in forcing him to talk to her; he would open up when he was ready to.

"Okay, okay. Just remember, I'm here if you ever want to talk about it," she said, before kissing his cheek. Her little boy was quickly becoming a young man—a complicated, awkward young man. She wished Peter were here. Amber had thought more about him than she had in awhile, not that he didn't enter her mind daily, but she tried not to dwell on his death.

Amber rose off the couch slowly. She needed to shower and wash away the sweat and smell of food that clung to her. She planned on writing in her journal. It was how she got through her grief, and it helped her organize the jumbled emotions in her mind. Before Peter died, Amber had written for fun. She had started blogging when it had become all the rage, and she'd found she was quite good at it and could actually make a little money doing at it. Then, when her world had grown dark, she found solace in writing. Amber found her voice when she wrote— the words she was too afraid to actually say, the feelings she didn't want to really confront. Now she had gotten into a routine of writing before bed; it helped her cope with the highs and lows of the day.

"Are you hungry?" Amber asked as she started for the kitchen.

Dylan shook his head. "Grandpa and I had some soup. I'm good, thanks."

"Okay, well, I'm going to go check on Grandpa and go shower. You going to go to bed soon?"

Dylan nodded again. "Hey, Mom…"

Amber turned back around and looked at him. "Yeah?"

"Is Grandpa going to die?" His young face was creased with worry.

Amber sat next to Dylan and hugged him from the side. "I don't know, sweetie. But it's a good thing we are here."

"It's just terrible, I mean, to move back because someone is dying."

Amber understood what he meant. It was awful to think she could have moved back to Birch Valley after Peter died and spent more time with her parents. But she had been crippled with grief, and she hadn't wanted to uproot Dylan, as he had been struggling with his own sadness.

"I know, but we're here now, and let's just make the most of whatever time we have."

Dylan looked down. "Mom, I miss Dad."

Amber squeezed him tightly. "I do too, sweetie." She fought back the tears that were threatening to

67

spill.

"Mom…"

"Yes?" Amber waited for Dylan to speak as she continued to hold him. She relished this moment, sad as it was, because as Dylan got older, he wanted less to do with her, where she only to spend more time with him. He was her only child, and all that she had left of Peter.

Dylan moved away from her, and he looked at her sheepishly. "Do you think we might ever see that Mr. O'Brien guy again?"

There it was. She had sort of been curious if her son was going to ask about Patrick. Amber had thought of him more than a couple of times and knew it was only a matter of time before they would run into each other again. She would jump that bridge when she crossed it.

But her mind was filled with a lot of other worries. For starters, they'd barely arrived and were trying to get somewhat settled, all while learning that her father wasn't just a little sick, but had cancer. Amber was still trying to process the fact that her father might die. She was a little more than upset that her parents hadn't shared his diagnosis with her until after she arrived. Things were a little strained in the house because of it, and that was partially why she brought up moving into a rental. Besides, she and Dylan couldn't live in her parents' house forever.

"You know he lives here in town. I'm sure we are bound to run into him again."

"He seemed really cool."

Amber agreed that he did, but he was also a large

slice of gorgeous too. She couldn't help but notice that he had only gotten more handsome since she had left. How was that even possible? When he had climbed out of his SUV, she had forgotten how tall he was, and that threw her a little off guard. If she hadn't been so panicked about the trailer tire, she could have enjoyed the view a little more. There would probably be more time for that in the future, but for now she needed to figure things out on the home front.

"Well, I'm going to hop in the shower. You better get ready for bed soon," Amber ordered softly, giving Dylan a peck on top of his shaggy brown hair as she got up from the couch.

On her way to the bathroom, she caught a glimpse of her parents in their bedroom, which neighbored hers. She could hear the soft whispers and could make out the outline of her father in their bed. Amber paused briefly and tried to listen, but their tones were hushed and too muted for her to make out anything. She continued to the bathroom and readied herself for a quick shower. Her mind was already spinning with everything she planned to journal about.

***

Patrick

The week drifted by, fairly easy and uneventful. Patrick was out in his yard Friday evening mowing the thick carpet of overgrown grass. He enjoyed the task quite a bit, as his riding lawnmower hummed and the scent of freshly shorn grass pervaded the air. He also just loved being outside. Patrick actually liked being outdoors far more than anyone realized. They just assumed that he was all books and numbers, but he liked getting his hands dirty. He looked forward to going out on job sites with Daniel, and appreciated seeing a project become complete. Patrick drove the mower another lap. The grass looked immaculate. The small bit of property was beautifully landscaped and was, in a way, a reflection of how Patrick maintained his business.

After showering, Patrick started to make dinner. He placed a frozen pizza into the oven, which wasn't the smartest idea considering how terribly warm it was in the house. He didn't feel cooking, and the boys loved pizza, which was well worth the sacrifice.

"Daddy, can we watch this movie?" Finn held up a plastic DVD case with a large dog on the cover. Fridays had unofficially become movie night, a tradition they'd started only a year earlier, where they would eat popcorn and watch any movie the boys could agree on. Patrick loved it and hoped it would be something they would continue to do for years to come.

"Yeah, I want to see that one with the big doggy on it, Daddy," Connor added as he tugged on Patrick's leg.

"Well, let's eat some pizza and then we can watch that movie." Patrick smiled at his two sons, who were looking up at him with hopeful blue eyes.

Both boys cheered and ran off toward the living room. He didn't have the heart to tell them he had barely put the pizza in, so they still had nearly thirty minutes until they could start the movie. Patrick set about preparing a small salad to accompany the pizza. He also poured some milk for Connor and Finn, right as they raced back inside the kitchen.

"Is it movie time yet?" Connor whined.

"Almost. Let's go wash up and eat." Patrick ushered the boys to the sink and assisted them with washing their hands. Each boy took a turn standing on a stool so they could reach the sink. There was more splashing and playing with the soap than actual washing, but Patrick figured it was better than nothing.

Once they were as clean as they were going to get, Finn and Connor ran to their seats and watched as Patrick brought over their favorite overly colorful plastic plates. Patrick seated himself across from them and nursed a beer as he chewed on the frozen pizza. It wasn't nearly as satisfying as a pizza from Steve-O's, but it filled the void.

The twins picked at the cheesy pizza and ate some of the salad. After getting the boys into the bath and into their pajamas, they finally nestled themselves on the couch and in front of the large TV. Patrick had a boy tucked on either side, each snuggled close with their fleece blankets. He was overheated; their small bodies radiated warmth, which made Patrick sweaty and a tad uncomfortable, but he wouldn't trade it for the world.

They sat together, the boys watching an enormous, slobbering dog on the screen getting into all sorts of shenanigans. The scene, which was playing in front of them, showed two young kids trying to give the dog a bath, which leapt out of an overly sudsy tub, practically mowing down an overwhelmed mother. Finn and Connor laughed in unison.

"Daddy, that dog is being bad," Connor noted, and giggled with delight.

Finn tugged on Patrick's shirt. "We should a get a big doggy like that one. Can we get a dog, Daddy?"

"Yeah, we want a doggy. Can we each get a doggy?" they started to beg.

"Guys, maybe someday," Patrick relented, but the boys continued to assault him with pleas of wanting a pet. They shouted out possible names and even where the animal would sleep.

Finally, Patrick was able to get them to return their attention back to the movie, but it wasn't long before Finn asked another question. One that was far more difficult to answer.

"Daddy, will we ever get a mommy?" Finn's eyes were wide with curiosity. Patrick decided it was best to just redirect his son's attention for now by insisting that he was going to miss the best part of the movie. He was grateful his son didn't press for an answer and happily returned his gaze to the TV.

Patrick could see their eyelids drooping as the movie continued to play. His own attention wasn't on the troublemaking dog or the comically stressed-out family. No, his mind had wandered far away. He let out a heavy sigh. He wasn't quite sure what to tell his sons, and he knew he wouldn't be able to keep avoiding their questions. Beth knew this was going to happen eventually, she knew everything, even as she lay dying. That's why she'd made him promise.

Chapter Six

Amber

"Amber, dear. Come over here, please," Lynn called out.

Amber grabbed a dishtowel and dried her hands as she headed toward the sound of her mother's voice. The diner had finally slowed down, well, just enough to get caught up before the dinner rush hit.

"Yes?" She had come through the swinging doors that led from the kitchen to the serving area by the front counter. She spotted her mother and smiled as she moved toward her.

"There she is," Lynn said. She was standing as usual with a coffee pot in hand, near the closest table to the serving counter, where three women sat. "Ladies, this is my daughter, Amber," Lynn announced, wrapping her arm around Amber, bringing her closer. "Mary, you probably remember her. She was in Liam's grade."

"Oh yes, that's right." Mary gave Amber a wide smile. Her hazel eyes were kind, and Amber vaguely remembered her, but it had been ages since she had seen Mary O'Brien.

"Amber, you remember Mary O'Brien. That's her daughter, Maggie, and that's Liam's fiancée, Rachel," Lynn introduced Amber to the women.

"Nice to meet you all," Amber responded politely, giving them a small wave as she continued to dry her hands nervously. She couldn't quite place Maggie's face but knew she had been the youngest of the O'Brien children. She wouldn't have even attended school with Amber, and as for Rachel, she was a completely new face altogether. Pretty and confident, she smiled back at Amber and extended her hand across the table.

"Hi, I'm Rachel Montgomery." Her tone was polite and direct, and there was a hint of authority. "I'm the principal at Birch Valley Elementary."

"Really? Mr. Anderson finally retired," Amber responded. She wasn't all that surprised; the man had been in charge of that school since she was a student and had to be well into his seventies.

"Yes, I started after the first of the year," Rachel added, and then her cheeks blushed a pale pink. Amber quickly did the math in her head and realized right away that Rachel hadn't been in Birch Valley more than six months. And she was already engaged? It must have been love at first sight.

"And you're getting married to…Liam?"

Rachel nodded, a happy smile playing across her lips. "Yes, actually in two weeks."

"Wow, well, congratulations. A Fourth of July wedding, how neat is that?"

Lynn and Mary remained quiet as Rachel and

Amber continued to chat. Maggie finally joined in the conversation, asking, "So, why did you come back home, Amber?"

The question, though well intended, felt like a swift punch to her gut. She looked at her mother, her expression marred with panic. They had agreed to keep her father's illness quiet for awhile. With the way the town spread gossip like a raging wild fire in the dead of summer, they weren't ready for all the comments, suggestions, and endless food that would more than likely be brought over. It was best to not to say anything until they knew exactly what they were up against.

"Do you have any children?" Maggie asked, taking a sip from her glass of ice water.

Amber stood there and carefully answered her. "Well, I came back to help out around here. My son and I, well, we lost my husband, Peter, a couple of years ago."

Maggie's eyes dropped down toward the table, her cheeks flushed with embarrassment as she lifted her glass and took a sip.

Mary frowned sympathetically. "Oh my, I remember when your mother told me. I'm so terribly sorry for your loss. He sounded like a wonderful man."

Rachel quickly chimed in and steered the conversation in another direction, but she wore a confused look on her face. "How old is your son, Amber? Does he attend the elementary school?"

"No, junior high. He's going to be thirteen soon."

"I have a little girl, Melanie, she's six. We're

expecting another little one this fall." Maggie's head pointed down to her belly, but the table was blocking the view of her stomach.

"That's wonderful news. Congratulations to you as well," Amber chirped. She glanced at her mother, almost asking permission to join the women at their table.

"Amber, dear, come sit. Lynn, you could do with getting off your feet for bit as well," Mary insisted sweetly.

"Don't mind if I do," Lynn replied, motioning for Amber to take a seat as well.

The women sat and visited until customers started to trickle in for dinner. Amber felt like she'd hit it off with Rachel fairly easily; they were the same age and found they had quite a bit in common. Maggie seemed a little reserved and distant, but friendly enough, and asked Amber if she would like to grab coffee sometime. Maybe she just needed to warm up a little to her, but Amber hoped they could get to know each other.

It felt odd, sitting there with this group of women. She had lost contact with most of her friends after Peter died, since she'd retreated so far into her cave, only venturing out to get food and to take Dylan to school; she'd become somewhat of a hermit. She hadn't realized how much she missed having friends. Just some female companionship to chat with about normal stuff. Maybe moving back wouldn't be so awful if she could make friends again.

***

Patrick

The family was all seated around the large table, all in their usual places. It was loud, slightly chaotic, but suffused with love as the O'Brien family celebrated Father's Day. Mary had prepared an incredible feast, almost Thanksgiving-like. She roasted a turkey to absolute juicy perfection, and she'd made her signature dressing and candied yams—basically all the trimmings imaginable.

Patrick eyed his sons and his brother, Daniel, as he noticed the makings of mischief and a possible mini food fight. Why Daniel insisted on being the one to instigate trouble and teach Finn and Connor the worst table manners was beyond Patrick. He loved that his brothers were the best uncles he could ask for, but Daniel tried his patience, especially during family dinners. "Boys," he said in a firm tone, causing Finn and Connor to return to their food momentarily. Patrick gave Daniel a pleading stare, silently asking his brother to stop messing around.

Rachel and Maggie were chatting about the wedding. They were on the countdown now; only two more weeks until his brother, Liam, tied the knot. Rachel had shared earlier that her family was being a bit difficult about attending the ceremony, to the point where she was worried that they weren't going to be coming at all. But her best friend, Chelsea, and her brother, Ethan, would be attending. Patrick nearly cringed when he'd heard Chelsea was coming up next week to help with the final wedding preparations. That woman had a hard time understanding the words "no" and "not interested". Granted, she was a cute little thing, but definitely not his type. She didn't cause the reaction inside of him the way Amber had, that's for damn sure. He still hadn't seen her since the day he changed that blown tire on her trailer, partially because he'd been avoiding the diner, which was not his usual style. He and Daniel used to get breakfast there daily, sometimes even popping in for lunch or a bite to eat after being out on a job site all day.

He was so caught up in his thoughts he almost didn't hear Grandpa Paddy say, "So, Patrick, my boy, I want to raise my glass to you, raising two fine little lads, Happy Father's Day to ya."

Patrick smiled and thanked him. Grandpa Paddy, with his glass still lifted, said, "And to Liam, may you have many happy days and a lot of luck as a father." He paused briefly before saying, "Michael, you have done a beautiful job with my wee lass over there…" Melanie giggled and stared at Michael with loving admiration. Grandpa Paddy looked wise with his shock of white hair and continued in his thick brogue. "May you and Maggie have many more blessings and a healthy baby this go around."

"Aww, thank you, Grandpa Paddy." Maggie had a wet sheen to her eyes. She got up from the table and gave her grandfather a kiss on the cheek.

Their father, Pat, cleared his throat, raised his own glass, and not to be outdone, said, "To my children, you have all made me so proud. It's an honor to be your father."

All the O'Brien siblings rose from their seats and gathered around Pat, all hugging him and showering him with affection. Even Rachel and Michael felt so moved by the toast that they wanted to show their appreciation for these men, who had a tremendous part in raising their significant others. As Patrick returned to his seat, he saw his mother dab her eyes with the bent corner of the linen napkin she clutched. In the O'Brien household, tears were shed often, mostly from laughing so hard until their sides ached, but sometimes it was the emotional moments such as this that showed the deep-rooted love that cemented their family together.

***

Amber

"Dad, did you want any more water, or can I get you anything at all?" Amber asked softly.

The morning of Father's Day started out rough and only seemed to grow worse as the day progressed. Her father had spent most of the night ill beyond anything she had ever witnessed. The after effects of chemo were hard and violent, the process brutal. Her mother had already left for the diner, after Amber reassured her countless times that she was happy to look after her father and that it would do her mother good to get out of the house. Lynn had hesitated, but Amber insisted to the point where she started to push her mother out the door. She had also sent Dylan to go help out for the day, as she thought is was probably better for him to not see his grandfather in his weakened state.

Her father shook his head, his eyes closing from the exhaustion of spilling out the contents of his stomach for hours. His softly weathered face was ashen and pale, his gray hair matted and wild. This man, Dean Herrick, who Amber remembered had been strong and vital on their last visit when they came down to Portland for the holidays, was now reduced to a shell of his former self. She reached for his blanket and pulled it up, tucking it securely around his body. She removed the damp wash rag she had used to cool him down earlier that afternoon when the fever had relentlessly tormented him. Looking down at him, Amber had felt almost maternal toward the man who helped create her, who'd helped raise and protect her, who now needed her more than ever before. As she spent Father's Day alone with her father, tending to him during this challenging time, and with the unknown outcome looming over them, she'd said a silent prayer. He didn't deserve this; no one did.

Amber sat comfortably on the couch, her laptop balanced on her thighs as her fingers danced along the keys, words flowing in a fast rhythm, and she found herself escaping to the place she loved. A place where she could pour those bottled-up emotions out and turn them into something well, prettier than how she truly felt inside; that's why her blog meant so much to her. It made her happy. She was swarmed by people eager to read her thoughts and ideas, who didn't know of the raw and frayed emotions that had been welling up inside her. This was her alternate life, one that she had only dabbled in before Peter died, and one that she had fully immersed herself in when he was gone. She was editing a blog she had just created moments earlier, scanning it for errors and battling her self-doubt, when the front door opened. Her mother and Dylan worked their way past the small entryway and into the living room.

"Hi, guys," Amber greeted them, looking up from the bright screen and readjusting the reading glasses that were perched on her face.

"Hey, Mom." Dylan plopped down next to her on the couch. He looked utterly worn out. Her son wasn't used to hard work, and running a business like the diner was one of the hardest jobs out there. He barely could keep his room clean, but an experience like this would hopefully teach him the benefits and rewards of hard work. Besides, she didn't want her mother to be without an extra pair of hands.

Lynn stood there, a worried expression apparent in her eyes. She had called to check on how Dean was doing throughout the entire day. "How's Dad?"

"He's resting now. Not much has changed since the last time you called."

She hung her head, visibly disappointed. "Okay, I'm going to go peek in on him."

"I made soup. I had hoped to try to get something in him, but he wasn't really able to eat. So there's extra if you didn't eat yet," Amber offered. Her mother gave her a grateful nod and turned to go to the bedroom where Dean was resting.

Amber turned to Dylan. "You hungry, buddy?"

"No, I ate there. I'm so tired," he complained as

he yawned and scowled.

"It's hard work, I know. That's what I grew up having to do."

Dylan tossed her a scared look. "Like, you had to do this all the time? God, Mom, that's awful."

Amber laughed. "It wasn't all that bad. Looking back on it, I sort of miss it."

"Well, I wouldn't."

Amber frowned. "Sometimes we don't have much choice. It's important to help your family out."

They sat on the couch quietly, Dylan staring at the wall directly in front of them as Amber tried to finalize her blog post, but she was distracted by having Dylan next to her, knowing he wasn't very happy. "Mom…"

"Yes, sweetie?" Amber answered without looking up from her screen. Her brain was having a difficult time processing what she was reading.

"I miss Dad. I'm also really worried about Grandpa," he explained. "Is he going to get better?"

Releasing a deep breath, she closed her laptop and moved it to the coffee table directly in front of them. After removing her glasses, she faced her son and pulled him into her arms. He was rigid at first, resisting her, but seconds later he melted into her chest and unleashed an army of angry, sad tears. He was swallowing and gulping to catch his breath; the crying was hard and caused his small shoulders to shake. Amber rubbed his back and whispered soothing words, all while fighting back the urge to let go and join him.

Were things ever going to get any easier? Just

when they had somewhat moved on to a different stage of grief, one where they had finally been getting into a better place, at least mentally, they had been hit with this issue. It was hard not to feel overwhelmed.

Amber wiped at her own silent tears and pulled back, looking down at Dylan. "I have an idea…"

She led him out to the small detached garage next to the house. Inside, Amber turned on the single light and located her shiny green bicycle and Dylan's sporty BMX.

"A bike ride?" Dylan asked, not overly impressed by her grand plan to turn this night into a win.

"Why not? It helps me clear my head, and we haven't gone for a ride since we moved here," Amber explained as she fished out his bike and rolled it near the opening of the garage.

"I guess so," Dylan grumbled. He grabbed his bike from her and mounted it. She could tell that he wanted to ride. He was more than a tad moody, and this would be just the cure.

Amber steered her bicycle out of the garage and gingerly slung her short legs over the frame. Her bicycle had taken her more miles than she could count, providing so much joy and freedom. Riding bikes had also been an activity that she and Dylan enjoyed together. Peter had loved riding with her; they would cruise along the many trails that were designed just for bicyclists in Portland. After Dylan was born, Peter had strapped on a baby trailer to his bike and they would go out as a family, even just around a couple of blocks in their neighborhood or to a nearby park. She had kept his bicycle, as she didn't have the heart to donate or sell it. Amber wanted to give it to Dylan when he was bigger and able to ride it.

They left the driveway and started to pedal down the street. The sky was almost dark, the street lights softly illuminating the quiet streets. Amber breathed in as she felt the air hit her face; it was warm and lightly scented with all the delicious smells of a summer night. She had missed this. She looked over at Dylan, who was on her right side. She could see his tormented worries from earlier disappear, replaced with contentment as he pedaled faster and sped past her, his laughter echoing. She was more than up for the challenge as they raced down the block. Her legs started to burn slightly, tingling as she pushed them harder to catch up with Dylan. Her boy was quickly proving to be a little more difficult to beat these days, but she couldn't help but smile. Sometimes it took a little physical strain to push past the emotional pain. Amber's smile grew wider; this had been exactly what they both had needed.

They returned to the house exhausted, drained, and happy. Amber and Dylan walked inside to find the home quiet and dark; only one table lamp had been left on. Amber put her finger to her lips, a silent warning for them both to be quiet.

They started toward their bedrooms when Dylan paused. "Thanks, Mom," he whispered and hugged Amber tightly. She squeezed him close, feeling positive for the first time since they had arrived. She realized in that moment, that together they would find a way to get through all of this.

Chapter Seven

Patrick

The temperature was rising. Even the morning had started out hot. Patrick grimaced as he and Daniel unloaded some wood planks out of their work truck. Daniel kept wiping away the beads of sweat that ran down his face.

"God, it's hot," Daniel complained as he hefted the heavy wood up unto his broad shoulder.

"Well, it's almost summer. It's only going to get hotter."

Daniel rolled his eyes and again wiped more sweat away. They were at the Belsky family farm, and they would soon be finishing up another large shed on the property. Patrick caught sight of a few goats grazing in the distance. The property was massive; there were several large fields that had been divided and were growing different crops. Another large patch of land had hay, which was being cut and left in organized piles, drying out in the sun and waiting to be baled. Patrick could only imagine how incredibly hard it must be to maintain a property of this size. But they were doing it, and they were successful at it. Patrick had learned, after talking to Mr. Belsky, that he sold a good deal of his crops to some major markets; they also jarred their own honey and sold a ton of produce and homespun goods at the local farmers' market. Mr. Belsky had several sons that helped run the farm, but he also provided jobs to some of the local guys. He also had two daughters, and they were notorious for their soaps and quilts. Patrick knew his sister wanted to purchase one of the quilts for the nursery she was setting up.

Patrick and Daniel worked until late afternoon; the sun still perched high in the sky, beating down hard on the earth and on them. Working inside the sheds was miserable; the enclosures corralled the heat, making both Daniel and Patrick cranky.

"You about ready to call it a day? I don't think I can take much more," Daniel asked as he drank from another bottle of water. He had just chugged two in a row and was almost done downing the one he held.

"Yeah, look on the bright side, we got a lot done today though." Patrick admired their handiwork. The building was almost complete.

As they both started gathering their tools, they heard the delicate footsteps of someone entering.

Patrick and Daniel both looked up and saw that one of the Belsky daughters had come in. It was Hannah, the older of the two, and she was carrying a tray with two glasses and a pitcher.

"My mother wanted me to bring this to you."

Her voice quivered with shyness, and she looked terribly nervous. Seconds later, her sister, Nina, entered. Her long, blonde hair cascaded down her shoulders, a bright yet mischievous smile on her face as she entered. It was obvious that Nina was gorgeous, and she knew it. She strutted inside, almost pushing past her sister. She gave both Daniel and Patrick an appreciative glance as she approached them.

"How's it going in here?" Her voice was overly sugary and almost high pitched. She batted her mascara-covered lashes. Patrick watched as Daniel swallowed. His brother was so easily affected by women, especially one as attractive as Nina. Patrick almost laughed as he watched Nina move in closer. She seemed focused in her movements, purposefully swinging her hips, puffing out her ample chest, and almost stalking them with her eyes, clearly craving their attention. Daniel seemed frozen, hypnotized even. Out of the two sisters, Nina had the looks of a super model. She was thin, tall, and graceful. Hannah was of a more sturdy build and quite a bit shorter, and had a simple beauty, not overstated or overly made up with make-up.

"Daniel, you want to help me carry this stuff to the truck?" Patrick tried to break his brother's stare.

"Oh, y-yeah, s-sure," Daniel stammered.

"Do you need some help?" Nina offered, a smile playing on lipstick-stained mouth.

"I think we got this, but thanks," Patrick replied as he turned his attention to Hannah. "Thanks for the drinks. We'll be right back to enjoy them.

Please tell your mother we appreciate it." Hannah nodded, giving him a close-mouthed, polite smile.

Nina looked confused and slightly disappointed. Patrick wasn't as easily moved as his brother; he was used to women flirting with him regularly and learned how to deflect their charms. Daniel moved his eyes away from Nina and lifted a heavy toolbox to take to the truck.

"Wow, Nina sure is pretty," Daniel commented once they were away from the shed and loading their tools into the back of the work truck.

"Yeah, but you can get into trouble with a girl like that."

"I'd like to try," Daniel teased back, causing Patrick to laugh.

"Well, let's go have that drink that Hannah brought in. Try and behave," Patrick said.

"Behave? Patrick, behaving isn't nearly as fun," Daniel joked.

Patrick knew that Daniel talked a big game, and that he tried to act like he was this Casanova, when in actuality he was terrified of women and had crippling self-doubt. It was a shame, really. Daniel was a great guy, but he always seemed to feel rejected by women. Patrick remembered that when Rachel's friend, Chelsea, had visited, Daniel was totally into her, and Patrick could understand why. Chelsea was hot, simply put. So of course his brother would be easily smitten, but her snobby attitude and aggressiveness didn't sit well with Patrick. As the thought of her crossed his mind, he couldn't help but feel a bit worried. Chelsea would be arriving at the end of the week, and he needed to try and keep his distance. Daniel was welcome to try his hand at getting her attention again.

Maybe this would be a great time to pay a visit to Amber. He had been thinking about her a lot the last couple days and was tempted to stop into Herrick's and possibly ask her out. He really didn't know what he wanted to do. He still found himself wrangling with guilt about even wanting to get to know Amber. But what would a cup of coffee hurt?

***

Amber

She was wiping the counter with a towel doused in warm bleach water, the heavy chemical smell making her nose tingle, when she heard the bell on the door chime. Amber turned her head and saw Patrick O'Brien walk in. His tall body filled the doorway. He paused and seemed to be looking around, almost searching. Then his eyes caught hers before she had a chance to dart hers away. A sexy grin curled on his lips, and she felt the insides of her stomach knot nervously. How was it possible for this man to cause such an array of reactions inside her?

He moved toward the counter with ease, almost gliding across the dining room. He was dressed in jeans and a crisp white polo shirt, which enhanced his tanned skin. Amber swallowed as she drank him in. She tossed the towel back into the small bucket of water that was near her and tried to smile as he approached.

"Hi, how's it going?" Her voice was shaky, and she almost didn't recognize the sound of it. So much for her feeble attempt at trying to act cool.

"Not too bad, yourself?" Patrick stood by the counter, his thick black lashes highlighting his twinkling green eyes. She could see the dark stubble on his jaw and made the mistake of looking at his lips. Instantly, she was curious what they would feel like on hers.

"I'm good," Amber managed to answer, unintentionally licking her lips; her mouth had suddenly gone dry.

"So, how are you and Dylan settling in?" Patrick asked as he took a seat directly in front of her. She stared at the fine black hair on his toned muscular forearms, which he had placed on the counter.

"We're starting to get reacquainted with the area. He's struggling to make some friends at school," Amber admitted.

Patrick's brow creased with concern. "Well, I'm sure he will make some. It's hard being the new kid. How's your dad doing?"

Amber sighed. "I know, you're right. Just with school letting out next week, I really had hoped, you know? That way he could have buddies during the summer." Amber made no mention about her father and hoped that Patrick wouldn't press the issue.

He nodded and leaned back against the back of the stool. She eyed his long torso, trying desperately not to imagine what he would look like without his shirt on. It had been a long time since she had felt any stirrings of desire, and the flame was causing her skin to feel suddenly flushed.

"Did you want to order anything?" The diner was eerily quiet, but Amber had enjoyed the peace. She'd been using the time to catch up on cleaning and prep work.

"Actually, I was wondering if maybe..." He paused. She could see him hesitate and wondered why. "Maybe you would want to go out sometime?"

Well, she had not been expecting that. She was floored that Patrick O'Brien, the best looking guy in school, probably in all of Birch Valley, was now asking her out. Amber tried to control all the spinning emotions that were whipping around inside her. *Play it cool, Amber.*

"Yeah, that might be fun." She wasn't so sure that her wobbly voice sounded as nonchalant as she had hoped.

"Great." She could see relief wash over his face, and she found it odd that a guy like Patrick would even be nervous about asking someone out, let alone someone like her. Not that she was some hideous creature, but he could have his pick of much more attractive women. *Had he dated since Beth died?* Her mother had shared with her, after they had visited with Mary O'Brien, some of the details about Beth's death, among other things. Amber's heart had immediately broken for Patrick. She vaguely recalled her mother mentioning that Beth had died years ago, but she wasn't aware of the circumstances. "So, when's a good time for you, I mean, for us to get together?" Patrick asked shyly.

"Um, hmm..." Amber wasn't sure why she was stalling, probably because she hadn't been on a date in over two years and found herself nervous around Patrick.

"Hey, it's okay if you don't want to go out."

Amber frowned. "No, that's not what I'm saying. I just...well..."

"What?" His eyes sparkled with curiosity. She could see a serious tightness in his jaw as he cocked his head to the side.

"Okay, honestly, I haven't been asked out in like two years. I guess I forget how this works, you know?" She couldn't believe she had just let out those words, but it was best to be honest. She hoped that, if anyone would understand, it would be someone who knew what it was like to lose a spouse.

A mysterious grin formed on his face as he replied, "I can't even begin to tell you how much I get what you are saying."

"Well, so you want to go for drinks or something?" Amber offered softly, proceeding cautiously.

"Yeah, I have an idea. Are you free tomorrow evening?"

"Sure."

"Great, how about you meet me at my house, say around six?" Patrick suggested.

"Okay, that works." Amber wasn't quite sure how she felt about meeting him at his house, but it was probably better than him picking her up at her parents' house. The less questions, the better.

Patrick told her where his address was and gave her his number. As he went to leave, he turned and gave her a sexy grin. Amber felt her body buzz with excitement and was worried she might be in a little overhead.

***

Patrick

Patrick dropped the boys off at his parents' place. He was relieved that he wasn't questioned about his plans or sudden need for babysitting. His mother was not the best at minding her own business and liked keeping tabs on all of her children. He was just grateful that she didn't suspect anything.

As he raced home, he set a plan in motion: he decided to pack a picnic dinner and take Amber for a drive. He chose this as their date for several reasons: the first being that Birch Valley was a small town, and if they were spotted together, it would be front page news. Patrick hadn't tried his hand at dating at all since Beth passed, and after the fiasco with the online dating which his sister had tried to set up, he wanted to keep this whole thing quiet until he figured out what it was that he was doing. Patrick had no idea what he was doing. He knew that he was the most nervous he had been in a long time, but he felt excited at the thought of getting to be around Amber.

When he saw Amber in the diner yesterday, he couldn't explain the sudden desire to kiss her. She'd looked scared when he had asked her out. But it made sense why she would react that way: they were on an equal playing field in a way; neither had dated for a long time. Patrick didn't know what had happened in her marriage, probably divorce or something, but two years was a long time to be single. But then again, it had been four years for him.

Patrick inhaled deeply as he pulled into his driveway. He glanced at the clock on the dash on his SUV; he still had almost an hour before Amber was to arrive. He had to pack the food he had gotten from the deli at the lone grocery store in town. Patrick wasn't certain what she liked, so he bought a variety of crackers, cheeses, some fruit, and anything else he considered somewhat romantic. That was what he hoped this would be, right? He wasn't quite sure what he wanted it to be, but right now he was looking forward to spending the evening with her.

***

Amber

Amber fussed with her hair. Should be she put it up or leave it down? She had no clue what to expect that evening. Her nerves were a jumbled-up mess, her stomach in tangled knots. She shyly tried to apply mascara, which caused her to run the wand across her eye. She tried wiping and flushing her eyes out with water to remove the giant black smudge, but now her eyes were red and puffy. Great.

Her outfit was a whole different ordeal. It was warm again today, but she also didn't know where they were going or what they would be doing. She should have asked more questions to get more of a sense on how to plan for this date. Amber stuffed her legs into a pair of jeans, but then instantly felt hot and uncomfortable, so she shucked them off, then tried on a skirt, but it just felt too fancy and dressed up. She wanted to make an excellent impression and really wow Patrick, but at the rate she was going she should probably just cancel. Amber huffed. She was beyond frustrated and annoyed, her nerves were shot, and she couldn't find anything to wear that didn't make her look fat. Everything was suddenly too tight or making her skin irritated. But worse, she was cranky.

Amber dove onto her bed, lying there with her face in her pillow. What was she even doing? Why was she putting herself through this torture? She had forgotten what it was like to dress up for a man, especially someone as delicious looking as Patrick. Her husband was a fine specimen as well but had nothing on Patrick. There was just something extra special about him; he had this mysterious aura, which he'd always had for as far back as she could remember. She was so out of her league here. Amber just wanted to scream into her pillow. Maybe she wasn't ready for this? She should cancel.

***

Patrick

He eyed the clock; she was already about ten minutes late. Maybe she changed her mind. She did seem uncertain about the whole thing when he had asked. But she would've called, right? Patrick paced the kitchen, double checking that he had packed everything. It was like the fifth or sixth time he had checked, but he didn't know what else to do while waiting for Amber.

Just when he was about to lose all hope, he heard his doorbell. When he opened the door, there she stood, her dark mahogany hair wrapped in a loose knot, several strands hanging near her neck, and he had to fight the urge to touch them. Her eyes were bluer today; her turquoise top enhanced their bright color. Her legs were tan against the off-white Capris she wore, but his attention was drawn to her ankles, where a thin gold chain surrounded one, and then to her feet, which were barely covered by thin strappy sandals, her toes painted a delicate shade of pink. Patrick had thought she was gorgeous the first day he laid eyes on her; now she was stunning, and he had to catch his breath.

"I'm so sorry, Patrick," Amber apologized, her hand moving to her neck as she grabbed at the loose strands of hair. He could tell she was anything but comfortable, and he immediately wanted to reassure her.

"Oh, it's fine, I'm glad you made it. Did you want to come inside while I grab everything?" Patrick offered. She nodded and stepped inside.

***

Amber

When she rang that doorbell, she had to do everything in her power not to throw up. She felt sick, then once Patrick opened the door and she was greeted with those enchanting eyes and seductive face, her knees went weak and she melted inside. Was this really happening?

He offered for her to come inside while he gathered some things. Well, now she knew they weren't going to be eating there. Which was probably for the best, because the moment she entered into the large home, she was hit with a defining female presence. The home was beautifully decorated, and it was warm and inviting. But it shouted Beth. Amber felt almost as though she was entering another woman's territory; it didn't sit too well with her already nervous and queasy stomach.

"Go ahead and make yourself comfortable while I grab the stuff I packed." Patrick started off toward the kitchen. The floor plan was open, so she could see the dining room and the kitchen from the living area.

Amber wandered slowly into the living room. There was an enormous fireplace, two dark forest green couches sat in an L-formation, and a large entertainment center stood proudly against one wall. Amber instantly imagined how nice it would be to sit on either couch; one was perfect for cuddling in front of a fire, the other for snuggling close to watch a movie. Her eyes gravitated to the large prints on the wall; they were scenic portraits of locations that looked very similar to Birch Valley. Upon closer inspection, Amber was certain that one, which showed a barn standing alone in a field, with some rugged hills as the backdrop, was for sure in Birch Valley.

"Patrick, these pictures are incredible. They look like Birch Valley," Amber called out.

"That's because they are. Beth took those." He had entered the room, a large canvas cooler slung over his shoulder. "You ready to go?"

Amber took in a deep breath and smiled as Patrick ushered them out the door. The palm of his hand found the small of her back. *I could get used to this.*

Chapter Eight

Patrick had insisted that they take his car, and as she climbed into the SUV, the reality of their date started to hit her. She was actually going out with a guy, someone who wasn't Peter. It felt weird and a little emotional. After loading the food and a large blanket, she learned they were going on a picnic.

When they first started driving, there was some awkward silence, but Patrick tried to break the ice by telling a terrible joke that had them both laughing at his sad attempt. As they cruised outside of the main part of town, driving past the diner and the cozy little neighborhoods, they were soon on the single lane highway. They drove for almost thirty minutes until Patrick started to turn down a quiet country road, not much different than the one she had found herself stranded on. The asphalt turned into gravel, making the drive bumpy and loud. He pulled into an open meadow with tall grass. A small body of water shimmered in the distance; the spot was beautiful.

Amber got out of the car and offered to help

carry something, but Patrick refused. He gathered everything and led them down a path that had been carved by wildlife going down to the water. There were several trees, mainly birch and a couple weeping willows. Patrick chose a large, flat spot that was partially shaded under an enormous willow but gave a magnificent view of the water. Patrick set the cooler down and fanned out the large blanket. The setting couldn't be more romantic, and her head spun with the notion of just how intimate the setting was. This was their first actual date, and here they were out in the middle of a meadow, with nothing but the sound of nature surrounding them. The sun beamed its rays down, and the shade of the willow was a welcomed relief.

Patrick crouched down, taking his place next to Amber. It felt so natural sitting next to him. She could smell hints of his spicy aftershave wafting on the breeze, and inhaling it deeper only made her want to be closer to him. He unpacked several containers filled with food. Amber was impressed at the thoughtfulness and care he had put into planning the picnic. Amber was a simple woman; she didn't need to be wined and dined in a fancy restaurant. But this was perfect.

It wasn't long before they found themselves engaged in easy conversation, mostly sharing a lot of about themselves. They were both surprised they had so much in common.

Patrick's long legs were stretched out, and Amber had hers curled under her. They sat there, each staring out at the water, surrounded by a comfortable silence, the kind that was usually formed after years of being together.

"This is really nice," Amber said as she was handed a wheat cracker with a thin slice of smoked Gouda cheese on it. Slipping it into her mouth, she relished the creamy texture of the cheese but tried to shield crumbs from falling onto her blouse.

"I'm glad you like it out here. We could have went somewhere else, but this way there are no distractions as we get to know each other." Patrick's eyes focused in on her, causing her to shift her weight on the blanket. She suddenly became very aware of his gaze and the intensity behind his green eyes.

"No, this is perfect." She could sense his movement, and before another word slipped from her mouth, she could feel Patrick's lips on hers. The warm and soft texture surprised her as she offered more of her mouth to him. He deepened the kiss, causing her to moan. She had never experienced a kiss like that—the way Patrick's tongue traced her lips and then ventured into her mouth.

Suddenly, she felt him pull back. He looked dazed. "Amber, I'm so sorry. I don't know what came over me." He must have caught the hurt in her eyes. "I mean, I wanted to kiss you, it's just that…well…"

"I know." Amber looked away, still reeling from the kiss. She brought her hand to her lips; they were still tingling. She turned her focus to the slight breeze that flew through the trees, making the willows move with grace and beauty.

"Amber, I haven't dated or been with anyone since Beth."

She turned back to him and watched sadness fill his eyes, which broke her heart. "It's okay, I understand completely." Amber reached and stroked his arm, trying to comfort him.

"Do you? How long have you been divorced?"

"Divorced?" Amber was confused but then realized she had never really shared her past with him. She knew about Beth because of her mother telling her.

"Yeah, isn't that part of the reason why you and your son came back?"

"No, we came back because my dad's sick." Amber paused briefly, careful not to disclose that her father was actually sick with cancer. "My husband died two years ago."

Patrick's eyes grew wide, and his mouth gaped slightly open. "Oh, Amber, I had no idea. God, I feel stupid. I just assumed, you know?"

"It's okay, you didn't mean any harm. I just thought you knew. But it's not like I told you. Just with this being Birch Valley and all, I figured everyone knew."

"I know what you mean, especially if your mother is the one and only Mary O'Brien."

That made Amber laugh. Even though Mary was well known for knowing all the bits of gossip and news in town, she was such a lovely woman.

"Well, it's fine, Patrick. You didn't know, and now you do."

***

Patrick

Talk about putting your foot in your mouth.
Patrick felt like an ass. He had no idea that she was
widowed as well; that leveled out their playing field
a little more evenly. He also couldn't believe he just
went and kissed her like a hormonally charged
teenager. It felt incredible, he couldn't deny that,
but it was as if he had no hold on himself, no self-
control. That scared him a little.

He watched Amber stare toward the water as
they sat there absorbing the quiet. He hoped he
didn't move too fast and ruin something before it
even started. Patrick was enjoying his time with her;
she was funny, witty, and so damn beautiful. The
worst part was that he found himself wanting to
touch her.

"So how did your husband die?" Patrick asked as
he grabbed a handful of green grapes and waited for
her to tell him the story.

***

Amber

Amber's shoulders sagged, and she felt her gut
twist. She hated retelling the story of how Peter had
died. She relived it with each retelling, knowing that
no matter how many times she talked about it, that
it wouldn't ever change what happened or bring him
back.

"Peter was a police officer in Portland. That's
where I have been for the last fifteen years,

roughly," Amber started off, wanting to gauge his reaction. He was completely listening, his full attention on her every word. She continued. "Well, he came from a long line of law enforcement guys. He loved it. He was a cop before we met, and I knew that it was a pretty dangerous job," Amber explained. She took a sip out of the bottle of water that was lodged safely between her legs. "Two of his buddies came to the door and told me that Peter had been killed. It was a traffic stop, fairly routine, and then shots were fired."

"They nabbed the guy that did it, right?"

Amber shook her head. They hadn't been able to find the man who had gunned down her husband. She had spent her time wading through the different depths of grief. She had been angry; she'd felt robbed and devastated. She had to make peace with the fact that the man who took her husband's life might never be found, and she had to come to grips with that. Ultimately, she found acceptance somehow along the way.

"I'm so sorry, Amber." Patrick pulled her toward him, bringing her to his chest, resting his head on hers. She felt herself mold against him. She hadn't felt this protected and secure in a long time. How was it possible that, after only spending a couple of hours together, sharing some cheese and crackers, she could feel this connected and close to someone? The kiss. That's what she would blame it on.

***

Patrick

He wasn't sure why he wrapped her up in his arms, but instinct told him to. She looked wounded, and Patrick wanted to banish those dreadful feelings. He knew exactly how she felt—the hollow feeling that no one else understood, unless they too had lost a spouse.

Patrick enclosed his arms tighter around her, the plush softness of her body causing him to ache in ways he had forgotten. She twisted her body so that she could look up at him, her eyes swimming with questions. His eyes were fixed on her mouth, which was lush, full, and swollen from their earlier kiss. He threw caution to the wind, polite manners out the window, and bent down, capturing her mouth once more with his. The ache only intensified.

***

Amber

Amber leaned against her car, Patrick's mouth on hers again. He towered over her, making her feel tiny and small and ultra feminine. The way his hands held her at her hips eliminated any space between them. She needed to come up for air. Her lips almost felt bruised from kissing him so much. They had spent a couple more hours in the meadow, talking, laughing, and kissing—lots of kissing. It had been over two years since she'd kissed someone, probably longer. But God, it felt good. She felt more alive now than she had in a long time. The only problem was that this was moving fast, like warp-speed fast, and that worried her quite a bit.

"I'd better go," Amber reluctantly said. She looked up at his handsome face, caught in the evening sunset. How was it possible for him to be more gorgeous now than he was just moments ago?

"Can I see you again?" His voice was seductive, but there was an underlying shyness.

"Yes, I'd like that a lot." Amber meant it too. Her brain starting to act silly, conjuring up notions about them together. She had enjoyed his company, she admired his passions, his love for his sons, and felt that there was far more chemistry than either of them knew what to do with.

He leaned in again. Amber placed her hand flat against his chest; she could feel the strength under his shirt, and her mind went to a dangerous place. "I need to go. Otherwise I fear we won't stop."

He raised his eyebrows and said, "Would that be such a bad thing?"

She could tell he was teasing, or at least she hoped so. "Patrick, behave. Maybe we can get together again this week?" she asked hopefully.

Patrick bent lower, and his mouth hovered just above hers, "Are you sure you want me to behave?"

Amber playfully slapped at him and weaseled her way out from under him. "Thanks for a really nice evening."

"I had a good time too." Patrick moved out of the way of her driver's side door, and he wore a smile on his face as he waved goodbye.

Amber got in and started her car and slowly backed out of his driveway. Replaying the events of the date, she was a little mortified at her behavior, but she was nearly thirty-five. She also knew that life was fleeting and sometimes things, or people, got snatched away. Oh, who was she kidding? Amber knew she was in way over her head with Patrick O'Brien.

***

Patrick

Patrick let himself inside his home, and as soon as he closed the front door, he fell back on it. His brain was rehashing the details of their entire date. He hadn't expected it to go the way it had, a part of him was ashamed at how out of control he had allowed himself to act, but Amber brought out a side of him that he had lost touch with for a very long time. Patrick almost felt like he was young again, out there in that meadow. He couldn't explain their chemistry, but it was wild and intense. Wicked thoughts slipped into the workings of his mind, and though he couldn't stop them from entering, a piece of him welcomed his new feelings.

He grabbed his car keys and headed out the door again, this time to retrieve his sons before it got too late. The drive over to his parents' house felt quicker than usual, probably because his mind was overloaded as it tried to process everything.

"Daddy," Connor squealed to Patrick the moment he entered the living room, where his sons were down on the ground playing with Daniel.

"Hey, buddy." Patrick scooped him up and

headed to where Finn was. His son was busy trying to pin Daniel, and he barely looked up at Patrick. Daniel seized this brief lapse in concentration and playfully grabbed Finn, tickling him and causing him to laugh hysterically.

Once released from Daniel's grip, he charged. "No fair, Uncle Daniel," Finn cried as he used every ounce of his small body to tackle Daniel, who easily became pinned.

Patrick didn't hear his mother enter but felt her wrap her arm around his waist. "Hello, son. I wasn't sure when you'd be by for the boys, so I gave them a bath." Her eyes were full of questions as she met his eyes with hers.

"Thanks, Mom." Patrick sat Connor down, who immediately took advantage of Daniel being pinned.

"So what were you doing? You were gone a bit longer than I thought," Mary questioned. Here it was; he knew he wouldn't get away so easily. Not if Mary O'Brien had anything to do with it.

"I just had a ton of errands to run, I went grocery shopping, cleaned the house..." Patrick tried to create a fictional list of tasks. "I appreciate you watching them and giving them a bath. I'd better get them home."

"Okay, dear." Mary gave her son a final hug and then wandered away toward the kitchen.

"Come on, boys, we need to head home." Patrick helped peel Finn off Daniel.

Daniel slowly got up off the floor with a slightly pained expression. "Thanks, man, they are getting a lot stronger."

"Either that, or you're getting older," Patrick

teased. "I'll see you at work tomorrow."

Daniel smiled and nodded.

Patrick couldn't help but feel relieved once he was back in his car and headed home. He felt a tad guilty lying to his mother, but he'd much rather avoid the family from knowing anything about him seeing Amber. He didn't want to deal with the pressure of having to answer questions from everyone, not just his mother. It was best if he kept Amber a secret, at least for now.

Chapter Nine

Rachel

"Aww, I have missed you so much." Chelsea squeezed Rachel hard. They stood outside the baggage claim at the airport in Spokane.

"I missed you too," Rachel said. She tried grabbing Chelsea's suitcase.

"Uh, no you don't." Chelsea snatched it back. "You're preggers, remember?"

Rachel rolled her eyes toward the baby blue, cloudless sky. "Yeah, but I'm not disabled."

"Whatever." Chelsea got into the passenger side of Rachel's silver BMW. The paint glittered in the bright sunlight.

Rachel slipped into the leather seat of the driver's side. "Are you hungry?"

"Um, sure, I could eat. Anything good around here?"

Rachel looked at her side mirror and carefully pulled out of the spot she was parked in, though the airport was not terribly crowded. Nothing like LAX or any of the other southern California airports she used.

"Well, it's up to you. Spokane has pretty much everything," Rachel explained.

Chelsea's blonde hair was pulled into a loose knot on top of her head, and it bounced when she spoke. "I don't know, you are the pregnant lady. Shouldn't we go somewhere with pickles and ice cream or something?"

Rachel laughed as she merged easily onto the freeway. "So far the only thing I crave is sleep. I get so tired." She felt herself fighting a yawn.

"Rachel, you have two people living inside of you right now." Chelsea scrunched up her face. She'd had the hardest time accepting Rachel leaving Newport Beach and moving up to Birch Valley, but she had an even more difficult time accepting that Rachel was pregnant.

The BMW zipped along the non-congested freeway, and she got off on the Division Street exit. They were sure to find something suitable to eat before they made the over sixty-mile drive to Birch Valley.

"See anything you want?" Rachel asked when they were stopped at a red light.

"Ooh, what about that Thai place over there?" Chelsea pointed excitedly.

"Perfect." Rachel looked over her shoulder, got into the right lane, and then turned into the parking lot. It was fairly packed with cars, but she located a spot right near the front entrance of the large building.

Once inside, they were greeted with enticing

aromas and a beautiful atmosphere. They were led to a booth near a window and were offered some tea.

"This place is sort of fabulous," Chelsea commented as she perused the menu.

Rachel scanned the room. It was decorated in remarkable fixtures that caught her eye, and there was lots and lots of gold everywhere. "Yes, it is. I bet the food is amazing."

The waitress came back with their tea and took their order, leaving them alone again.

"So, how are you feeling?" Chelsea asked as she nervously fiddled with her silverware. Rachel picked up on her friend's discomfort. It would have been different had Chelsea been the one that was pregnant. She was competitive and didn't like to be showed up.

"Not bad, I mean the morning sickness is gone, thank goodness. So, I do feel human. Well, kind of."

"How are things going with Liam? I mean, you guys have a big day coming up pretty darn soon."

The whole reason why Chelsea was visiting was so that she could help Rachel with all the last minute details of their small wedding. It was still unsure if Rachel's parents were going to be attending, and her brother, Ethan, was scheduled to fly in a couple days before the event.

Rachel blew on her tea in hopes of cooling it down. "We are super excited and doing really great. I love him so much, Chelsea."

Chelsea gave her a weak smile. "I wish I had someone so awesome like him." Her eyes twinkled. "How's Patrick?"

Ah, there it was. When Chelsea had visited earlier in the spring, she got to meet the O'Brien family and instantly fell hard for Patrick. Who could blame her? The man was gorgeous and something of a mystery. Unfortunately for Chelsea, Patrick didn't seem quite interested, but Rachel hoped that maybe they could all go to dinner together and see if there could be sparks.

"Hey, I was thinking, it would be so fun to go out."

Chelsea's head perked up at the suggestion. "Go out, like, double date or girl's night?"

"Double date," Rachel answered quickly. They both saw their food arriving, and Rachel's stomach made an audible gurgle. "I guess I'm hungrier than I thought."

Chelsea delicately picked at her plate. "So, like with Patrick or that other brother, what was his name again?"

"Daniel. But yes, I'm thinking Patrick for sure. I know you thought he was hot."

"Um, yeah, because he is. I know you are all gaga for Liam, but come on, the man is fine." Chelsea slipped a piece of the spicy food into her mouth.

"Well, yeah, but that's besides the point. This way, maybe if you meet someone, like say Patrick, then you would consider moving up," Rachel said shyly.

"I don't know, Rachel. I mean, yes, to the whole Patrick thing. But I'm not so sure I'd want to live in Birch Valley."

"I know, that's why it's just a thought."

"Well, if I hit it off with Mr. Tall, Dark, And Terribly Sexy, we can talk. Until then, it's a no for me moving here. I love you and all, but I can't do tiny, small towns."

"Like you said, let's just wait and see."

***

Rachel's car pulled into the long gravel driveway that led to the cabin.

"So you moved out of that cute little house?" Chelsea asked.

"Well, I mean it made sense for us to move in together. Besides, it's beautiful here, and it is the venue for our wedding," Rachel added happily.

"Wait, what?" Chelsea's tone didn't match the cheerful pitch it had been just moments ago.

"Yeah, why not? He proposed right there on that lake." Rachel pointed out her window at the shimmering water in the distance.

"You can't be serious, Rachel. I mean, who gets married outside, like next to a swamp?" Chelsea huffed as the car came to a stop. Rachel sat and considered what Chelsea was saying. She didn't think of it as some hideous place; she loved it. It was quiet and serene, Liam was there, and it was now home. She had been adding her own personality to the cabin and felt comfortable being there. She had worried she would feel like an intruder, but it was the exact opposite. Liam had begged for her to move in; he claimed that having her there made his place feel complete.

"Well, this is where it's taking place. Trust me,

when you see the plan of attack I have for it, you will totally get it then," Rachel tried to reassure Chelsea.

"Hey, it's your wedding." Chelsea got out of the car as Liam emerged from the house. Rachel's eyes instantly connected with his. He jogged over to the BMW.

"Chelsea," Liam said. He hugged her tightly and then moved over to Rachel, planting a kiss on her cheek and pulling her to his side.

Rachel looked up at him. The evening sun was setting behind the neighboring hills and small mountains that surrounded the cabin. The tall pines cast quiet shadows on the ground around them, their rich scent filling the air. Rachel inhaled deeply, appreciating the moment. She felt her heart fill with even more love for Liam as she saw how kind he acted toward her best friend.

"Chelsea, how was your flight?" Liam asked as he moved to the rear of Rachel's car. He unlatched the trunk and grabbed Chelsea's suitcase.

Rachel watched Chelsea. Her friend was examining Liam with her eyes, possibly even undressing him. She wouldn't put it past her friend.

"It was good. Thanks for asking," Chelsea answered as she toyed with her long, blonde hair, which had found its way out of its knot. "Liam, I can get my bag."

"Oh, it's no trouble." Liam started for the front door, and Rachel and Chelsea followed.

Chelsea was quiet once inside the cabin, a first for her. Rachel suddenly felt nervous, waiting for her friend to give her opinion on the house.

"It's cute in here, really cozy and woodsy. That fireplace is to die for," Chelsea said as she went toward it, touching the large river rocks that lined the wall and went straight toward the ceiling. "This is beautiful."

It was the centerpiece of the cabin. Rachel recalled the first time she had seen it. Granted, she was terribly upset with Liam at the time and didn't get to take the time to appreciate it until much later on.

"Hey, babe, did you want me to put this in our room?" Liam asked as he lifted the suitcase up.

"Sure, thanks." Rachel and Liam had decided since they only had a little over a week until they were to be married, that Chelsea was going to stay with Rachel in their bedroom, and Liam was going to go stay at Patrick's house. It was Liam's suggestion. He wanted Rachel to catch up with her friend; he understood how close the two were and he wanted her to enjoy this visit.

"Wait, why am I going in there?" Chelsea spun around and asked. "Don't you guys have a guest room?"

"Well, we did." Rachel rubbed her stomach. It was starting to bulge out more. Her days of having a flat stomach were numbered.

"So, where's Liam going to stay?"

"With his brother. Liam thought it would be nice for me and you to spend some time together."

Chelsea looked at Liam and smiled. "You are so thoughtful." She turned back to Rachel. "He's a keeper."

Rachel laughed and nodded. "I think so."

Liam rolled his eyes and went off to drop off the suitcase, mumbling something as he walked away.

"You want anything to drink? We can sit outside on the deck, if you want?" Rachel asked.

Chelsea followed Rachel as she moved to the kitchen. "Wow, this is a really nice kitchen, I'm surprised."

"Why?" Rachel asked, grabbing three glasses from the hickory cabinets and setting them on the granite counter.

"Well, you know, because he's a guy, and usually they have no clue how to make it fabulous. This is pretty fabulous." Chelsea ran her hand along the smooth surface of the counter. "He actually has really good taste."

"Thanks," Liam said as he entered. He stood quite taller than both Chelsea and Rachel. He went over to Rachel and gave her another kiss.

"We thought maybe we could go outside and visit. Sound good?"

Liam nodded. "Sure. You need me to carry anything out?"

"No, Chelsea and I have it. Thanks, babe." Rachel reached up on the tips of her toes and kissed Liam on the cheek.

He left the kitchen. Chelsea peeked around the corner to make sure he was out of earshot.

"Wow, so aren't you little Miss Domesticated?" Chelsea laughed.

Rachel had fallen into the comfortable role of being the future Mrs. O'Brien. It was a huge change to how she used to be. She had actually been learning how to cook, thanks to the real Mrs.

O'Brien. It felt so much bigger and more real than just playing house with a boyfriend. This man was going to be her husband, the father of her children.

"Someday, you too will be like this, and you will love every minute of it." Rachel smiled and grabbed a tray to carry the tall glasses of lemonade.

Chelsea rolled her eyes and giggled.

***

Liam

Liam was sitting in Patrick's living room, Finn and Connor both snuggling on either side of him.

"Crazy to think you're going to have twins too, huh?" Patrick commented. He was stretched out on the opposite couch. He snacked on some popcorn, his eyes on the screen in front of them.

They had been watching a movie with the boys, per their Friday night ritual. Liam had been staying with them for a couple days. Rachel and Chelsea were back at his place; he'd wanted to give Rachel some much-needed time with her friend, but God, he missed her. Waking up alone in a strange bed the first morning had been rough.

"Yeah, but this is pretty cool." Liam's arms covered each boy. The warmth of having them next to him made him eager to hold his own children. He had been terrified once Rachel announced she was pregnant, but then when they learned they were having twins, he couldn't fully wrap his head around it. He knew he wanted to be a father someday, but he didn't expect things to move so fast, and the thought of two babies scared the hell out of him. Luckily, he had seen Patrick survive, and his circumstances were far worse. It made him respect his brother that much more.

They continued to watch the movie until the boys fell asleep against Liam. Patrick turned off the TV and peeled Connor from Liam, depositing the small boy in his bed. As he was coming back, Liam already had Finn in his arms. After both boys were tucked in, the two men ventured to the kitchen.

"You want a beer or something?"

"Sure," Liam replied. Patrick bent down into the fridge, removed two dark-colored glass bottles, and motioned for them to sit outside on the deck.

Liam took a seat in a patio chair. He extended his legs and inhaled deeply. He felt relaxed, not like a man that was getting married in a week. He had been asked by different friends and people he would run into at the store or gas station if he were getting cold feet yet. His answer was always a simple no. Now, he couldn't explain why he wasn't nervous. Maybe, that's just how it was when you find the right one.

Patrick sipped his beer and let out a long sigh. "Nice out tonight."

Liam nodded. It was; the evening was warm, but pleasantly so. The sun was starting to hide behind the mountains, and the sky was a burnt orange color, with lavender clouds stretched out like taffy.

"You getting nervous yet, man?"

Liam shook his head and answered. "No, that's what is so weird. I'm actually excited. I miss her right now."

"Well, that's good. I'm happy for you, Liam." He took another swig from his bottle. "I had my doubts, I mean to get pregnant and married, sort of all at once. That's a lot."

"Yeah, it wasn't ideal to have it all happen like that, but you know, I'm totally good with it." Liam took a sip from his own bottle. He relished the rich flavor.

"So, Chelsea's here. How's that going?"

Liam turned toward Patrick. "Actually, I'm glad you brought her up."

"Really? Why?"

"Well, Rachel thought it might be fun for the four of us to go out one night. Kinda like a double date, you know?" Liam waited for his brother's reaction. He hadn't been completely sold on the idea himself when Rachel mentioned it. He knew that Patrick wasn't really into Chelsea; hell, his brother wasn't into dating at all. Liam wished that Patrick would meet someone. It would be great to go out on dates together.

"Oh, Liam, I just don't know." Patrick had a faraway look in his eyes.

"Ah, it won't be that bad, might be fun actually. You could always take her as your date to the wedding," Liam suggested.

"Uh, no thanks," Patrick said quickly, a distinctive hint of irritation in his voice.

"Why? What's wrong with her?"

Patrick rolled his eyes. "Nothing, I'm just not into her."

"Well, let's just go out this weekend. Maybe you will change your mind. You might actually like her,

Patrick."

"Highly doubtful." Patrick wore a scowl and put the bottle back to his lips.

***

Rachel

"Chelsea, you want some more coffee?" Rachel asked as she refilled her mug. She had been trying to break herself of her caffeine habit, but so far the habit was winning.

"Sure." Chelsea yawned. She was curled into the corner breakfast nook in the dining room. The morning light filtered in. It was early, and today Rachel had plans for them to work on wedding stuff. "Tell me again, why we are up at the crack of dawn?"

"Oh, please, it's after seven." Rachel laughed as she brought the mugs to the table.

Chelsea nibbled slowly on the blueberry bagel that was in front of her. "Thanks," she said as she accepted her mug. "So, tell me, what is the game plan for today, Rachel?" She returned to pinching off small pieces of the bagel and eating in a bird-like fashion. Rachel knew how much Chelsea hated consuming carbs. It was something that Rachel had learned to get over. Now she enjoyed food and found comfort in actually cooking.

Rachel considered the question. She started thinking of the list of things they needed to accomplish in less than a week. The wedding was the following weekend. Chelsea had already been there for a couple of days, and now Rachel was missing Liam terribly. Every morning she had woken up, she thought it was him next to her, but it was only Chelsea.

"I was thinking today we could meet up with Maggie and Mary, maybe work on some of the decorations and stuff."

Chelsea rolled her eyes, and a smirk followed. "I don't really want to deal with Maggie."

"How come? She's really awesome."

"I'm glad you guys get along so well." Chelsea's tone turned cool as she moved her eyes away from Rachel and sipped her coffee.

"Oh, don't be like that. She's nice, and I'm lucky because not every sister-in-law is. Same goes for Liam's mom. She's amazing. I couldn't ask to be getting married into a better family."

"Yeah, I liked her. But you know who I liked more?"

"I know. Trust me, I know. Liam is going to see about us going out together. I thought maybe tonight," Rachel added, lifting her mug to her lips.

"So I have to endure the torture of hanging out with Maggie in order to see her brother? Not sure if it's worth it."

"Chelsea, first, it's not torture. Second, maybe you've forgotten just how hot Patrick is." The best friends looked at each other, grinning, and burst out laughing into their mugs, each reveling in their close moment.

Chapter Ten

Patrick

He wasn't sure how he was tricked into going, but he wasn't happy about it. Not one damn bit. Liam kept smiling at him, silently trying to encourage Patrick. Why? He had no interest in Chelsea. Sure she was pretty, but she wasn't Amber. But of course, he wasn't about to tell his brother about that. He had been doing a good job keeping that whole thing under wraps, which made it all sorts of exciting.

"So, Patrick, pretty wild that these two are getting married," Chelsea said as she motioned with her head at Rachel and Liam, who were happily seated across from them. He smiled and nodded. There was no sense in egging her on; he had no desire to get to know her, and he felt like this was a huge waste of time. A waste of both of their time.

Rachel looked at Liam, and he could see his brother shrug. Rachel's intentions were great, but Patrick would much rather be doing something else, anything else than sitting there, tucked into a booth at a restaurant in Spokane. He was thankful they suggested they go out of town to have dinner; he couldn't risk Amber seeing him with this beautifully blonde, tanned, beach babe. Granted, Amber and he had not made anything official or staked a claim on each other. Patrick just wanted to finish their food and head back home.

After dinner, they all rode together in Rachel's BMW, zipping around and exploring the busy downtown district. The tall and beautifully designed buildings shielded them from the early evening sunlight. Liam and Rachel decided it would be fun for them all to take a walk around Spokane's Riverfront Park. It was home to a raging river that could be watched from a bridge. It was a must-see for anyone visiting the area, and Rachel insisted they show Chelsea, who seemed fairly unimpressed.

The air was still rather hot, even though the sun had started to set; it had cooked the concrete city all day. The mist rising up for the water was a welcome relief as they stood gazing at the sheer force and power of the river.

"Pretty incredible, right?" Rachel commented in complete awe as she stood, her eyes fixed on the water.

Chelsea nodded and said, "But it's not the ocean, Rachel. Remember how crazy that would get? Especially if there was a storm coming."

The water was so loud, Patrick had a difficult time hearing Chelsea and Rachel, but that suited him just fine. He was eager to go home. His sister was keeping the boys overnight, which surprised him because she seemed a little irritated more than usual when he had asked her to babysit. Patrick was pretty sure it had something to do with Chelsea; the two just didn't click for some reason. Not that Patrick could blame his sister for being rubbed the wrong way by Chelsea; she was nice enough, but there was a terrible snottiness about her that didn't sit well with him. That's what made him adore Amber that much more. She was easygoing and was happy doing simple things. They had seen each other a couple times that week, the chemistry was growing between them, and they found it difficult not to be kissing or touching. They hadn't taken things to the next level yet, but Patrick's body was more than ready to. He craved physical contact with her. Whether it be his hands or mouth, he needed to touch her. Patrick had sent a text to Amber earlier that day, asking if they could get together later. She had finally agreed. Maybe tonight they would be able to explore their chemistry a little more.

"We probably should head home soon," Patrick announced to them.

Liam agreed and started to usher Rachel back toward the direction of where they had parked. Once inside the car, Chelsea, who was seated in the backseat alongside Patrick, leaned in closer to him. "It was nice going out tonight."

"Yeah, it was," Patrick lied and then continued, choosing his words carefully. It was best to get any notion of seeing him again out of her head. "I think you're really great, but I'm just not ready to really go out."

Chelsea pouted and placed her hand on his

khaki-clad thigh. "I think we could've had a lot of fun."

"I'm sorry, it just…"

She cut him off, quickly taking ownership of the conversation and removing her hand. "I know it has to be hard, because like, didn't your wife die or something?"

"Yes." Her voice annoyed him; her tone was dismissive and not genuine at all. He was eager to get home and hoped that the hour drive home went by quickly. He turned and looked out the window as the trees whizzed by, then threw a glance at Liam, who was driving. Patrick willed his brother to step on it.

***

Amber

It was nearly nine by the time Amber pulled into Patrick's driveway. She sat there for a minute after turning her car off. What was she even doing here? Of course she liked Patrick, a lot, in fact. But she had a feeling that tonight they were going to probably explore this whole thing, whatever it was, a little more. They had a spent a couple of dates together, mainly just going for a drive and then engaging in some heavy making out. Not that she minded; her lips had gone unkissed for about two years, and it felt wonderful being wanted and desired again. She just couldn't shake the feeling that she was somehow dishonoring Peter—it felt like borderline cheating. In her heart, she knew he would want her to love again and to be happy.

Amber was more than attracted to Patrick, but she just wanted to sort of know where this relationship was headed. He hadn't really suggested that they were going to be dating or become an actual couple, hell, she had no idea how this all worked, and she doubted that he did either.

Letting out a huge sigh, she gathered her inner strength to get out of the car. She had shaved her legs after all, so she knew very well what the plan was for tonight. She just hoped it was the right decision. *I guess I'll find out.*

She rang the doorbell, and Patrick opened the door after a minute or so. As he stood there, she felt her body warm. The length of his tall body filled the doorway, his black hair wet from showering, she could detect the light smell of soap and his aftershave, the one that made her crazy. His eyes, which were full of mischief as they scanned her body from head to toe, matched the sinfully sexy smile he greeted her with. He had all the looks of a man that had been waiting for his prey, hungry.

He didn't even utter a word; he just bent down and mashed his mouth on hers, taking what he had been waiting for.

Amber tried to catch her breath after he pulled away. "I'm glad you're here."

"Yeah, I can tell," Amber said as she licked her sensitive lips.

Amber followed Patrick inside. It was quiet. She had been told that his sister, Maggie, was keeping his twin boys for the night. Dylan was at home with her parents. He was playing a computer game she had just purchased for him, so she knew he was more than happy and wouldn't want her around. She swallowed hard; her mouth had gone dry. She was completely nervous.

Patrick placed his hands on her hips, guiding her closer to him. "I missed you."

They had just seen each other the other day, granted, but she thought about him every moment. Patrick captured her mouth once more with his, this time less gently and with far more need. She could hear him moan inside her mouth and could feel the tightness of his body as he brought her even closer to him.

"Amber, I swear, you have no clue what you do to me." His eyes were dark with lust, desire apparent on his face. He wanted her. Amber raised her hand to his jaw, tracing the outline of the black stubble covered skin. God, he was a sexy creature. The shade of his skin was slightly tanned from working outside in the elements, causing his already mesmerizing eyes to stand out even more. Her body was melting. If he tried taking her to his bedroom right now, she knew she wouldn't resist. She was half tempted to drag him there herself.

***

Patrick

God, he wanted her. Patrick couldn't escape the rush of desire that coursed through him, racing like a flash flood during rain season. His body was quickly losing control. He needed her more than anything. His brain was firing off instructions, telling him what he needed to do. It pleaded with him to haul her off into the bedroom and strip every last bit of fabric from her creamy skin. He grunted deeply as he grabbed her again. This time he wasn't going to be able to let her go.

They stood near the living room, just outside the entryway. Patrick looked over at the couches. Those were closest, but a bed would be so much better.

"Oh, Patrick, I think I need a little air." Amber whimpered against his chest, her breath ragged.

"No thinking right now. Only feeling." He possessed her mouth with his, probing deeper, tugging at her lips as he left her mouth. His hands began to roam her body, the swells and curves; he mapped them all out in his mind and desperately wanted to see them naked.

"Should we slow down?" Her pink lips were swollen and quivered as she spoke.

"No." Patrick couldn't. He needed her. He wanted to explore every last inch of flesh. He scooped her up and carried her to his bedroom. Amber clung onto him tightly, her teeth nipping softly at his neck, driving him to be more wild and reckless.

He gently put her on the bed as he went down with her, eliminating any space between them. Clothes were in the way of where his hands wanted to be. He loved the way she matched his desire. Equally hungry, they both began to shed their clothing. Patrick relished the silkiness of her body, his eyes eating her very being, all of her. Her body was plush and full, with rounded curves that begged to be grabbed and adored. He left her mouth and went in search of all her treasures. He wanted to discover what made her writhe on the mattress. He needed to learn everything about her, how to satisfy her, how to send her over the edge, and how to conquer her. Patrick wanted nothing more right then than for her to have this moment scorched on her brain. He knew he would never be able to forget.

***

Amber

Oh my God! Her body was on fire from the way Patrick touched her, kissed her body, and licked every inch of her skin. It was driving her mad. He caressed her one moment, would act wild with need the next, then he would go back to teasing her. He would play with her like she was clay, massaging and kneading her supple flesh. Patrick was wicked, and she was in more trouble than she could have ever possibly imagined. Her heart fluttered as she tried to close her eyes and feel all the ways he was loving her.

Moaning under his touch, Amber couldn't begin to sort out all the feelings her body was experiencing. She felt tremors of pleasure, which were brought on by Patrick worshipping her body in ways she hadn't known were possible. Every now and again Patrick would pause to look up at her, his green-eyed gaze connecting with her own, burning straight into her soul.

He seemingly wanted her to see what he was

doing to her, to watch her reaction to every possible sensation that he alone knew he was responsible for creating. Never in all her years would she have thought that she would be naked and under Patrick O'Brien, the most gorgeous man in all of Birch Valley.

She admired his naked body, the strong, hard, yet deliciously smooth muscles which covered and shaped his semi-lean form, the fine black hair that lightly covered him—all the makings of someone, who, in her opinion, should not be allowed to wear any clothes, ever. He should be walking around showing his gifts to the world. On second thought, he could just stay naked for her eyes alone.

Not one to be outdone, she turned the tables on Patrick, pushing him to the side of the large bed, where she then took control. Two could play this game, and that is what it had become—a lust-filled battle. She slithered along him, goose-pimpled flesh left in the wake of her traveling fingers. She treated each area that she kissed and nibbled on with the utmost care. He kept reaching for her, each time vying to be the winner of their game of seduction. Amber could hear him groan as her lips met the sensitive skin of his hip as she worked her way down his body, showering him with the same gratifying and torturous attention. She aimed to win, but Patrick was equally competitive, more than she realized as he maneuvered away and easily flipped her on her back. The white, flat sheet was now twisted around their legs, locking them together. Patrick pinned her, and time froze as he moved above her, hovering as he drank her in with his eyes.

Amber's hands were splayed against his back. She licked her lips as she saw the taut muscles of his flat stomach, his muscular chest and arms clenching slightly as he supported himself over her. Without hesitation, her body took over, passion seizing her at her very core as she wrapped her legs around him. A devilish smile played across his lips that seemed to say, *I won.*

***

Patrick

His arm was nearly numb as he spooned with Amber, but he didn't want to remove it. He inhaled the smell of her hair; it was light and fruity, simple and clean.

Their lovemaking had been intense, and they both were deeply exhausted. One thing that confused Patrick, as he basked in the afterglow, was how connected he had felt with her. It had been four years, four awful long years, without any type of intimacy. He wasn't sure if it was the lapse of time, or if there were anything real between him and Amber, but he couldn't help the waves of emotions that were surfacing. His brain was too busy trying to figure out how to handle this situation, because now he didn't know quite what to make of whatever their relationship was. Patrick wasn't all that sure he wanted to be in a relationship. The carnal need had been fulfilled, and he couldn't deny his attraction to her, but to try and love again, he wasn't so sure he could handle that.

He listened to the rhythm of her breathing; it was hypnotic and peaceful, and it stirred bits of leftover desire. He moved closer to her, wanting to steal more skin-to-skin contact. He gingerly kissed her exposed neck. As his eyes grew heavy and his brain finally tired, he let himself fall victim to sleep. But before he was completely gone, Patrick knew one thing for sure: he wanted more of Amber.

His eyes shot open in the dark room. Everything was black, and Patrick felt disoriented. His arm was wrapped securely over a body. *Beth?* His brain was confused and his thoughts muddy, as he whispered, "Beth?" There was silence, no response, then came the stirring of the figure next to him. Patrick switched on the small lamp on the nightstand next to his side of the bed and turned back to the body that was sharing his bed. His heart squeezed when he saw the dark tresses sprawled out on the pillow. His stomach dropped as he started to recall the events from earlier in the night. He was hit with a sudden sadness and guilt. For a brief second, he was certain it was Beth, that the last four years had merely been a nightmare. Reality burrowed into his mind and heart. No, Beth was still gone. The figure next to him turned over, looking up at him, and he saw eyes that didn't belong to Beth.

She smiled, but her brow twisted into confusion as she stared at him. "Patrick, are you okay?"

He was anything but. He felt hot tears pooling up in his eyes, and a hard lump formed in the back of his throat as he tried to swallow.

"Oh, Patrick." Amber sat up in the bed, letting the crisp white sheet fall from her nude body and pulled him to her. He resisted at first, but she tugged a little harder, and finally he allowed her to hold him.

The instant he nestled his head on her chest, breathing in her scent, he began to feel at ease. She rubbed his back tenderly, whispering soothing words, reassuring him that everything was going to be fine. But was it? Patrick wasn't so sure.

***

Amber

She held Patrick, smoothing her palm across his back in soft circles. Her heart broke for him. Amber was confused by this sudden outburst of emotion but then quickly realized he hadn't shared a bed with anyone since Beth's death. Not that Amber had either, but the toll it was taking on Patrick sent off warning signals in her brain. She knew they had moved too fast. It was one thing to kiss and share dinners; it was a whole different matter when sex was involved. When you share so much of yourself, you completely left yourself open and vulnerable. Maybe Patrick wasn't aware of that risk; maybe he didn't take in account the side effects of making love. Neither had shared any kind of love since they both were robbed of their soulmates, their lovers.

Amber closed her eyes. She felt lips moving along her collarbone, and then those kisses trailed down to her breasts, along with his large hands. Apparently Patrick had his own way of figuring things out. She just hoped they could figure this out together, that maybe he could acquire some sort of peace. Hell, Amber was still in shock herself. Once that passed and reality set in, who knew how she was going to react? She knew that, since the moment they'd met again, she felt herself drawn to him. She hated even daring to think that she might feel more deeply connected with Patrick than Peter, but it was almost cosmic, the way they'd found each other. Maybe she was just being swept away with all these new feelings that had been dormant for so long. Amber sighed, and she tried steering her mind away from overanalyzing things. Her body was too busy enjoying other sensations.

Gathering what bit of sense she still had, she pulled away from Patrick and stared into his shining, emerald eyes. "Patrick, we don't have to do this."

He lowered his mouth on hers, causing a deep warmth to spread through her. "Yes, we do."

Chapter Eleven

Rachel

Rachel could feel her tears threatening to spill over as she stared into the full-length mirror. She wasn't the only one. She stared at her reflection and could see Maggie, Mary, and Chelsea sitting behind her, each holding a tissue and dabbing their eyes, but the smiles that were plastered on their faces told her that the memory being made was a happy one. Her only regret was that her mother wasn't here to share in this. Rachel took a deep breath and saw the bride looking back at her in the mirror. The white gown she wore was classy, yet simple and understated—it was perfect.

She smoothed her hands over the fabric and turned around carefully to face Mary, Maggie, and Chelsea. "What do you guys think?"

This was Rachel's final fitting before the wedding that coming weekend. She was taking the week to get everything ready and was thankful that school was out for the summer so she could spare the time and attention to all the last-minute details.

"Rachel, love, you're beautiful," Mary said as she rose from her seat and came to the bride-to-be. She touched the dress and gathered Rachel into her arms. "My boy is so lucky."

"It's me who is lucky, Mary. Liam is the best thing in my life."

Maggie and Chelsea sat together. Neither one of them had spoken much to the other throughout the day; they were polite but hardly friendly. It bothered Rachel to see them at odds; she really had hoped the two could get along and actually become friends. Rachel loved Chelsea but knew that she could come off as a tad too much, but she had a heart of gold. As for Maggie, Rachel had felt an instant connection with her after they shared that impromptu cooking lesson with Mary. Now with them both pregnant and Rachel marrying Liam, they were more than friends; they were family.

"It's gorgeous," Maggie commented and rose from her spot and came over to Rachel, standing next to Mary. Chelsea stood up, looking slightly pouty as she went to stand on the opposite side of Rachel.

Rachel could see them all in mirror, smiling at her. Her brain was taking mental snapshots of the occasion. Again, she couldn't help but wish her mother had been there. Not that she was terribly close with Evelyn; it was more the principle of the matter—the fact that this moment should be shared between a mother and daughter.

"You are a vision, dear. This dress couldn't be more perfect," Mary commented as she stepped aside to let the saleswoman place a veil on Rachel's head.

"Veil or no veil?" Rachel asked the ladies. She wasn't so sure she liked it; she worried it made the dress more formal.

"I think it's lovely," Mary quickly replied.

Maggie and Chelsea both looked hard at Rachel and said in unison, "No veil." That's why she was happy to have them here, not that Mary's opinion wasn't great, but she was far more traditional, whereas Chelsea and Maggie were younger, more modern, and they knew what type of look Rachel was aiming for.

"Really, girls?" Mary asked as she fluffed the veil, spreading the thin, delicate white material out. "I think it makes her look like an angel."

"Well, that's pretty much a given, and we all know Rachel, don't we? Hardly an angel," Chelsea teased. Rachel playfully turned to slap at her. "See what I mean?" Everyone laughed and crowded around the bride-to-be.

"Thanks, guys, it means so much to have you here with me." Rachel developed tears in her eyes again, this time from laughing and being surrounded by people who loved her. Mary, Maggie, and Chelsea gathered her into a hug. How was she going to handle her wedding day? She now knew she was going to be a blubbering mess.

***

Rachel had a piece of ranch-covered lettuce in her mouth and almost choked on her salad when

Chelsea asked, "So are we going to have a bridal shower for Rachel? I mean, what about wedding night lingerie?"

Maggie winked and said, "I think whatever she wore last time worked."

"Oh God, stop you two!" Rachel cried in utter embarrassment. She could feel her cheeks grow warm. Mary gave her a knowing look that said it all.

"Well, Maggie actually has a point," Chelsea replied as she forked a small bite of salad into her mouth.

"I'm just teasing." Maggie patted Rachel's hand across the table.

They'd gone to eat at a gorgeous Italian place in downtown Spokane, which was only a few miles from the bridal shop. They were seated outside, enjoying the warmth and sunshine of the midafternoon sun. Chelsea was enjoying a glass of wine, which made both Rachel, and probably Maggie, a little jealous.

"Well, I'm not," Chelsea said firmly. She took a long sip of her wine, looking a little too hard at Rachel, which made her shift uncomfortably in her seat. "If you were in Newport, you know what kind of bridal shower we would've had." Rachel sighed. She knew it would be some grand affair, but if she had been in Newport, she wouldn't be marrying Liam.

Rachel sent Chelsea a warning glare as she felt both Mary's and Maggie's eyes on her. "I guess we can have a little wedding shower, but honestly, I would much rather save it for the baby shower."

"Babies," Mary corrected with a happy smile.

Rachel nodded and started to rub her belly under the table. It was still semi-flat, but she knew there was not one, but two lives growing in there. "Exactly, it's not like Liam and I need anything for our wedding."

Chelsea rolled her eyes. "A wedding is a big deal, Rachel."

"So is having a baby, let alone twins," Maggie added with a little more attitude than necessary.

Rachel watched as tempers started to flare. Mary looked over at her, her eyes pleading.

Chelsea snarled back, "Well, being a bride is something that a little girl plans for and dreams of about her whole life. So this is really the more important day."

"Really? Because why do you suppose those same little girls play with baby dolls? Because we all dream of being a mommy," Maggie shot back.

Chelsea huffed. "I'm just saying that Rachel deserves to have a bridal shower and that if she lived back home, she would've had one. A fabulous one."

"Yes, that might be so, but she's not back home, she's here."

Rachel felt her nerves tightening. She didn't like them fighting over her like this. This game of tug-of-war made her feel lousy. "Guys, please just stop." Rachel turned to Chelsea, who wore an irritated scowl on her otherwise smooth and perfectly made-up face. "Chelsea, I know you mean well. Honestly, this whole marriage and motherhood thing has happened so fast, I hadn't even thought about either shower. I have been so focused on just finishing up the school year, not throwing up, and planning this wedding before everyone sees this baby bump. It sort of slipped my mind." She then turned her focus on Maggie. "Mags, we're lucky, we get to both be pregnant at the same time, but I think Chelsea was just looking out for me and making sure that we celebrate me being a bride too. We did always talk about our wedding plans as kids."

Maggie looked over at her mother and then focused on the distance, pretending to be distracted by it. Rachel could see the anger rising in her green eyes; she had seen that same anger in Liam's before. The O'Brien shade of green would grow dark and piercing. The O'Briens all wore their emotions in the eyes, whether it be happiness, anger, sadness, or desire.

"You're right, Rachel. This is supposed to be about you, and you just need to tell us what you want or need," Maggie finally uttered, still not making eye contact.

"Oh, dear, you girls just need to knock off all this silliness. Chelsea, we all know that you miss your best friend, and for you, love, I'm sorry. As for my daughter, Rachel has become her friend too, so it's hard when the first friend comes along and has different ideas or plans. But we must bear in mind that it's Rachel who you both care for. So, let's compromise. Rachel, how about a fun bridal shower brunch?" Mary offered.

"Oh, Mary, I'm getting married in a week. That's not enough time to plan for that."

Mary's tone was sugary sweet but almost

intimidating. "Rachel, my sweet, do you not recall when you moved up and took Mr. Anderson's place at the school? Did you forget how quickly Karen and I, and even you, got that cafeteria looking like one of the best retirement parties in all of Birch Valley? Don't worry about time to plan, dear. You leave that to us."

***

Liam

"What do you mean her mom and dad aren't coming? You can't be serious," Daniel exclaimed loudly. Liam and his brothers were sitting out by his lake, fishing. None of them had caught anything, except for a light buzz from the partially warm beer they had been drinking in the sun for several hours.

"I know, right?" Liam responded as he cast his line out into the water. "I think it will just be nice when this whole wedding business is over and done with."

Patrick shook his head. He was now seated in a forest green, canvas camp chair, his fishing pole tucked loosely in his hand. He had just put the twins down for a nap, and things were finally quiet. He could enjoy some down time with Liam and Daniel.

It had been a guys' day, but with two little boys added to the mix, that made things interesting. More talk about dinosaurs and trains than women. Now that Finn and Connor were sleeping, Patrick and the others could talk about women, and Daniel had wasted no time. Just moments ago he had pestered

Patrick about dating, saying that they should see if the Belsky sisters might be up for going out.

"Yeah, what's the deal with her family? Are you sure this is something you want to get roped into?" Patrick asked as he stared out at the water. The lake had the look of dark glass today, and it mirrored the cloudless, bright sky, as well as the pines and tamaracks. When they cast their fishing lines out, gentle circles rippled on the surface of the water, but there was no other activity.

"Well, to be completely honest with you guys, her parents sound kind of snotty and more concerned with their own lives. But her brother is coming up in a couple days, so he can't be that bad. At least he'll be here for her. As for getting roped in, yes, Patrick, I'm ready to be hog-tied."

"Not the least bit surprised." Patrick grinned at him and went back to viewing the water.

The whole thing pissed Liam off. He hated seeing Rachel upset and stressed out. The wedding was meant to be a ceremony of love. He was thankful that his family had pretty much adopted Rachel, and so she felt loved by everyone, especially his mother. She had become fast friends with his sister, and now with both of them pregnant, they were always hanging out. Even today, she had taken his mother and sister with her and Chelsea to pick up her wedding dress. Liam and his brothers had taken the opportunity to spend some quality time together. Unfortunately, Michael was busy with a small case he had agreed to take on, and Melanie was feeling a bit under the weather, so Michael had stayed home to work and take care of his daughter. But it was great when all of them were hanging out. He couldn't ask for a better group of guys to have in his corner.

"It just seems a little weird, like imagine if our mom and dad refused to go. So what's her brother like?" Daniel sent his line out into the water again. It was obvious he was growing frustrated.

"Yeah, we know her taste in friends isn't so great," Patrick commented snidely as he took another swig from his bottle.

"Chelsea's not that bad," Liam said, defending her as he took a sip out of his own bottle and tried to hide the smirk on his lips.

"She kind of is. A real snob," Daniel added.

Liam sighed. They were right. Chelsea wasn't his favorite person. His sister had her own soiled opinion of Chelsea, and that didn't help matters. Liam tended to side with Maggie on a lot of issues. It had even been a sore spot between him and Rachel a couple of times. But Maggie was his baby sister, and he was used to protecting her. Now, with Rachel in the picture, he found he had to learn to balance it out a bit more.

Daniel turned toward Patrick and Liam and said, "But, Patrick, you actually went out with her."

"Uh, no, forced to go to dinner is more like it," Patrick quickly replied and raised his bottle.

"I didn't get asked to go. How come, Liam?" Daniel pretended to pout and bat his eyelashes.

"Really, Daniel. That's why right there, you goofball." All three brothers started to laugh.

The air was a little too warm, the fish weren't interested in any of their bait, and now that the beer was gone, they were finally tired of fighting the mosquitoes.

"Time to call it in," Liam announced as he started to grab some of the gear.

"Yeah, I need to get the boys home," Patrick said. He folded up his chair.

"Hey, Liam, do you think after you're married…we can still hang out like this?" Daniel asked. Liam looked at him. His brother seemed so young and almost sad. Liam sometimes forgot that his brother didn't have a girlfriend or someone to spend his time with. He relied on his brothers for company and friendship.

"Of course, it's not like I'm moving or going anywhere. Besides this is the best lake in the area for fishing," Liam reassured him.

"Yeah, you can tell by our haul today, real plentiful," Patrick teased as he grabbed Daniel's shoulder and gave it a squeeze. Liam could see that Patrick also sensed their brother's loneliness.

Liam loved being able to spend time with his family, especially his brothers. He couldn't imagine ever moving away. He often wondered how Rachel had been able to. To leave your family and set off in an unknown area, not knowing a soul—that took some guts. Thinking more about her family, he felt the nagging irritation rising inside of him again. He hoped that her brother, Ethan, was a cool guy. At least he was willing to come up and support Rachel. Liam knew that Ethan was less than thrilled that his sister had left, gotten pregnant, and now was getting married. He knew that if Maggie had pulled that same stunt, he'd be a little mad. Oh, that's right,

Maggie had done the same exact thing. Maybe that's what little sisters did.

***

Rachel

The BMW quietly hummed along the highway. There was little to no traffic after they left Spokane. No one was really talking, and the tension in the car made Rachel nervous, making it difficult to concentrate on driving. Mary and Maggie sat in the back, each gazing out their small windows. Chelsea had her arms folded across her chest and appeared to be pouting.

Rachel thought lunch had gone badly, but that was nothing compared to when they decided to go shopping at a couple of stores for some last-minute ideas for the decorations. Rachel was game for the fun suggestions from Mary and Maggie; Chelsea was not. She ran her mouth a bit too far, claiming that the ideas were tacky and just plain horrid, and how could anyone even consider them? It was probably best that Rachel failed to mention that they were going to be using hay bales for the seating at the altar. Rachel found it to be quite charming—a country wedding in the evening. She had visions of mason jars filled with tea light candles, strings of white lights in the trees and around the deck, and at the tables there would be the beautiful floral centerpieces with red, white, and blue dyed roses that she had already ordered. She tried to convince Chelsea of how lovely and simple it was all going to be. But her friend wasn't having it and broke down into a miniature tantrum. Rachel had been shocked; Chelsea wasn't acting like herself at all. That wasn't how her best friend of almost twenty-five years acted. What was going on with her bestie?

"How much further?" Chelsea asked quietly. Her friend wasn't known for being silent, and Rachel knew that the lack of speaking had to be killing her.

"We're almost home," Rachel lied. They were still a good thirty minutes away.

Mary's eyes connected with Rachel's in the rearview mirror, and Rachel offered her a weak smile. What was she supposed to do? Chelsea had been her friend since they were little kids. Granted, that didn't give her the right to belittle or insult Maggie, or especially Mary, who took the brunt of Chelsea's earlier explosion. Something was definitely going on with her friend. Maybe it was all too much, knowing that Rachel was getting married and having babies, all things that Chelsea was certain she would do first. For the most part, through their entire friendship, Chelsea was the first one who was willing to try anything. Not Rachel. Her overly cautious nature kept her out of trouble. That was, until she moved away and met Liam. The rest of the drive consisted of Rachel getting random glances from everyone in the car. There were a lot of scowls, and they were all pointed at her. How could she fix this? Her wedding was coming up quicker than she imagined, and to make things more complicated, she needed all of their help to decorate and set up everything, and that meant they would have to work together. If that wasn't enough, her brother was flying in and she was insanely worried about how he was going to behave. Ethan was a pretty intense guy, and knowing that he wasn't so happy about the whole married and pregnant thing, she feared how he and Liam would get along. To top it off, she still wasn't sure if her own parents were going to come up for the ceremony. She had little hope that they would, but miracles did happen. Adding to her list of impossible things to get through during the week, she had an ultrasound at the start of it. Mary and Maggie were there last time. Considering how today went, she doubted it was a very good idea to have all these women in the same room, especially one as cramped as that one.

This whole wedding could turn into a giant disaster, and now Rachel wished they had just eloped. Vegas would have been fantastic. The wedding jitters she didn't think she'd have? Well, they had taken root and were growing stronger by the minute.

Chapter Twelve

Amber

Amber was chatting with two customers who had quickly become her favorites. They were two women, best friends, and the funniest ladies in all of Birch Valley. She had learned their names only a couple days prior—Donna and Andrea. They had been coming to the diner every morning, insisting on their coffee, also affectionately referring to it as "survival juice," since it was made a little hotter than how it was normally served, and they ate basically the same breakfast every day. Amber got the biggest kick from the jokes that they shared with her. They sat in the same spot at the counter. It gave them a perfect view of anyone entering the diner, which they quickly gossiped about. That morning, the mailman came in, and the ladies went on for about twenty minutes after he had left about his legs and how he looked in his uniform. Amber had never laughed so hard or enjoyed customers as much as these two fabulously entertaining women.

Hearing the chime of the bell hanging on the tired weathered string, Amber glanced up. In walked Patrick and who she believed was his brother and Maggie. Her belly started to flip flop. She hadn't seen Patrick for a couple days, and she was starting to miss him, terribly. She quickly grabbed three menus and trailed behind them as they headed for a booth near one of the windows. Patrick's eyes met hers. He looked almost scared to see her, and that confused Amber. Because they hadn't seen each other for a couple of days, self-doubt was settling in all of a sudden, but he had sent her a couple of text messages. Were all her fears coming true? Was Patrick now realizing that sleeping together that night had been a colossal mistake?

As she watched them slide into their seats, she avoided Patrick's eyes. She had seen his dart away too, and that was not a good sign.

"Hi, what can I get you guys to drink?" Amber asked, her voice coming out a tad wobblier than she had hoped. She tried clearing her throat.

"Hey, Amber, how's it going?" Maggie smiled brightly at her.

"Great." She kept her response short. She just wanted to get their drink order and then have her mother or another waitress take their table.

Maggie nodded. "Glad to hear that. You know, I think I will have the lemonade. I've been craving it."

Daniel laughed and looked up at Amber. He had the same green eyes; they twinkled with a happy glow. "I'll just have an iced tea. So obviously you

151

know my sister. Thanks, Mags, for introducing me, by the way," he teased playfully as he turned around to look at Maggie, who was tucked in next to him by the window. "I'm Daniel." He waited for her to say something, and her mind froze for a brief second. Feeling Patrick's presence was creating a stormy cloud of confusion.

"Amber."

"Well, Amber, it's really nice to meet you. Are you new here?" he asked, the twinkle in his eyes growing brighter with interest. Amber surveyed his joyful face. His coloring was closer to Mary's, and even Maggie's. He looked nothing like Patrick, except for his eyes.

"Actually…" As Amber was answering, Maggie quickly cut her off.

"Nope, her parents are the Herricks. She's been here now for a couple weeks, right?"

Amber nodded. She snuck a glance at Patrick, who smiled politely and looked out the window. This was so incredibly awkward. Amber wanted to run and hide.

"Well, that's great. So you work here then?" Daniel continued to question her, prolonging their conversation far longer than Amber would have preferred.

"Yep, just helping out for a while. Let me get those drinks for you guys. I'll be right back." She had no intentions of coming back to their table. She hoped that her mother or the other waitress on shift could take it. As she moved to leave, she caught a glimpse of Patrick looking at her from the corner of his eye. Why was he acting this way?

***

Patrick

He felt like the biggest jerk, ignoring her like that. He just couldn't risk Maggie or Daniel finding out just how serious he was with Amber. Patrick watched her walk away—more like run and hide. He doubted she would even come back to the table, and he sort of wished that she wouldn't.

"Wow, she's cute," Daniel declared as his stare followed Amber.

"She's pretty nice too. Rachel and I got to talk to her one time when we were in here with Mom." Maggie looked at Patrick, studying him. "You acted a little rude, though."

"I wasn't being rude. You guys were talking to her," Patrick replied, again looking out the window at the sparse traffic in order to avoid eye contact.

"Well, I think you were. But whatever." Maggie huffed with mild aggravation and then turned to Daniel. "You should ask her out, Daniel."

That got Patrick's attention, and apparently Maggie noticed too. "What do think, Patrick? Should our darling Daniel ask her out?"

Daniel's face lit up, and that made Patrick feel even more like a jerk. "Should I?"

"I don't know, man. She does have a kid," Patrick said, trying to sound nonchalant about the whole matter when a bite of jealousy started to chew at him.

"Why would that matter?" Daniel questioned him as his eyes sought out Amber.

Maggie cocked her head to the side. "Patrick, just how do you know that?"

Patrick swallowed. He had to think quickly. "I think Mom might have mentioned it."

"Hmm…I don't think so," Maggie pressed him. She clearly knew something was up.

Right as she opened her mouth to say something, their drinks arrived, and they weren't brought by Amber.

"Here you go. Who had the lemonade?" It was Lynn Herrick, Amber's mother. Patrick could see the resemblance, though Lynn had a mixture of gray hair and a couple extra pounds.

"I did, thank you." Maggie raised her hand and then glared at Patrick.

Lynn passed out the last two drinks to Daniel and Patrick. "Do you know what you'd like yet, or do you need a little more time?" she offered sweetly.

"I'm ready to order. Are you guys?" Maggie looked at her brothers. They both nodded. "Okay, well I think I will just take the chicken salad, and…" She flipped the menu over and debated out loud so that everyone heard her. "You know what, can I also get an order of onion rings? They sound really good right now."

"No problem, honey, and they are good any time." Lynn laughed as she turned to Daniel, her order-taking pad ready. "What about you, sweetie?"

"Well, Lynn, I think I will take my usual." Daniel didn't even bother looking at the menu.

"Okay, patty melt then, you want the regular fries, or seasoned today?"

"Surprise me." He winked at her.

Patrick rolled his eyes. His brother could be such a ham. In mid eyeroll, Lynn turned to him, her face a little less happy. "And for you?" Her tone was polite but definitely not her usual playful and sweet self.

"I'll just have what Daniel's having, I guess."

"Okie dokie." She smiled as she turned and left with their orders, but Patrick knew that Lynn must know something. He hadn't considered that Amber might tell people, since they had been sort of seeing each other.

"Okay, something is up," Maggie said. She shook her finger at Patrick. "Lynn is always sweet as pie to you guys. What is going on?"

"Did you go out with Amber or something? Because Mags is right. You acted kind of weird," Daniel added, his tone cool and slightly aloof.

Patrick sipped on his drink, his brain trying to conjure up a plausible lie. "Um, no, I ran into her a while back. She had a blown tire." Best not to lie. His siblings could smell out a fib, but he could afford to not divulge all the details of the last couple of weeks.

"Yeah, really?" Daniel asked. "I don't recall you mentioning that before."

"Why would I?" Patrick snapped.

"Because that's what we do. We talk and share things that go on in our lives, like when we meet people, especially really friggin' hot ones. Sorry, Mags." Daniel was starting to turn a light shade of red, his anger apparent on his pale skin.

"Look, that's part of the problem with this family. No one minds their own damn business."

"Oh, please, are we bringing that up again, Patrick?" Maggie hissed.

"What, having you guys pry into my life isn't enough reason for me to not want to tell you guys every last detail of who I run into or who I meet?"

Maggie's glare burned him. "Patrick, you don't get it. We are a family, and members of a family share what is going on in their lives. You try so hard to push us away, and honestly, I'm tired of it. I get that you have been through some stuff, pretty damn bad stuff, but you aren't the only one."

Daniel raised his eyebrows. Patrick could tell his brother agreed with her but was a little shocked by the confrontation that was brewing. "Come on, you guys. Oh, look, food's coming."

Lynn balanced the plates on her arms with a skill that only came from years of practice. She placed each one in front of them. Patrick was shocked to see that his patty melt and fries were noticeably smaller than Daniel's. She bent down toward Patrick's ear and whispered, "Don't hurt my daughter again."

Wow. Well, at least he knew it hadn't been his imagination that Lynn was upset with him. Patrick sighed. He needed to talk to Amber and soon. As much as he would love to jump up and go to her now, he couldn't.

"Well, looks like you got what you deserved for just changing a tire," Maggie added as she nibbled on a crusty onion ring.

Daniel focused on his patty melt. He clearly wasn't comfortable when any of them fought. He never really started arguments and sure didn't enjoy being a spectator at them either.

"Maggie, just eat your salad." Patrick pulled the older sibling rank on her. He wasn't in the mood to keep fighting with her. He just wanted to eat his stupid patty melt, get back to the shop, and then figure out a way to fix things with Amber. He hoped it wasn't too late.

***

Amber

"Mom, it's fine. I'm okay, I promise," Amber begged, hoping her mother would stop talking about Patrick.

"Well, I think it's wrong. Why would he act like that? Patrick's a good guy."

"Mom, it's nothing, honestly," Amber tried to explain as she swept the tile floor of the kitchen. They had closed the diner about thirty minutes ago, and she just wanted to finish cleaning it so she could get home to Dylan. She had been feeling as though she hadn't spent enough time with him, between working at the diner and spending time with Patrick. She knew that her schedule was going to be a lot more open now. She wasn't going to be ignored or be treated like she didn't exist. His treatment of her this afternoon had hurt. She didn't know what to expect, but having him pretend that he didn't see her or that they hadn't been together, to act like that in front of his family, had just rubbed her the wrong way. Maybe Patrick O'Brien wasn't as fantastic as she thought he was.

"You ready to go then?" her mother asked.

"I will finish up here in a few and ride my bike. You really should check on Dad." Amber frowned. That hadn't been going well either, and Patrick had been a nice diversion from all the other pressing issues in her life.

"Okay, sweetie." Lynn hugged her. "Don't let that boy get to you. Best to know what kind of guy he is now, before you get too involved or bring Dylan around him."

"I know." Amber hung her head, focusing on a chipped section of tile, silently pleading with the build-up of tears to hold on until her mother left.

"See you at home." Lynn left through the front door, and the bell chimed, echoing in the empty, dark diner.

As soon as Amber confirmed that her mother had driven off, she plopped down in a booth and held her head in her hands. The tears finally came. They weren't gentle streams; no, these were raging rivers of angry, ugly tears. Amber felt suddenly dirty and just angry with herself. Why did she sleep with Patrick? Granted, it was some of the hottest and best lovemaking, if you could even call it that, but it was so much more than that. It was a grief-driven, soul-shattering, lust-propelling type of sex. With unstable combo, it's no surprise that someone would end up getting hurt. Considering all the emotions that were expressed just in that single night, what did she expect? Maybe he was a good guy, someone who could teach her that it was okay to love again. She thought she had found that with him. It has been difficult to move past the line she had felt she had crossed even being with Patrick; it felt almost like she had cheated on Peter. Why did Peter have to die? He should be here with her and Dylan. Life was so unfair.

Wiping the tears away from her cheeks with a defiant swipe, she tried to catch her breath and pull herself together. She had survived far worse than anything Patrick had dished out. She was stronger than she often gave herself credit for. Amber lived through a husband being killed, having to raise their son single handedly, and coming home to find her father practically dying. Having Patrick act like they didn't share one of the most incredible nights of her life, that was so minuscule. She would be able to get past this; she'd find her footing again and carry on, like she always did. She was a Herrick, and they were not ones to lie down and take it. The world had given them their fair share of hard blows, trying to knock them down, yet they were still standing.

Amber shook off the rampant torrent of emotions and finished up. She wheeled her green bicycle out of the diner, then locked the heavy, glass door. She inhaled the appealing scents of summer night-time, the warm residue of pines that had been cooked all day from the searing sun, the smells of grass which had been mowed in the evening, and the delicate aroma of the flowers hanging in large baskets all through town, permeated the air. She looked up toward the sky, her eyes focused on the outline of the mountains that surrounded Birch Valley, their shadowy figures protecting the tiny community. She had to admit, she did love it here. It had a simple, understated beauty. She just wished that Peter was here to enjoy it with her. As she spoke to God, in her mind, she thought she heard her name. She spun around and quickly realized who had called her name. It was Patrick O'Brien. He was leaning on his car, his long body angled in a way that she hated herself for being attracted to.

"What do you want?" Amber asked as she stood firmly, squaring her shoulders, and holding onto her bike for support. Her knees were turning into jelly; no surprise there, that was how her body reacted when she was around him. It didn't matter if he was twenty feet or two feet away; the result was always the same. Right now, she hated herself for being so easily affected and hated him for just being so damn sexy.

"Amber, I want to talk about today." His eyes pleaded for her to listen. "I want to apologize. The way I acted was just terrible. I was a complete jerk."

"That's one word I would use to describe how you acted." Amber put one hand on her hip, giving him a hard look.

He went to her, towering over her by almost a foot. He bent to place his forehead on her head, connecting them softly. "I'm sorry."

"You should be." She could feel her resolve breaking away.

"Forgive me?" Patrick's eyes met hers. His lips pouted in a way that was hard to resist. God, she hated him right now. Amber wanted to stay angry; she didn't want to crave his lips on hers or imagine his hands on her body.

"Patrick, we need to really discuss why you treated me like you didn't know me in front of your family," Amber demanded.

"It's sort of a long story. But I just didn't want them involved in my business," Patrick answered. He traced the side of her cheek with his hand. "I'm sorry, I really am. I should have explained all that to you. You didn't deserve what happened today. It's my issue, not yours."

"But Patrick, they are your family. I mean, why wouldn't you want them to know what's going on in your life? I told my mom I was sort of dating you."

"Is that what we're doing? Dating?" Patrick eyed her playfully.

"Well, we were. Now I'm not so sure. I mean, I have met your sister. She's nice. Daniel, he seems super friendly."

Patrick smirked and rolled his eyes. "Yeah, he was almost going to ask you out."

"Well, maybe he should have," she snapped. "At least he wouldn't be so shy to introduce me to the family, or maybe he wouldn't act ashamed of me when they are around. Unlike another O'Brien boy that I know, and even slept with, possibly even started to really care about," Amber spat. She didn't know what had come over her. One moment she was almost bending to his will, the next she felt fiery and angry again.

"Amber, I'm sorry. I'm not ashamed of you. You're wonderful." Patrick brushed his lips along her neck. "You're right about everything. I guess I wanted to keep this to myself a little longer. Trust me, I think about you all the time. I just wanted to…"

161

"See how it all played out? I mean, I get that. I'm not asking for you to pledge your undying love to me, nor am I even asking to be invited over for dinner at your family's house. It would have been nice for you to have acknowledged me, that's all." Amber tried to back away. She needed a little space so she could think.

"I know, again, you win. I don't want to fight." Patrick seized the moment when she wasn't speaking, took hold of her head, and planted a firm kiss on her lips.

Amber instantly felt her body flood with desire; she felt it betray her as she heard herself moan into his mouth. His hands ran along her back as he pulled her closer and deepened the kiss. It was like he was making love to her mouth, taking possession, and marking her as his own. Patrick wanted all of her, and she was gladly giving it to him. She felt herself release her grasp on her bicycle and heard it fall to the ground.

God, not only did she hate him right now, but herself too.

Chapter Thirteen

Rachel

"Remember, this might be a little cold, dear," the nurse said as she applied the jelly to Rachel's stomach.

Rachel grimaced as the nurse moved the ultrasound wand over her, pushing a little too hard for Rachel's liking, onto her stomach. She looked over and saw Chelsea mesmerized by the grainy images that started to appear on the tiny monitor. Rachel tilted her head up and smiled at Liam.

The sound of two fluttering heartbeats echoed loudly in the room. Chelsea's face went bright with wonder. "Oh my God, is that them?"

Liam and Rachel nodded. The nurse smiled as well and continued to roll the wand over Rachel, probing further into her skin. The discomfort almost made Rachel's eyes water, but watching the two little beans on the screen wiggle and dance was well worth it.

After several minutes of the nurse taking

163

measurements, tapping away at a keyboard entering the data, she grinned happily. "Well, I will get Dr. Salinger to come in and visit with you for the rest of your checkup." The nurse excused herself, leaving the door slightly open.

"That was so cool, you guys." Chelsea squealed. "It really makes it seem, well, real, I guess." She laughed.

"I know, that's how it was when we came in last time. It made me realize that they were really in there." Rachel could feel the tears burning in her eyes. *Pregnancy hormones are the best. I love feeling overly emotional all day long,* she thought sarcastically.

Chelsea stood up and walked over to Rachel, who was lying down, her belly still half exposed as she tried to cover up with the paper blanket. Chelsea wrapped her tan, thin arms across Rachel's chest. "I'm so happy for you."

"Thanks, Chelsea." Rachel squeezed her back.

Chelsea moved over to Liam and threw her arms around him. "I know I haven't been the easiest to get along with…"

Liam cut her off. "No, Chelsea, it's okay. It has to be difficult, I mean, losing Rachel. I couldn't imagine her moving away. So I know that has been hard on you. She's your best friend. You guys are as close as sisters."

"Liam, I appreciate you understanding, but that doesn't give me a right to act the way I do. I really am happy for both of you, and you guys are going to be great parents."

"Thanks, that means a lot," Liam replied, kissing

Chelsea on top of her head, treating her like she was part of their family. The simple gesture of kindness warmed Rachel. They were her two favorite people, and she just wanted them to get along.

"Can you believe we've got a wedding to get ready for in, like, a couple days?" Chelsea cried. Her smooth and perfect face was genuinely happy. This was the first time she felt that Chelsea was genuinely thrilled for her.

They heard a soft knock at the door; Dr. Salinger peeked in from the other side.

"Hi, Rachel and Liam." Her smile was a little too big for her face, her black hair always in a tight knot. Her blue eyes shone as she greeted them. "I'm Doctor Salinger." She extended her thin arm and petite hand to Chelsea.

"I'm Chelsea, Rachel's best friend. I'm visiting from California."

"Well, pleasure to meet you, Chelsea."

Turning her attention back to Rachel, she asked, "How have you been feeling, lady?"

Rachel had been starting to form a friendship with Dr. Mallory Salinger. They'd run into each other at the only grocery store and hit it off. Rachel learned that Mallory was from southern California as well, and her story was very similar to her own. Mallory had left because the rat race had grown to be far too much, and she found herself in Birch Valley completely by accident. She had been on her way to Canada to visit a close friend, who had moved to Grand Forks. Mallory had considered flying but decided she needed a real vacation, and what was better than a road trip? On her way to

Grand Forks, she passed through the rural town of Birch Valley. Instantly, she fell in love with the charming old buildings and the friendly community. Never in a million years would she have thought she would find herself in such a place. On her way back from her visit, she ran into a bit of car trouble and ended up having to stay the night. That changed everything; her whole life had been steered in a different direction. She learned that the town was in desperate need for another OBGYN, and she fit the bill. But did she dare consider leaving everything in Los Angeles to come up to a town in the middle of nowhere, knowing absolutely no one? Yes, because Mallory had been in search of something, just as Rachel had been. Now the two were forming a fast friendship. They'd exchanged numbers and planned on having lunch together.

"I feel pretty good, not really sick anymore," Rachel answered.

"How about movement?" Dr. Salinger looked over at her and then Liam.

"Sort of, I mean, I usually think it's gas or something else. It's not like I'm getting strong kicks or anything."

"Well, it's still early, but I just want you to try and be aware of any changes. The kicks will get more noticeable. Thinking that it's gas, completely normal. Everyone tends to think it is, especially this early on." She smiled at Rachel and Liam. Her demeanor was calm; she exuded a sense of serenity and was just plain mellow. Rachel considered for a moment that her new friend and doctor must be doing yoga or something to keep her this eerily calm.

Dr. Salinger turned her attention to the computer that was to side of Rachel. As she sat on the stool, she read out her findings. "So, by looking at some the results here from the ultrasound, things are progressing nicely. Both babies seem to be around the same size, heart rate is good, fluid looks fantastic." She then grabbed a cardboard wheel with a bunch of dates on it.

"What's that for?" Chelsea asked. Her curiosity always had her asking questions.

"This..." Dr. Salinger held up the cardboard disc. "This is a way for us to track her due date. Basically, we use it to show the date of the last period, then I like to go back after an ultrasound and compare the findings, to see if the size and the date match up," she explained. "In Rachel's case, I'm seeing that her due date and the size of the babies are following pretty close together. So we are still looking at a tentative due date of November, still unsure on the exact day. Babies love to come when they are ready."

"So November still? Great," Liam said. "I think Maggie is due in late September or something, right?" He looked down at Rachel.

"I think so. She's already getting huge," Rachel commented.

"Well, you will too. Give it time." Dr. Salinger laughed.

"Oh, I almost forgot, I wanted to invite you to our wedding. I know you and I discussed it the other night when I called you. Do you think you will be free for the Fourth of July?" Rachel asked sweetly. She really liked Mallory and wanted to make her feel included. After all, she knew what being an outsider, especially from California, felt like. This would give Mallory the opportunity to meet more people and to celebrate the Fourth.

Dr. Salinger squinted up toward the ceiling. It looked as though she was looking through some mental planner, seeing if her schedule was open. "Yeah, I think I might be on call for the hospital that night, but who am I kidding, I'm always on call."

"We are having the ceremony and reception at our home. We live about five miles out of town. You could give the hospital our land line number so that they can reach you," Liam suggested as he stroked Rachel's arm. She loved how he made her feel so cherished and cared for, and he even was trying to convince her new friend to attend their wedding. This guy was too good to her.

"Yeah, they sort of need to reach me on my cell, but thanks for the offer."

That's when Liam, Rachel, and Chelsea laughed. The service was terrible out at Liam's property. Chelsea had been complaining nonstop about it since she arrived. Rachel had learned to live with it being so awful, relying on their landline more than her cell.

Dr. Salinger frowned. "Well, I will try to go out there, even if for just a little while."

"Great, I will call you later with the details. My brother, Ethan, he'll be there. He's an ER doctor," Rachel babbled. She wasn't quite sure what made her tell Mallory about Ethan. She'd already said she would try to make it; Rachel didn't need to sweeten the deal more by adding her brother.

"Oh, really? He's from California too?"

"Yes, he lives near me actually," Chelsea piped in. She had always been a little obsessed with Rachel's brother. The two had even attempted to date, but Ethan just wasn't into Chelsea; he looked at her more like a little sister. Rachel couldn't blame him; they had all sort of grown up together and had had same circle of wealthy friends.

"Well, that's great. Yeah, I'm from Los Angeles," Dr. Salinger added. She gave Chelsea a soft look.

"Really? How did you end up here?" Chelsea's arms motioned all around them, and she crinkled her face.

"It's not that bad. I actually love it here," Dr. Salinger answered.

Rachel laughed. "That's what I keep telling her. I love it here too." Liam bent down and kissed her forehead.

"Yeah, but that's your reason right there," Chelsea said as she pointed to Liam.

Rachel couldn't deny that, not for a minute. She looked up at him. Yes, he was definitely the reason why she loved being in Birch Valley.

***

"So we are seriously using those for the seating?" Chelsea's face said it all as she pointed at the stacked hay bales. She was shocked and slightly disgusted. Rachel had expected this but had hoped maybe her friend could see the simple beauty behind it.

"I think it's cute and very practical," Rachel pointed out. "Besides, we are covering them in some lovely white fabric that Mary came across."

"That's supposed to help somehow?" Chelsea teased. "Hey, it's your wedding."

"Come on, think country chic," Rachel added as she shrugged her shoulders. She was wearing a pale pink tank top with thin straps. Her goal was to get a little extra sun and have a natural tan on her wedding day. Chelsea was wearing short denim shorts and had a lime green tank on, her long legs absorbing the sun as they both stretched out on the deck.

"So what are you wearing to the ceremony, Chelsea?"

"Well, I brought a couple of dresses. I wanted to get your opinion. I'm thinking something more casual now but festive. I have a sexy little red dress. Think Ethan might like it?"

"Why must you torture me with your lustful thoughts of my brother? Eeeww," Rachel groaned as she leaned back further on the lounge chair. The sun's rays felt amazing on her skin.

"You just need to make your brother fall in love with me. You know I would be your favorite sister-in-law."

"Oh, Chelsea, honestly, you don't want to be with Ethan. Trust me."

Rachel loved him, but he was a spoiled egomaniac who thought that the world belonged to him. He was cocky, arrogant, and while he could be charming, he was too wrapped up in himself to really care about anyone deeply. She worried about him; she knew the sweet side that lurked somewhere deep inside Ethan, but she didn't know of any woman who was ever able to reach in and pull it out. He kept that tucked away and hidden. He didn't need to be sweet; women clamored all over him—they always had. Ethan was gorgeous, well, according to every single friend that Rachel had ever known. They were in awe of his hotness. Rachel just saw Ethan for what he was—her brother. Her thoughts went to Patrick. Rachel still didn't quite know him, and she didn't fully understand that moody brother of Liam's. But the moment she had met him, she saw that he was gorgeous as well, and he too had always been told how handsome he was. Women fell all over themselves to be with him. Maggie had told Rachel just how it had been growing up with the best-looking guy in town being your brother; she had to be leery about who wanted to become her friend, as they usually had their sights on Patrick and would use Maggie to get a little closer to him. Rachel could relate, hell, her best friend of almost twenty-five years was still obsessed with Ethan and would use Rachel in a heartbeat if it allowed her the chance with him.

"Well, I will be the judge of that. When does his flight come in?"

"Tomorrow, actually. I figured you and I can pick him up. Maybe take him to lunch."

"Are you sure you shouldn't maybe pick him up yourself? I mean, you and him kind of need to talk, right?" Chelsea wore a funny expression. It made

Rachel a little nervous.

"Yeah, but since you wanted to see him so badly, I just figured you'd want to go," Rachel said.

Chelsea's eyebrows raised. "Under normal circumstances, I totally would. So I will just hang back and do the last of the party favors or something."

Now Rachel felt a little uneasy. How mad had Ethan really been?

***

Rachel tapped her steering wheel nervously as she waited for her brother. She sat in her silver BMW, the air conditioner blasting. A sudden heatwave had taken hold of the area. She finally spotted him, his blonde hair perfectly styled in a hip fashion: short on the sides but longer on the top. He wore expensive sunglasses, a comfortable but faded USC college t-shirt, khaki cargo shorts, and flip-flops. He looked every bit of a Californian. He looked around. She honked and stuck her arm out the window to wave at him. Rachel undid her seatbelt and got out to greet him.

Ethan was only about hundred feet away when Rachel quickly walked up to him. He smiled, his stark white teeth bright against the golden tan of his perfect and smooth skin. She noticed the start of a beard, which hadn't been there before.

"You made it," Rachel cried as she embraced him. He had a backpack slung over one shoulder, and a rolling suitcase.

"I did." Ethan squeezed her and looked around.

"No Liam? Or Chelsea?"

"No, I figured I would just pick you up." Rachel led the way back to the cool comfort of her BMW. The sun was making the concrete sidewalk hot; she could feel the heat radiate from it, which almost burned the bottoms of her sandal-clad feet.

"God, it's hot here. Thought you said this place was cold?" Ethan scowled and wiped a small bead of sweat from his forehead.

"Well, it is cold, like in the winter and spring, but they all say it's unusually warm for this time of the year. We are actually in the midst of a heatwave." Rachel popped her trunk and let Ethan put his baggage inside. They both got into the car, and Rachel carefully pulled away and left the airport.

"So this is Washington, huh?" Ethan asked once they were headed eastbound on the I-90 and headed into the heart of Spokane.

"Yep, what do you think so far?" Rachel asked. Not that it mattered much, but she was curious what her brother's opinion would be of the area. She had tried to gauge his reaction by watching his face. His darn sunglasses didn't let her see his true feelings.

"Well, the traffic isn't bad."

Rachel was hoping for a little more of an answer as she merged toward the Division Street exit. "I know, I was really surprised the first time I drove on this freeway."

"Yeah, so that's cool. How close are we to your place?"

"You hungry? I thought we could grab something to eat. We still have like over an hour drive home."

"I could eat, I guess. I could really use a drink, though." There it was. Rachel knew that he had acted slightly cool. He was probably worried about meeting Liam. She had been fearing their meeting all morning. It was now early afternoon, and those feelings had only wound up tighter inside of her. Rachel prayed that her brother didn't come at Liam, guns blazing, mouth running, and saying things he might regret. She hoped Liam could see her brother's position. They had talked about it several times, and he reassured her that he would listen to whatever Ethan had to say and that most likely they'd end up buddies by the end of it all. Ethan didn't really have buddies. He was more of a lone wolf. That's what made him excellent at being an ER trauma doctor. He was cool, calculated, he handled pressure with ease, and he knew how to lead. But he didn't bother with feelings; he always teased that they got in the way.

Rachel drove toward the red light. "What do you feel like eating? And drinking?"

"More drinking, less eating. So you figure out what you want to eat," he answered, his head turned toward the window. He was quietly taking in the scenery, or at least that was what she hoped he was doing. His body language didn't give off the impression that he was terribly upset, but she never knew with Ethan.

She spied a fun looking bar with outdoor seating. The brightly colored umbrellas appealed to Rachel, so she slowly drifted over and tried to locate a spot near the bar.

"How about this?" she asked Ethan once she finally parked.

"Yeah, this works."

Once they rounded the corner from where they had to park, they walked into the entrance of the bar. It was bright and a little noisy, considering it was mid week and early afternoon.

Rachel watched as Ethan removed his sunglasses. He surveyed the room, getting a lay of the land. A cute blonde practically ran up to him and offered to seat them. The hostess completely ignored Rachel; it was as if she was invisible. She led them outside to a fairly open seating area after Ethan requested the best table they had. The patio had several tables and even an outdoor bar. The atmosphere was far different than inside; it was relaxing with the small fountain and plant arrangements, and you couldn't quite hear the traffic. There was even a peek-a-boo view of the Spokane River. Then with the large overhead canopy providing just enough shade from the blistering sun, it was perfect and could rival any of their favorite bars in California.

The petite blonde stumbled over her words as she asked Ethan if there was anything he wanted to drink. He threw on the charm, ordered his drink, and asked for water for Rachel. He winked at the hostess as she hurried away.

"Gosh, this is why going out to dinner with you was always so frustrating."

"Oh come on, she seemed nice," Ethan said, smiling as he avoided Rachel's stare and looked over the menu. "You want like a meal or just something light?"

"Ethan, I'm pregnant with twins. I need food," Rachel joked and then watched his face drop, the smile completely removed.

"About that…"

Rachel put her hand up. "I know. But first, I need you to remember a couple things. One, I'm in my thirties, two, it's not all Liam's doing."

"Well, he sure had a big part in it, if you want to know my opinion." Ethan played with his sunglasses on the table.

"I know, but I am just as responsible for the whole thing as he is."

"Rachel, does he have a sister?"

Rachel tilted her head in confusion. She was trying to follow what he was getting at. Of course, she understood that he was a little upset, but she was a grown woman, not some teenager. Granted, she didn't act like a sound-minded, mature adult when she had wound up in the predicament. "Yes, Maggie is Liam's sister. Why?"

The waitress carried a tray with their drinks and set the beverages on the table in front of them. Ethan gave her a grin and another wink. He turned back to Rachel, all his playfulness gone. He grabbed his glass and took a long drink. "If he has a sister, he knows full well what to expect when I meet him."

Chapter Fourteen

Patrick

"So, are you a little nervous to be meeting Ethan?" Patrick asked as he drove. Liam was seated next to him, a pained expression on his face.

Liam shrugged. "I don't know. I hope we get along."

"Man, you got his sister knocked up within like two months of knowing her."

"Thanks for pointing that out, Patrick." Liam looked away, out the window.

They were headed to the diner for lunch; Patrick had tried to convince Liam for them to eat at Antlers, Steve-O's, really anywhere other than Herrick's. He had partially mended things with Amber the other night, but he wasn't in the mood today. The boys had been difficult earlier that morning when Patrick dropped them off with his mother. They probably sensed the anxiety and wild energy that was buzzing with all the wedding preparations. Liam offered to help out at the shop if

Patrick bought lunch. Daniel was out at the Belsky farm. He'd claimed he wasn't hungry when they all decided to break for lunch. Patrick knew very well that Daniel wouldn't pass up a meal, but obviously he wasn't about to miss out on entertaining a beautiful Russian girl either.

"But I love his sister, and hopefully he will be able to see that," Liam said.

They arrived at Herrick's, which was busy as usual. The parking lot was filled with trucks and cars, even a couple Harleys from bikers passing through, which was fairly common during this time of the year, with the beautiful scenic highways. Who could resist a cruise? Patrick located an empty spot and parked the work truck. He hesitated briefly. He wasn't so sure he wanted to go inside. It wasn't that he didn't want to see Amber. He really liked being around her; it was just that he didn't want anyone, especially anyone that was an O'Brien, to get wind that he and Amber might be a little closer.

"What's up, Patrick? You seem weird," Liam asked as they both got out of the truck and started for the front entrance of the diner.

"Nothing." Then he saw Amber, her smiling face looked up at him the moment they crossed the threshold. That damn bell had alerted her to his presence.

Liam led the way to a couple of bar stools that were available by the counter. Amber stood behind the counter, but she turned her attention back to the elderly customer she had been chatting with. Patrick soaked her in from a distance; her dark hair was tied back and gave her a youthful look, she was wearing jean Capris that showcased her legs nicely, and he couldn't help but notice the how the dark green shirt made her eyes bright, more green than their usual blue. Her eyes were darting between the two brothers. Patrick knew he needed to say something or else he'd be in trouble with her again. She walked over and stood in front of them, as if daring Patrick to make the first move.

Liam was unaware of the silent battle that they were engaging in; he was too busy viewing the menu.

"Liam, have you met Amber yet? She just moved back a little while ago," Patrick stated. Liam looked up at her and gave her a kind smile.

"Didn't we go to school together?" He wore a confused scowl as he tried to place Amber's face.

"Yes, we did," Amber answered. She tossed Patrick a sultry look. He knew he was going to be rewarded later.

Liam and Patrick ordered their lunch, and Amber spent her attention on other customers, giving Patrick the space she knew he needed.

Patrick's eyes had followed everywhere Amber had been; he watched her head into the kitchen, he saw her wait tables, and he heard the many customers laugh as they spoke with her. She had a way with people; they just couldn't help but fall in love with her.

They ate their hamburgers, chatted about the upcoming wedding and a little more about Rachel's brother. When there were only a couple of fries left and partial bite of burger left, Liam excused himself to use visit the restroom.

Amber saw Liam get up and seized this moment to talk to Patrick.

"Hey, you. How was the burger?" She stood in front of him with her hands on her hips.

"It was great. But I'm still hungry." Patrick grinned at her, then licked his lips.

Amber bent over the counter and shot a look from one side then the other, then she quickly kissed Patrick. "Want to get together tonight?"

"Yes." Patrick swallowed. He felt his body responding to her daring sassiness.

"How about dinner? I'll cook for you," he offered, craning her neck to see if Liam was headed back yet.

"Yeah, I'll see if Maggie or my mom can watch the boys for me."

"You know, I don't mind them being there."

Patrick shook his head. "Not yet, they would have too many questions, and God knows they would run and tell their grandma."

"It's fine, I understand." Her voice grew quiet.

Patrick didn't want to hurt her feelings, but he still wasn't quite sure what they were doing yet. He had been plagued with another terrible dream about Beth just the night before.

"Hey, you almost ready to get back?" Liam had returned. He fished out several dollars from his wallet to leave on the counter.

"Yeah, we'd better get back. Didn't you mention that you and Daniel are going out tonight?"

"Yeah, his buddies wanted to play poker. You want in on the game?"

"Nah, I'm good. I need to call Mom and see if

she can take the boys tonight," Patrick mentioned as they walked away from the counter.

Liam paused and called out, "Good seeing you again, Amber."

They went through the door, the distinctive chime of the bell signaling their departure.

"Why do you need Mom to watch the kids?" Liam questioned as they got into the truck.

Patrick walked around to the driver's side. He could kick himself for slipping up. He hadn't meant to say anything; he just wondered how much longer he could keep Amber a secret.

Once he slid inside the cab of the truck, Liam glared at him. "So why do you need Mom to watch the boys?" he asked again.

"Oh, uh...I was going to go grocery shopping and stuff."

"Patrick, I've been staying with you for over a week. We just went to the store and loaded up on stuff. Come on, what's going on? You've been acting weird, even for you," Liam teased.

As they pulled out of their spot, Patrick considered what his brother was saying. Had he been acting weird or different? He had been trying desperately to appear as normal as possible, but it was hard when he felt so happy. That was a strange thought; he was actually starting to feel something, and that it would be happiness of all things. But that was the effect that she had on him; she made him laugh, she understood what he was going through, and their chemistry, well, that was unreal and unlike anything he'd ever experienced, even with Beth. That guilt laden thought pierced his belly like a knife.

Patrick knew that if there was anyone in the family he could open up to, it was Liam. He never was one to let out a secret, and he really didn't badger or try to pry into anyone's life. Patrick respected that his brother was pretty much the only O'Brien besides himself that left well enough alone.

They drove down the quiet streets back to the shop. Children were riding their bikes and mothers were pushing strollers. With the weather being warm with a touch of a breeze, the people of Birch Valley wanted to be out in it. Patrick gripped the wheel tighter and said, "Well, here's the thing..."

Now he had Liam's attention.

***

Amber

Well, she was certainly glad that Patrick acted the right way this time. Maybe he truly was sorry. Either way, his simple act of introducing her to his brother had made a dent in the tension between them. As she scrubbed the pots in the back sink, she heard her mother round the corner. They were almost closed for the day, and the cook who had been helping out was busy cleaning the grill, his back to Amber.

"Sweetie, here are a couple more." Lynn placed several dirty dishes to the side of Amber.

"No problem," Amber said as she reached for a food-encrusted plate, slipping it into the hot, soapy water.

"So I noticed Patrick was in here earlier."

"Yes, he was." Amber knew what her mother was getting at. She didn't want another lecture. Lynn had made it perfectly well known that she didn't care for how Patrick acted and that Amber shouldn't waste her time. "Mom, remember, Patrick and I talked the other night. He was wonderful today. He introduced me to Liam."

"Here's the thing, dear. Don't think that Patrick's the only fish in the sea. There are plenty of wonderful men out there."

"Mom, this area is more like a lake than an ocean, so pretty slim pickings here. Besides, I really like Patrick." Amber let out a happy sigh.

Lynn put her hand on Amber's shoulder. "I know that he's gorgeous, hon. I'm not blind. I can very well see why you are attracted to him. I just don't want you allowing any man, no matter how damn good looking, to treat you like you aren't important."

"I know, Mom." Amber turned and kissed her mother on the cheek. "I appreciate you having my best interests at heart."

***

Patrick

"So you don't mind watching them? I really appreciate it, Mags," Patrick said on the phone. He had found out that his mother had a book club meeting that evening and wouldn't be able to watch the twins. She had offered to cancel, but Patrick didn't want her to suspect that him going grocery shopping wasn't what he was really doing.

"No, it's fine. You going to go play poker after all?" Maggie asked.

Patrick swallowed as he felt the lie leave his lips. "Yeah, I figure I might go check it out."

"Well, good, you really should. Michael and I are going to order pizza and watch a movie with the kids. I'm feeling like ice cream sundaes too."

Of course she was, she was pregnant after all. "You want any pickles with that sundae?"

"Eeeww, gross. I don't like pickles normally. They're not going anywhere near my ice cream."

"Well, I appreciate you looking after them," Patrick said again.

"I love getting to watch them. Besides, Melanie is thrilled. So it's like a slumber party for her."

"Good, I'm glad." He didn't realize the boys would be staying over at his sister's house. Now he planned to make full use of his night of freedom. That stab of guilt jabbed him as he listened to Maggie talk.

"Besides we all are getting together tomorrow, lots of last-minute stuff going on. Mom is going to do a little brunch shower for Rachel, then we have the rehearsal dinner tomorrow night. Has Liam met with her brother yet? He flew in today, right? Where is he staying at?" Maggie bombarded him with tons of questions.

"You know, I really don't know. Liam was helping out at the Belsky place with me and Daniel this morning."

"So when are you dropping off my munchkin

nephews?" Maggie's voice turned sugary sweet. She adored Finn and Connor and tried to spend as much time with them as possible since she left Seattle. This was how he had always pictured it would be, except there was a vital piece missing—Beth. He quickly pushed the thought out of his mind.

"I'll swing by in like twenty minutes or so?"

"That works, see you when you get here." Maggie hung up, and Patrick went to pack an overnight bag for Finn and Connor.

The two boys were rolling toy cars on a carpet that had several streets and a track embroidered on it. Patrick walked in to hear a lot of vrooming and tires screeching.

"Hey guys, Aunt Maggie is going to have you over for a sleepover," Patrick explained.

"Yay!" they both shouted in unison.

"She even told me a little secret."

Their blue eyes grew large with anticipation. "What, Daddy?" Connor asked, barely able to contain his excitement.

"Daddy, tell us," Finn begged.

"Okay, but you didn't hear this from me. But Aunt Maggie is making ice cream sundaes."

"Yay!" they shouted again and then started rolling on the carpet, attempting to do somersaults.

Patrick laughed and joined them on the floor, where they quickly pounced on him. God, he loved being a dad.

***

185

Amber

"Are you sure you don't need me to stay?" Amber asked Dylan.

"No, I'm fine, Mom," Dylan replied with more attitude than Amber would have liked. When she came home from the diner, Dylan was acting every bit the hormonal pre-teen boy you would expect. She still struggled to find her footing with this new phase in parenting.

"We can hang out together, if you'd rather," Amber softly offered. A huge part of her wished that she could bring Dylan along. Maybe he needed another male influence besides her sick father. That poor man had spent the entire week in bed again after a recent trip for more chemo. He was finally able to eat and drink, but he was wasting away in front of her eyes. Amber would give him one thing: he still was as ornery as ever. They all took that as a good sign and kept praying that he would beat this cancer.

"Mom, it's fine. I'm just bored," Dylan complained. "There's nothing to do here. I really wish we were back in Portland."

"I know, sweetie," Amber tried to soothe him. She missed Portland less and less, but she understood where her son was coming from. He hadn't had the chance to really make any friends yet. Summers could be long in Birch Valley, especially when you didn't have anyone your own age to run along with.

She just wanted to console him as they stretched out on her bed. He was tucked in next to her and was just about as long as her. Which wasn't saying a lot, she was only a couple inches over five feet, but it was a strange sensation realizing that her child was outgrowing her. Amber rubbed his back, making wide circles, gently lulling him to sleep. She felt almost sad as she realized how much he was growing; his body was getting bigger, he was quickly losing his baby fat, it was now turning into lean muscle. He was in that beginning stage of awkwardness, not quite a man or even a full-fledged teenager, but right at the threshold. No matter how tall or manly he might get, he would always be her baby. She heard him breathing deeply and steadily as sleep finally settled in. She brushed away his hair and kissed his forehead. He would always be her baby.

***

Patrick

It felt weird, but a good kind of weird. That was the only way Patrick could explain it as they pushed the shopping cart down the narrow aisle, pausing to sneak a kiss when no one was looking, but part of Patrick didn't care if they were seen. The exhilaration and rush from acting like two teenage kids in love was not lost on either of them.

Amber looked radiant tonight, wearing a pale yellow sundress with thin straps, exposing her smooth skin, making Patrick itch to touch it. He was dying to get home, but Amber had made this shopping trip to get their dinner fixings a game.

They both had been laughing and almost frolicking through the store when they rounded the corner and Patrick stared straight into Maggie's eyes.

"Hey Patrick, funny running into you here." Maggie gave him a hard stare but then turned to greet Amber. "Hi, Amber, how are you?"

"Great, thanks. How are you doing?" Amber's chipper response made matters worse in Patrick's eyes. How was he going to explain this? He watched Maggie eye the contents in their shopping cart, all the makings of a romantic dinner for two.

"I'm good. I was just running in because I realized we were out of chocolate syrup for our ice cream sundaes."

"Well, you can't have a sundae without chocolate syrup. Did you buy any cherries? Or nuts?" Amber looked up toward the ceiling. "Are you making banana splits? Those sound really good right now."

"Nope, I got a couple twin boys at my house right now who hate bananas. Maybe you guys should stop by for a sundae. I have chocolate syrup now," Maggie said as she held up the brown plastic bottle.

"Maybe another time, Mags," Patrick answered before Amber accepted the invitation.

"Too bad, your loss. Well, I'd better get back home, Michael is probably pulling his hair out by now." Maggie smiled at Amber. "Amber, we really should get together for coffee or tea sometime."

"I'd really like that. Maybe we can drag Rachel along?" Amber asked.

"Oh, that would be fun. I'll check in with you

next week. Have a great night, guys." Maggie shot Patrick one last look, which pretty much told him he had a lot of explaining to do.

After getting the rest of their groceries, Patrick tried to not let the encounter with his sister rattle him. The gears in his head were churning. How was he going to tell Maggie, who ultimately would tell their mother that he was seeing Amber, and that he was starting to really fall for her? Granted, he knew that his mother and sister would be thrilled to hear that he was dating, but for him to have kept it to himself, that's where he was in trouble.

***

The smells coming from his kitchen were divine, but then again, it was Amber who was cooking. The woman knew her way around a kitchen, and she was magical when it came to blending flavors and creating edible art.

Patrick wrapped his arms around her waist as she stood in front of the stove, holding a wooden spoon as she delicately stirred some sort of concoction. It was creamy and he assumed it was a sauce, but her concentration and focus on the mixture made him wonder if it were something more. A love potion, perhaps?

He nuzzled her at the nape of her neck, his lips nipping at her exposed flesh. "Stop, I'm cooking." He could hear her smile before seeing it on her lips.

"You weren't telling me that a little bit ago."

"That was then. I need to cook this is food. We need nourishment."

Patrick ran his hands along her sides, letting his fingers run down her arms. "We did burn a lot of calories."

Amber spun around to face him. "You are a wicked man, you know that, Mr. Patrick O'Brien?"

"Yeah, but you like me."

"A lot." She reached up and kissed him full on the mouth and then quickly pulled away. "But I have a sauce that needs my attention. Go pour us some more wine."

Ah, this woman drove him mad. He couldn't explain the feelings that he had; they confused him. Their connection was intense, being around one another felt natural and easy, but he couldn't quite peel away the nagging guilt that seem to cling to him. Beth told him to promise, and he was trying, sort of. This was the first time in four years that he was even able to feel alive.

***

Amber

Why were they so comfortable together? Why was Patrick so damn sexy and simply adorable as she watched him eat the pasta she had prepared? Why was she finding herself starting to fall in love with him? All these questions and more circulated in her brain.

Running into his sister had thrown Patrick for a loop; she saw fear in his eyes. Why? She still didn't quite get why he wanted to shield his life away from his family. Each family member who she had met seemed nice and genuinely sweet. The way Maggie looked at Patrick, she did almost feel bad for him. She knew that Maggie was going to be talking to him soon. Amber realized that Patrick must not have been as honest with Maggie about her watching his sons. She really didn't like the idea that he felt the need to lie or sneak around to be with her. But she knew Patrick was skittish, so he needed to take small, easy baby steps. She would figure out soon enough how to get him to see that they didn't need to hide this, whatever this was. She definitely would be taking Maggie up on that offer for coffee.

The air was starting to cool as they sat out on the deck and finished their meal, sipping the last swallows of wine and listening to the distant croaks of frogs and crickets. The sky had turned a blended mixture of purples, and tiny stars glittered the late evening sky. Amber couldn't explain how romantic it felt being there with Patrick. The glow from the candlelight was their sole source of light, casting mysterious shadows on Patrick's face.

He looked at her, almost lovingly, but there was that deep green, rich-with-desire stare again. It caused the quiet butterflies in her stomach to start flapping wildly. She rose to clear the table of their dishes, and he reached out to grab her hand. He rose off his chair. Silently, he grabbed the dishes and took them to the kitchen. Amber stood there, unsure of what she was supposed to do. She looked back and saw Patrick return. He picked up their glasses with one hand, and with his free hand he took hers and led her inside.

The lights were dim in the house; he had left on a single lamp on an end table in the living room. The kitchen light was also off, but they maneuvered with what little light was available. He set the glasses on the counter, turned to her and took her head in his hands, bending to reach her mouth. Amber parted her lips, savoring the tenderness of his kiss. He gently moved his hands, letting them roam down to her bare shoulders, stroking her skin. She could feel her body starting to burn, heating up with want. The power this man had over her scared her a little. She didn't know what to make of this romance, this attraction, this greedy lust. But on the flip side, there was a connection that was growing, anchoring itself. They were forming something. She just wished they could put a label on it. Amber just wanted to know what exactly it was. Her brain was tormenting her with questions, doubt, fears, desire, possibly love.

Patrick reached for her face, his large hands cradling her head, his eyes staring directly into her. She knew that look that illuminated in his eyes. It was pure, raw need. She silently hoped it would mean more eventually. *Baby steps, Amber.*

Chapter Fifteen

Rachel

"God, I'm so stressed," Rachel complained as she thrashed around in the large bed.

"Stop moving around so much," Chelsea ordered. She threw a pillow at Rachel.

Flinging the covers off with more force than necessary, Rachel sat up. "I have so much to do. What was I even thinking? I'm getting married friggin' tomorrow."

"Chill out, you said you weren't going to stress out. Knock it off," Chelsea demanded. "What time is it, anyway?" Her voice was groggy and laced with the remnants of sleep. She burrowed further into the comforter, almost completely hidden except a bit of pale blonde hair sticking out.

"What I said and what I'm going to do are two very different things."

Rachel had tossed and turned all night. She had watched Chelsea sleep soundly, and she had been envious and actually had been tempted to

193

"accidentally" kick her or knee her in the back. That made her a terrible friend, but at the moment she had far too much on her plate to really care. Her list for today was incredibly long, and as her brain started jotting down more things, the list kept growing.

Rachel groaned. "You need to wake up, Chelsea. I'll start coffee." She playfully swatted Chelsea's butt. "Let's go, get up," she called as she left the bedroom. Rachel heard Chelsea make some snide comment but chose to ignore it.

They were seated side by side in the breakfast nook. Rachel had out her notebook that had been filled with the various things that needed to be accomplished by today if this wedding was actually going to happen tomorrow. The most important thing was sitting right in front of them, two jumbo mugs of the strongest and richest coffee she could find in the cupboard.

"Okay, first thing…" Rachel was about to speak when she heard the phone ring. "Oh, let me go get that." She was frustrated. She didn't have time; literally every minute was accounted for.

Rachel grabbed the phone off the cradle. "Hello?"

"Good morning, dear." Mary's voice was far too perky this early in the morning.

"Hi, Mary," Rachel said. She hoped that this conversation didn't linger too long; there was far too much stuff that needed her attention. As she vaguely heard Mary speaking, her mental checklist was taking over. She needed to stop by the florist, make sure all the outside stuff was set up, paint her toenails, and she still had to wait for Ethan to come over and talk to Liam. They had the rehearsal dinner tonight at Maggie's house. Oh, the list was almost too much.

"Rachel, dear, are you there?" Mary asked with slight concern.

"Yes, I'm sorry, I didn't catch that." Rachel lied. She hadn't really hadn't been listening at all.

"That's okay, dear. Not to worry, we'll come to you."

"Come to me?" Rachel asked, but it was too late, Mary had already hung up the phone.

Chelsea gave her a confused look. "What was that about?"

"It was Mary. She said not to worry, that they would come to me."

Chelsea raised her perfectly plucked brows. "Well, that sounds a little cryptic."

***

Rachel was downing the last bit of her coffee, savoring the caffeine that she knew would finally kick in. She rubbed her belly and apologized to her babies for her weakness and assured them it was far better than some of the stuff out there. Rachel found herself talking more and more to her belly. Liam was too; he was the first one to actually talk to their babies. But now as they inched closer to their births, Liam and Rachel wanted to start really bonding with these unknown little people inside her.

Chelsea appeared from the hallway, fresh from a shower, her blonde hair wet and sticking to her.

"When is Ethan coming over?"

"I texted him a little bit ago. He is just hanging out at the motel until afternoon. To be honest, he's not in a real rush to come over here today," Rachel said.

"Well, I'm sure it'll work out. I mean, there's not a whole lot that Ethan can say. It's not like he can force Liam to marry you. That's already being done. So seriously, how bad can it be?"

"You're probably right. I guess I just really want Ethan to like Liam."

Rachel could feel anxiety building a thick wall around her chest. She was worried that everything was going to go horribly wrong. Then the doorbell rang. She opened the door to see a smiling Mary and a group of women she recognized all too well: there was Karen, her right-hand woman down at the school; she spied Sue-Ellen, her old neighbor; Janice was standing next to Cheryl; and Maggie was standing in the far back, appearing to be blocking something or someone. They were all carrying gift bags and boxes. Some held onto balloons.

"Hi, everyone." Rachel waved. "Please come on in." This is what Mary had meant—that darn bridal shower.

"Well, I told you, dear, we'd come to you. You sounded so stressed on the phone. I know your head must spinning with all the last-minute details. Well, after you are well fed and open a few gifts, you might start to feel better." Mary hugged Rachel. God, how did He make this woman so good and kind? Why couldn't her mother be like this? That's when she heard the squeal. Evelyn Montgomery was weaving her way through the tiny sea of people standing on the porch.

"Well, I made it." Evelyn was dressed as chic as always, wearing a navy blue, casual, cotton pant suit. Her champagne blonde hair was perfectly styled, and her trademark diamond earrings sent off glittery beams as she moved in the morning sunlight.

"Mom…" Rachel was in shock. How? When? So many questions, yet when she looked at Mary, she knew the answers to them all.

Evelyn pulled Rachel into an awkward hug, but Rachel craved her touch. She had missed her mother and was grateful that she was here.

The women all quickly migrated inside the house. Rachel stood there as Mary put everyone to work. "Okay, ladies, food over here, gifts there." Mary pointed to where she wanted everything placed.

Rachel knew right then she didn't need to worry about her wedding turning out perfectly. Mary O'Brien was proving she was meant to be a wedding planner. She told everyone what was on the schedule for the day as they dined on an array of her homemade muffins that Rachel still hadn't quite convinced her to start selling.

"These muffins are amazing," Chelsea said as she carefully nibbled at the large baked good on her festive party plate.

Mary nodded and smiled gently at Chelsea. "I may need to teach you how to make them. Well, actually, I think Rachel makes them better than I do." She winked at Rachel.

"Well, you were the one that taught me," Rachel admitted to everyone in the room.

Mary walked over to where Rachel was seated and bent to hug her. "Dear, I cannot tell you how happy I am that you wanted to learn." She rose and said to the room, "If she hadn't, she may have never fallen for my Liam." Rachel could see the tears developing in Mary's eyes, which fueled her own to start welling up.

Mary cleared her throat and took a deep breath before explaining what was next. "So, ladies, as you know, we are here because tomorrow that beautiful girl will marrying my handsome boy. I want us to help Rachel today. We need to finish getting this property looking like a proper place for a wedding." Mary paused and walked over to where the gifts had been arranged. "I think we should give Rachel our gifts."

Mary and Evelyn carried the gifts to Rachel and tucked them around her legs and feet. The packages were decorated with white bows, some fancy, some fun. The bags all had images of either wedding bells, cakes, doves, or flowers. All of it started to really soak into Rachel's mind—this was actually happening. She was going to be a bride.

"You guys really didn't need to do this." Rachel blushed as she looked around the room, which was full of women who cared about her. Those darn pregnancy hormones, making her all emotional.

She held up another gift; this one was from her mother. Evelyn looked thrilled, anticipation in her mocha-colored eyes, as Rachel reached into the small gift bag. She pulled out a large envelope, and when she opened it she saw two tickets. Her mother had just paid for their honeymoon.

"Mom…wow." Rachel was stunned as she clutched onto to the envelope.

"Well, I figure, after this wedding business, you and your new husband need to go on a real honeymoon. Or maybe, think of it as a babymoon. That's a thing now, right?"

"Yes, so this will kind of be for both of us. Thanks so much, Mom." Evelyn smiled warmly at Rachel. This was the nicest her mother had been to her since, well, ever.

Rachel continued to open gifts. Most were nice little things, but there were a couple of naughty things that made Rachel and Mary blush. All in all, Rachel couldn't have been happier. She felt well fed, overwhelmingly loved, and believe it or not, not stressed. Mary, the mother of the man she was about to marry, was right, yet again.

***

Patrick

"Well, when do you want us there?" Liam asked into his cell phone.

Patrick and Daniel were sitting outside with Liam, as they had just finished breakfast out on Patrick's deck. It was a relaxing morning as the guys ate slightly overdone scrambled eggs, limp toast, and nearly burnt bacon, all of which was evidence of Daniel's not-so-great cooking skills.

The day was promising to be gorgeous. Hot, but gorgeous. The sun was already sending a wicked sting of heat down to Birch Valley, and it wasn't even close to ten in the morning.

"We can be there soon, hon." Liam looked over at his brothers. "Why, is he there yet?"

Patrick leaned back and took a generous sip of coffee. Daniel was nursing a hangover from the poker game he'd gone to; he and Liam didn't come back home until after seven that morning. Patrick had slept in. With not having the boys at home, it had been deliciously quiet. He had slept the best he had in months, hell, maybe even years. Dinner with Amber had been incredible, and the food had been incredible too. He couldn't get the images of her body under him as they twisted together in his bed out of his mind. He could still smell her light fragrance on his pillow that morning. Amber was burrowing her way deep under his skin, and he didn't quite know what to do about it. Would this fast and hot relationship fizzle and burn out quick? Or was this the start to something more tangible and real? Patrick wasn't sure, but he enjoyed finding out.

"Hey, guys, we need to head over back to my place soon," Liam announced as he ended his call.

"So is Ethan over there?" Patrick asked carefully.

"Yeah, I guess so." Liam looked down.

Patrick knew his brother felt some guilt about the whole Rachel situation. It hadn't his intent for things to happen so quickly, but he knew for certain that Liam loved Rachel. He himself had doubted the relationship and just figured Liam was just trying to do the right thing by her. Patrick could see past that now; there was something between Rachel and Liam, something deep and real. But it still confused Patrick how people could fall in love so quickly, as he had known Beth almost their entire lives. So it wasn't a love at first sight type of romance, but one which grew over the course of childhood, then into their teenage years, and finally into adulthood. They were still figuring life out when they got married. Liam's situation, on the other hand, was more like love at first fight. He remembered how positively irritated his brother had been from the first encounter with Rachel. That had only been a little over seven months ago, and now, here they were on the eve of the wedding, pregnant with twins. Funny, how life worked.

"Well, Daniel and I will be with you. It'll be okay, man," Patrick tried to reassure him,

"Yeah, Liam, don't worry, we got your back," Daniel added.

Liam sighed. "I just wish it wasn't like this, you know? It would have been cool just to have met him and not know that he already hates me."

"You've got to see it from his point of view. I mean, his sister has been gone not even eight months, and he's here to attend her wedding while she's pregnant by some guy she barely knew for like two months," Patrick explained. He hated playing devil's advocate, but he just wanted to point out the facts to Liam.

"Yeah, but look at Mags. I was thinking about this the other day. She kind did the same thing, right?"

"Good point, Liam," Daniel agreed as he raised his coffee mug.

Patrick gave Daniel a quick glare. "I see where you are going with this, but it's different because

Rachel's his sister. Don't think for a minute I was thrilled when I found out about Maggie. She was so young too." Patrick grimaced at the memory. Granted it had all worked out, but barely. Only a few short months ago, his sister's marriage was in complete turmoil.

"Yeah, you're right. I just hate confrontation. Maybe it will go well. Who knows?"

"Sure, that's not a whole lot of wishful thinking, but let's go with it," Patrick teased; sarcasm was something of a gift for him. However, not everyone was so thrilled.

"Well, it's your funeral, I mean, wedding," Daniel joked, not to be outdone by Patrick.

Liam growled lightly and said, "It's now or never. Time to go face the music."

As they all reluctantly rose from their patio chairs, Patrick said, "Remember, we'll be there with you."

***

Rachel

Rachel stood looking at the partial transformation of their property—it was magical. She didn't think it was possible. But with the help of all the ladies who rallied together, they'd made it beautiful. They weren't quite done and were waiting for Liam and his brothers to show up. Her stomach crashed in uneven waves at the thought. Ethan was sitting on the deck, casually chatting with the ladies, as they were breaking from all the hard work they had been doing. It was nearly noon, and Mary suggested they grab something for lunch when they went to pick up the final floral arrangements. Typical Mary, always making sure everyone was fed and loved.

She could hear Chelsea's laugh, even though Rachel stood quite a distance away from the deck. She must be laying it on thick for Ethan. Why did her friend really think there was even a remote possibility of her and Ethan ever getting together?

Rachel viewed the shimmering water of their lake, after she had walked down the small hill that led her away from the deck. She glanced at the altar, a white arbor, which had an arch decorated with lights and flowers. It stood with the promise of what was to come. She stood in the middle of the aisle between the large hay bales, which were draped with white fabric. It really did turn out lovely, just as Mary had promised. An assortment of white flowers, tied with thick red and blue ribbons, were pinned at the end of each row, highlighting the aisle which Rachel would cross tomorrow evening to finally say her vows.

Hearing Chelsea's voice again, she turned her gaze up toward the deck. As much as she enjoyed staring at where the ceremony was going to take place, she needed to rescue her brother.

"There she is," Ethan said, a thankful and relieved look on his face once Rachel reached them.

"I was just checking out the set-up for tomorrow," Rachel commented as she heard the sound of Daniel's truck pull into the driveway. She peeked at Ethan's face; there was no hint given, but as he put his sunglasses back on, she prayed that her brother meeting Liam went okay.

Liam climbed out of the passenger side of the truck, and Rachel could sense from his body language he was nervous. He saw her and gave her a weak smile.

Rachel jogged over to him, leaving her brother on the deck. Liam bent down and kissed her cheek. "Good morning."

"More like good afternoon, mister," Rachel teased. She could feel how tense Liam's body was. He inhaled deeply, grabbed Rachel by the hand, and set off for the deck.

Rachel watched her mother and Ethan. They had looked at each other and then back toward Rachel and Liam. *Oh, please, Lord*, she silently prayed.

Liam released her hand, he extended his right hand to Ethan and said, "I'm Liam O'Brien." His voice was firm, yet friendly and not intimidating.

"Hello, I'm Ethan Montgomery." Ethan accepted the hand that was offered to him, but he didn't get up from his chair to meet Liam. His tone was cool, not much different than how their father acted. This upset Rachel a little; she expected more from her brother.

"You must be Evelyn. It's really great to finally meet you, both of you, actually," Liam said as he went to her mother, who rose slowly out of her chair and accepted the hug from Liam.

"Yes. Thank you. This property is quite lovely," Evelyn added. Rachel watched as her mother grew nervous.

"Why, thank you. We love it here," Liam

responded as he tossed Rachel a hopeful look.

"We have so much to do. Liam, your mom suggested that we grab some stuff for lunch. We have a hungry, hard working crew here," Rachel shared playfully.

"Leave it to my mother, Mary O'Brien, to feed you. You guys might end up ten pounds heavier by the time you leave," Liam joked. He turned to face Ethan and asked, "Ethan, would you mind helping me grab some things out of the truck?"

Everyone was watching and waiting. Patrick and Daniel were standing by, ready to protect Liam at a moment's notice.

"Sure." Ethan got up from chair and followed Liam off the deck. Rachel could hear the whispers as everyone watched the two guys walk away together.

Please let this go well.

***

Liam

"Well, I'm glad you were able to make it up. I know Rachel's thrilled." Liam faced Ethan at the back of his brother's truck. He tried to see past the designer shades; he wanted to get a read on what this guy was thinking. From what Liam could tell, this guy was holding back. He was trying to stay cool, but there was an underlying tension.

Ethan squared his stance as he looked at Liam. "I'm glad too."

Liam examined him. He looked a lot like Rachel,

205

the same sun-kissed blonde hair, tanned skin, the same slightly upturned nose, and almost flawless features. Ethan stood several inches shorter than Liam; he had an athletic build and had a cocky air about him. Liam wasn't too impressed.

"Let me be the first one to address what's happening here," Liam started. He leaned his arm against the truck casually and told himself, *Show no fear. You love Rachel.* Liam continued, "I know that this isn't easy, and I can only imagine what you are thinking. I have a sister, I get it. She did the same exact thing. But she's happily married to that guy, and I love him like a brother."

"That's real nice and all, but Rachel's my sister. So I can't stand here and lie to you. I'm not excited about this at all." Ethan's body was rigid.

"I know, man. But I hope you believe me when I tell you I love your sister more than I ever thought it was possible to love another human being. She's the best thing that has ever happened to me. I can't imagine my life without her in it."

Ethan nodded. "I can see that you seem to love her. I really have no say in the matter anyway. What's done is done. Time will tell if she made a huge mistake or not."

Liam grabbed his jaw and rubbed his chin thoughtfully. This guy was not going to make this easy, that's for sure. "I respect that, Ethan. I really hope that as time goes on, you and I can get to know each other. Maybe even learn to be friends." Liam paused as he looked over at the deck. He could see Rachel talking to her mother. "You mean the world to Rachel. Trust me, I know how much I care about my siblings. I just want her to be happy and not stressed that you and I are going to come to blows or something awful like that."

"I'm a little more civilized than that. Again, Liam, time will tell. I just hope Rachel hasn't ruined her life." Ethan went to move away from the truck but stopped mid-step. "Do you need me to help carry anything?"

Liam smiled. "Sure." He knew that they were miles apart from being close friends, but he knew that, as time passed, as Ethan saw that Liam really did cherish Rachel, that there was hope for them to quite possibly become friends, maybe even brothers. He had always been optimistic, even when things seemed like they were impossible. This would prove to be one of those times when his optimism would be put to the test.

Chapter Sixteen

Rachel

The sky was turning a deep shade of purple, the air was warm, and her stomach was threatening to let loose. Rachel sipped on ginger ale as she prepared to walk down the aisle.

"Are you just nervous, dear? Second thoughts?" Evelyn asked as she smoothed the elegant yet simple wedding dress.

Everyone had already taken their seats. Liam was waiting.

"No second thoughts," Rachel answered. She knew this was what she wanted; it was just the actual act of getting married that was terrifying her at that exact moment.

"You ready?" Ethan asked, offering his arm to her. He looked handsome in his gray suit. There was worry and concern on his face, but he tried to act happy for her sake. Rachel was upset that her father wasn't in attendance but was thankful that Mary had somehow figured out a way to convince

Evelyn to be there.

Rachel nodded and slipped her arm through her brother's. As they walked together, Rachel tried to absorb every last detail of her special day. As they passed the reception area, she saw the tables all lined up neatly, decorated with festive floral centerpieces on top of white table cloths; twinkling white lights were flickering softly, almost keeping time to the music which was floating in the air. Somehow, they had pulled this off, flowers, cake, the dress, everything. And it was beautiful. Rachel would never think of the Fourth of July as anything else but one of the best days of her life.

Ethan halted at the edge before the aisle. "Are you sure about this?"

"Positive. I have never been more certain," she replied as she squeezed his hand with her free fingers that weren't curled around the small bouquet of dyed roses.

"I just want you to be happy." Ethan's cornflower blue eyes were moist. That touched Rachel and brought on the sensation of tears, but she tried to blink them away.

"I am happy. Liam makes me happy."

***

Liam

He saw her standing there with Ethan, glowing with radiant perfection. The gown clung to her figure in a way that was classy and yet stirred desire in Liam. This gorgeous woman was going to be his wife. She was also the mother of their babies. He was going to grow old with her. How did he end up being so lucky?

The wedding march played, and he watched as Rachel seemed to glide toward him. He was standing near the shore, the water and mountains their backdrop for this ceremony. Rachel now stood only a few feet away, and Liam's heart squeezed tighter in his chest.

They stood facing each other. Ethan promptly handed over his sister, shaking Liam's hand, his grip firm and more of a warning.

"God, you're beautiful," Liam whispered to Rachel. He could see tiny trails of wetness move down her cheeks. He grabbed his handkerchief and wiped them away. "Those are happy tears, right?"

"Very happy tears," Rachel managed to say.

The exchanging of their vows was a blur, he didn't know what he had said, he was waiting to hear the final words announced, and with those he pulled Rachel close and kissed her with all the love he had. Cheers erupted from the hay bales where everyone stood. Overhead, several fireworks lit up the darkening sky, reminding them that this was also the Fourth of July. The fireworks continued, blasting over the still lake, which reflected the brilliant red, white, and blue sparks. Liam took hold of Rachel's hand—his wife's hand—and led her away.

"Wow, we did it," Rachel cried. Her eyes were wet as she reached up and kissed Liam. "I love you so much."

"Not nearly as much as I love you. Remember, I

was the one who knew I loved you first, Mrs. O'Brien," Liam teased as he scooped her into a tight embrace

"Is that so? Well, Mr. O'Brien, I think I loved you all along."

***

Rachel

"Ah, would you trouble having a dance with this old goat?" Grandpa Paddy asked Rachel as she neared the table he was sitting at with the other O'Brien men. She looked down at him, smiling at his thick accent, and stared into his emerald green eyes, which twinkled with the reflection of the candles.

"I would be honored," Rachel said as she extended her hand and as Liam assisted the elderly man up from his seat.

"Grandpa Paddy, now remember, she's mine," Liam teased.

"Aye, but the ink has not dried yet, my boy." He grinned at Liam as he walked with Rachel to the makeshift dance floor.

The guys had assembled some plywood and created a fantastic dance floor in the yard, with white lights hung high above, creating a romantic glow as couples swayed to the music.

Rachel rested her head on Grandpa Paddy's shoulder, and he held her lightly in his arms.

"You're a vision, lass," Grandpa Paddy said as they moved gracefully together.

"Aww, thank you. You are looking rather handsome yourself tonight."

Grandpa Paddy laughed. She could tell he was tiring from all the activity, but she cherished this memory of dancing with him. Liam must have sensed his grandfather's exhaustion and came to relieve him of his dancing duty. "I think I went too long without holding my wife," Liam said.

"I could do with a rest, but save me another." Grandpa Paddy left a sweet kiss on her cheek as he hobbled back to his table.

"God, he's such a dear."

"I know, I love that man," Liam replied as he took Rachel into his arms, twirling her and then finally flipping her into a dip. He pulled her up to kiss her.

The night was finally coming to an end as Rachel yawned; her eyes grew heavy as Liam held her close. They'd had the most incredible evening. There'd been food, laughter, dancing, fireworks, and Rachel couldn't have thought of a more splendid way to celebrate their wedding. To have all these new friends and family members in attendance made Rachel feel like everything had finally fallen into place. She was relieved that it was all over in a sense. The stress of planning the wedding had been rough and tiresome; now they could focus on just being together without the weight of the ceremony looming over them. Granted, they still had two babies to plan for, but that was a ways away still. For now she could breathe again and enjoy being a newlywed. Her, Rachel Montgomery, oops, correction, Rachel

O'Brien, was now a married woman. She sure hadn't seen that coming almost seven months ago.

***

Patrick

He swirled the last of the amber liquid in his glass and watched his brother dance with his new bride. The day had been hard for Patrick, as it broke out many dusty memories that he had kept tucked away in his mind. Memories of his own wedding came rushing back to him. He missed Beth. Patrick watched his boys run around and play with their cousins and other children that had attended the ceremony. Their carefree squeals of delight echoed in the air, which almost irritated him, and only made him feel more guilt as he swallowed the whiskey, burning as it slid down his throat.

"You okay, man?" Daniel asked as he nursed his own drink. He even had a solemn expression on his face.

"Yeah, just hard, you know."

"I can imagine. Even I am feeling a little bummed. I mean, I'm happy for Liam, but it would be nice to find someone too."

Patrick understood what Daniel was saying, and he agreed. His thoughts drifted to Amber, suddenly. After all the nostalgia and far too much to drink, he found himself not wanting to think about her. It was just too much right then to balance his emotions, thinking of Beth and Amber; they each brought with them different feelings.

"Well, maybe someday it'll be my turn," Daniel said as he polished off his drink. "I need another, how about you?"

Patrick shook his head. "I'd better not."

"I'm off for another." Daniel left the table and headed over to where the family had set up a beverage and bar station.

It was best that Patrick stopped drinking. The liquor was spurring his aggravation. He looked over at Grandpa Paddy, who had a faraway look. He was probably thinking about being alone, without his wife. Again, Patrick saw himself.

***

Amber

Sundays were always quiet in Birch Valley. Amber hadn't realized how much until she cruised around the main street on her trusty green bicycle. It was midmorning, and Amber decided to take a quick ride, forcing Dylan to accompany her.

"Mom, where are we even going?" Dylan complained as he hung back a bit behind her.

"Dylan, catch up. We aren't going anywhere in particular, just riding."

They started to pass the large Catholic church as it was letting out. People dressed in their best clothing were filing out and headed to their cars. Amber waved at Dylan to be cautious. You never quite knew if a car would see you. Parking lots with drivers hungry and tired from a long sermon might not be paying the most attention. Amber stopped before the mouth of the driveway as she saw a car pull right out without even giving her a second glance. That was exactly why she had instructed Dylan to be extra careful and mindful of the drivers around him; sometimes cars forgot that bikes had the right of way.

As Amber stood there straddling her bike, waiting patiently, she noticed a car slowing down next to them. The window rolled down and revealed Mary and Maggie.

"Hello, dear, what a nice day to be out for a ride," Mary commented with a cheerful smile.

The weather had changed drastically from how gorgeous it had been the day before. The sun was tucked behind some clouds, the air was a little cooler, and Amber could almost smell rain.

"Mary and Maggie, this is my son, Dylan, the one I was telling you two about," Maggie introduced her son. He gave a polite smile and wave.

"Nice to meet you, Dylan." Mary directed her gaze at him.

Maggie put the car in park and got out of the driver's side and walked around the car. "Hey, Amber, how's it going? I figure it's easier to talk like this than trying to see over my mother." Maggie laughed. Amber could tell that Maggie wanted to ask her a ton of questions, and they all probably centered around seeing her with Patrick at the grocery store.

Mary decided to get out of the car as well and join them. Their sedan was parked along the curb, traffic driving by slowly, passersby waving and greeting Mary.

"How was the service?" Dylan asked shyly.

"Very good, dear, very good," Mary replied.

"Are we keeping you guys from anything? We were just out for a ride. We don't want to hold you up," Amber nervously rambled.

Maggie grinned. There was no way that Amber was getting away that easy. "We are headed home to make Sunday dinner." Maggie got a strange gleam in her eyes. "I have a wonderful idea, Mom. Why don't we have Amber and Dylan join us?"

Mary's face glowed. "That's a terrific idea. Oh, yes, you two must come over. Now, I insist."

Amber snuck a glance at Dylan, and he nodded. "Well, as long as you are sure it's not too much trouble?"

"If it were, I wouldn't have asked you." Mary grinned as she started to get back into the car. "Should I have Patrick pick you up, or do you know where our home is?"

Amber looked at Maggie; the cat was definitely out of the bag. She couldn't help but feel a little set up.

Maggie started back to the driver's side of the car; she paused and smiled. "It will be great getting to know you."

"Dinner is served around six. You don't need to bring anything, just yourselves," Mary stated as she pulled her seatbelt over her.

Amber stood there, watching Maggie pull away, feeling bamboozled about going over for dinner. Her head was spinning. What was Patrick going to say? She needed to call him and let him know what was going on.

"So, they seemed nice," Dylan said as they rode back to their home.

"Yes, they are. That was Patrick's mother and sister."

"Yeah, his sister has the same eyes as he does. His mom seemed nice, kind of like Grandma." Dylan kept close by Amber as they pedaled through the neighborhoods. The weather hadn't changed much. Amber could still smell rain, but she knew for sure a storm was coming, and it didn't have anything to do with the weather.

***

Amber fussed with her dress. Was it too short? Why did it matter? She wasn't going over to the O'Brien house as Patrick's girlfriend. It's not like he was bringing her to dinner. Stress gripped her tightly, holding her hostage to her anxiety. She had been trying to reach Patrick all day, to give him some kind of warning, but had not had any luck. Now it was a little after five, and she and Dylan were getting ready to go soon. She dialed his cell again, willing for Patrick to answer, but it went straight to voicemail.

"What's wrong, Mom?" Dylan asked as he laced up his shoes. He had just gotten dressed after showering; he wore dark wash jeans and a brown polo shirt. He looked handsome and almost too grown up for her liking.

"Nothing's wrong, hon," Amber lied. A lot was about to be wrong, especially once they arrived.

Dylan eyes her suspiciously. "You're acting

weird. Do you not want to go to dinner?"

"Oh no, it's nothing, I promise."

He shrugged and continued to tie his shoes. "Well, I think it's pretty cool we are going to see Patrick. You said he'll be there, right?" Her son looked up at with a hopeful smile. Her precious boy, he needed to be around other men; sometimes being a mom was not quite enough. Sure, she tried to fill both positions as mom and dad, but a boy needed other men, some natural instinct which she didn't quite possess.

"I want us to leave soon. I'd like to stop at the store for a couple of things." Amber checked her outfit one more time in her full-length mirror. The dress was pale blue, with very feminine little pink flowers all over it. She wore a light white sweater to help cover her up, but she was now suddenly conscious of the thin straps and how exposed her arms were.

Her hair was a whole different matter, and she was beyond annoyed, as her dark hair was not cooperating. Amber ran her brush through it again. There was officially nothing it would allow her to do, so she just left it. But as she passed her dresser, she snagged a hair tie, just in case she couldn't stand it being down.

"You ready to go, kiddo?"

Dylan jumped up quickly from the couch. She hadn't seen him this excited for a while. She just prayed that tonight went well.

***

Patrick

The O'Brien house was always loud on Sundays, but this had to be some kind of new record. They were at capacity. Leave it to his mother to invite everyone to dinner. The one advantage was the enormous deck that allowed people to move about and not be isolated inside the home.

"Here, can you take this out to that table?" Mary pointed to an extra table that had been set up to act as a buffet.

"Sure, Mom." Patrick carried the large glass bowl that was filled to brim with potato salad. He watched the kids playing, laughing, and giggling. He was tempted to join them. Patrick felt oddly lonely today. Maybe it was the mild remnants of whiskey working its way through his system from the night before, but he felt out of sorts.

Rachel and Liam were sitting in their cloud of wedded bliss, chatting with her mother and brother. Things appeared to be going well, from the happy looks on all their faces. Chelsea was sitting as close as humanly possible to Ethan, ignoring Patrick completely. Maggie and their mother were busy in the kitchen. Michael and Daniel sat with Grandpa Paddy and their father. Everyone looked content and peaceful. Patrick just wasn't one of them. He felt his mood darken, and then he heard the distant sound of the doorbell. His mother had more people coming to dinner?

***

Amber

She pressed the small button by the door. She could hear it chime through the home, even with her standing on the porch of the adorable Craftsman-style home. Dylan was close by, holding some of the goodies she had brought with her. Her own hands were clutching a large bouquet of flowers—a delightfully cheery arrangement of sunflowers.

Amber watched the door open. Mary greeted them wearing an apron with American flags all over it. It was festive and adorable, just like Mary.

"My, those are lovely. Please come in," Mary said as she ushered them inside.

Amber followed her and stood at the entrance of an enormous living room. It could easily accommodate the large family, and Amber could only imagine all the memories they probably had made in that room. It was warm and comfortable, tastefully decorated in a rustic feminine manner that also made it feel cozy. The large brown leather couches had throw pillows of varied colors, all pleasing to the eye, and candles sat next to family pictures, encased in mix and matched frames on the mantle of the giant fireplace. Mary directed them to the kitchen, where Amber simply fell in love. The kitchen was beautiful, a cook's dream with the double oven, the large range, and the insane amount of counter space.

"Mary, your kitchen is incredible."

"Thank you, dear. I seem to like it." Mary smiled and reached to accept the flowers from Amber.

"I can only imagine having a kitchen this

amazing. Mine back in Portland was pretty great, but this, this is what I'm talking about. Oh, the baking I could do in here," Amber rambled.

Dylan nudged her and asked, "Hey, Mom, what about this stuff?" He gestured to the paper sack he had been holding.

"Thanks, sweetie, sorry. Mom was just admiring Mary's kitchen," Amber answered as she relieved her son of his carrying duties.

"Mary, your home is very nice," Dylan complimented, his eyes searching for something, or rather, someone.

"Why, thank you, Dylan. That's very kind of you." Mary squeezed his shoulder tenderly. "Everyone is outside. Let's go say hello, and then we can come back in the kitchen. Amber, I could certainly use your help." Mary weaved her way back to the hall they were in just moments earlier. They followed her to a door which led them to an expansive deck and onto the greenest grass she quite possibly had ever seen. Before she could take it all in or be able to survey who was there, her eyes connected with Patrick's. His eyes were wide with bewilderment, and he immediately walked toward her and Dylan. His expression was one more of confusion rather than anger.

"Amber, hi, what are you doing here?" He then looked at his mother, who had suddenly disappeared.

"God, I'm so sorry. I ran into your mom and sister. They invited us over." Amber wrapped her arm around Dylan, pulling him close to her side.

"Hi, Patrick," Dylan said shyly. He looked at the ground and asked, "Are you mad that we came?"

"No, buddy." Patrick softened his tone. He extended his hand to Dylan, who quickly reached for it. "I want you to meet my brothers." He tipped his head to look at Amber, winked, and dragged Dylan away. Her son was off to join the pack.

***

Patrick

He couldn't express the range of emotions that were bubbling inside of him right now. But seeing the possible hurt and rejection in Dylan's face somehow made him react completely opposite of how he wanted to. The poor kid had lost his father, and he was getting to that age where it was important for him to be around other men. Amber was a great mom; he never doubted her abilities for a second, her son had manners and respect, two things that showed Patrick that she had done a remarkable job raising him, despite their loss.

"Hey, guys, this is Dylan," Patrick announced as he approach where all his brothers were now sitting. Patrick gripped Dylan's small shoulder. "That guy there, that's Daniel. Watch out for him. That weird looking, tall guy, that's Liam. The guy that looks nothing like the ones I just pointed out, that's Michael. He's my sister's husband."

"Nice to meet you, Dylan," Liam said as he stood to shake Dylan's hand.

Daniel grinned and gave Dylan a more modern handshake. "Cool to meet you, Dylan."

Michael extended his hand and said, "Great

meeting you, Dylan. Care to join us?"

Dylan beamed, and his excitement wasn't lost on any of the guys. But they all wore a confused expression, except for Liam, who gave Patrick a knowing stare and playful grin.

After a couple of minutes of getting Dylan comfortable with his brothers, Patrick offered to get Dylan a drink, but what he wanted to do was find Amber. Then maybe his mother.

Patrick walked by the kitchen to find both his mother and Amber huddled over some food. It was an odd sensation seeing Amber there. She seemed relaxed and at ease around his mother as he watched them, not wanting them to realized he was only a few feet away. He wanted to see how they interacted. Could Amber fit into this family? Did Patrick even want that? After last night, he was so confused again, he felt like any progress he had made in moving on from Beth's death had been halted. Now, as he stood there, seeing Amber so perfectly at home, it worried him. Amber was no longer his secret. Now his family would become involved, pushing him to open up about her, to answer questions he had no answers to, at least not yet. The opportunity was now lost for Patrick to take the relationship at his pace, without the pressures of the family. Instead of being happy that Amber was being easily accepted, this almost had an entirely different effect. Now, he wasn't so sure that this was what he wanted.

Chapter Seventeen

Rachel

Saying goodbye was hard, a lot harder than she realized. Rachel and Liam were standing outside the airport terminals. Her mother had her Louis Vuitton rolling suitcase next to her, and Ethan had his backpack slung over one shoulder, his luggage next to him. Chelsea's eyes were hidden behind her large Hollywood-style glasses, her bags at her feet. Hugs had been exchanged multiple times; Rachel could feel tears threatening to spill each time she touched either of them.

"So, Mom, do you think you might be able to come back for the birth?" Rachel subconsciously placed her hand protectively on her belly, which was now starting to finally bulge. She had been grateful it had waited until after the wedding to start growing visibly round.

"You just tell me when those little precious darlings are to be born, and I will fly up," Evelyn promised as she hugged Rachel again.

"I'm so glad you made it up for the wedding. It meant so much to me." Rachel felt the tears; they were already running down her face as the words left her mouth.

Chelsea pulled herself hard against Rachel. "I'm going to miss you so much. But I'm so happy for you."

"You'll come up for the birth too?" Rachel asked as they clung onto each other.

Through bubbling sobs, Chelsea assured her that she would. "They need to meet their Auntie Chelsea. You guys are going to have the cutest babies."

"Aww, thanks. God, this is so hard. I hate goodbyes." Rachel struggled to talk, her chest ached, and her make-up was ruined.

Chelsea tried wiping the smeared eyeliner from under Rachel's eyes. "You are a mess. You need to stay pretty." Her own voice was sad and watery. They hugged once more.

Liam and Ethan stood a few feet away, and they shook hands, even making plans for hanging out in the future. Evelyn pulled back, sucked in her stomach, not that there was even an ounce of body fat on her, straightened her posture, and hugged Liam one final time. "You be good to her," she told him.

Rachel grabbed her brother one more time, forcing him to hug her."Come on, we got a plane to catch. Just make sure you are happy, Rachel. You can call me anytime if you need help," Ethan said quietly in her ear. She nodded and squeezed him once more.

They all faced each other in a semi-circle. This

was it. Rachel noticed Ethan started to wheel his bag and his mother's toward the automatic doors. Leave it to him to make the first move; that was his style. Chelsea followed closely behind them, turning back to give Rachel one final half smile and blew her a kiss. They disappeared through the large glass doors. Rachel stood there watching them as they fell into line with the other travelers. Liam wrapped his arms around her and kissed the top of her head.

"You want to get something to eat or go shopping before we head back home?" Liam asked once he was able to convince Rachel to get into the car. They had taken Patrick's large SUV, and now he was pulling away from the loading curb.

"I just want to go home." Rachel wasn't hungry, her stomach was in sad knots, and she felt depressed. She hadn't realized how much she had missed her family. She looked at Liam, who was staring straight ahead, watching the slowing traffic. Rachel focused on his handsome face; the light start of stubble along his jaw was already growing back despite having been shaved that morning. She reached over and brushed her lips against his cheek.

"What was that for?" He smiled at her. His green eyes darted toward her, then back to the road.

"Because I'm happy I married you."

"I'm happy I married you too," Liam said as he carefully switched lanes and then continued, "I know you miss them, Rachel. I am so glad they came up for the wedding."

"I do miss them. It's great we got to spend the time we did." She placed her hand on his thigh.

"But we're married now, and we need to enjoy it before these babies are born."

"Oh, trust me, I intend to." He shot her one of his famous sexy grins, the same one that got her there in the first place. The same one that would keep her next to him forever.

***

Patrick

It was Monday, again. He had slept terribly the night before, his coffee had not quite worked its magic yet, and the boys were fussing about their oatmeal; they had wanted waffles instead. It was going to be that kind of day, he could just tell.

It had all started yesterday. He'd woken up moody and irritable the morning following Liam's wedding; hell, he had been fairly miserable at that too. But he was pretty sure he knew why he had slept so awful again last night—Amber. Leave it to his mother and sister, who were again meddling in his life. They had invited her over, of course without telling Patrick. He knew it wasn't Amber's fault; she even told him that she'd tried calling to warn him. He did appreciate that, but unfortunately he hadn't checked his phone. The dinner itself was only partially uncomfortable and actually went better than he expected after being blindsided by Amber's arrival. She did her best to keep her distance from him; she understood his concerns and tried hard to not give the impression that they had anything romantic going on. During dinner, when the time had come to sit down and eat, Amber made small talk with everyone and really seemed to get on well with his mother. That scared him.

Patrick was headed to work, his brain still groggy as he pulled into the driveway of the shop. God, he needed more coffee. It was pointless to drink the stuff; he needed to have it intravenously, then he might actually get the much-needed caffeine buzz. He parked his SUV and walked up to the building. He could already feel the sun's heat bouncing off the metal. Today was going to be a hot one.

"Good morning, Patrick," Maggie called out to him the moment he stepped inside.

He nodded and hoped he could quietly retreat to his office, but he knew that she was going to hound him about Amber. Now it was just a waiting game. Maggie didn't approach Patrick about running into them at the grocery store; she didn't say anything after Amber left dinner last night. The whole thing made him uneasy. What was she waiting for?

"Hey, Patrick," Daniel said as he rounded the corner.

"Morning," Patrick muttered.

"Oh boy, someone's in a foul mood. What's going on?" Daniel asked as he leaned against the counter. Maggie left her desk and went to the counter.

Patrick swallowed. They were like raptors, working as a team to strike at him. "Nothing's wrong," he lied.

Maggie's lips curled into a smirk. "Well, I think we have a lot to discuss."

"Not now, Maggie." Patrick raised his hand up, hoping to stop her.

She placed her hands on her hip and cocked her head to the side. "Really? Then when?"

"Never," he answered.

She huffed, her growing pregnant belly moved as the air escaped her. "Patrick, what's going on? I mean, you lie to me the other night about watching the boys, I run into you at the store with her. Are you guys dating, how long?"

Daniel looked confused. "Lied? You saw them at the store together?"

Maggie turned to Daniel. "Yes, I ran into Patrick with Amber the other night. He'd said he was going to play poker with you guys. Apparently not."

"What?" Daniel looked at Patrick.

"Oh, get over it. You guys lie about stuff all the time. I just didn't want to have to explain myself," Patrick stated, his annoyance growing by the moment. He still hadn't had enough coffee to deal with this confrontation.

"I just don't get why you feel the need to keep things from us. I would have gladly watched the boys knowing that you were going to be on a date or whatever. I just don't see the sense in lying about it." Maggie directed her fiery glare at him.

"Because you guys get into my business, you hound me with endless questions, and honestly, I don't even know if I want to date Amber, or anyone for that matter. I just wish you guys would leave me alone."

Daniel rubbed his jaw; his skin was turning an off shade of red, silent anger clearly burning within him. Maggie swung her head back and laughed. "Are you seriously going to act like this? Amber seems really nice. I'm not sure what she wants with a guy like you, always moping around," she mocked him, making an exaggerated sad and pouty face.

"Real mature, Maggie." Patrick was beyond agitated now. He moved to go to his office. Daniel blocked his way.

"I think it's ridiculous, Patrick. Here you finally meet someone who's beautiful and sweet, and you act like you don't care if you even date her. How unfair is that to her? Now Mom invited her to the house, you introduce her son to us guys, and what, now you want nothing to do with her, because we might have a couple questions for you? That's just stupid, Patrick."

"Oh, you think so, do you?" Patrick squared his shoulders and planted his feet firmly on the polished concrete floor.

Daniel shook his head. "You got a lot of nerve, Patrick. We have been nothing but loving to you and supportive when Beth died. We gave you your space. We tried to walk on eggshells for years. Well, I'm fed up. This needs to stop. You can't treat us like this. It's not right after everything we have done for you." Daniel was seething.

Patrick knew his brother had a point, but he was not interested in hashing this out right now.

"Daniel, I get where you are coming from, but you haven't been in my shoes," Patrick tried to explain.

Daniel rolled his eyes. "That's right, none of us know. We'll never know how hard Patrick has it."

He swung his arms out wildly, his eyes burning with anger. "Pull yourself up by the bootstraps and get on with your life, man. It's been four years. It's time to move forward."

Patrick felt the frustration well up inside him. Daniel didn't understand the half of it. He hadn't even been in a serious relationship, let alone been married. How could he get them to understand? Not a single one of them had been where he had. "I'm not getting into this with you, Daniel. We're done talking about this." He shoved past his brother and stomped toward his office. Daniel trailed him, acting so unlike himself. Maggie stood there with her mouth open, completely shocked.

"So you think just because you say you don't want to talk about it, that's how it's going to be?" Daniel was in the door frame, his voice raised and his temper flaring.

Patrick stood there, staring at Daniel, who was growing more pissed off by the second. "Daniel, once you actually have been in a relationship, then you can talk to me about this. Until then, you can't possibly understand and really need to back off."

Daniel smacked the inside of the doorway, rattling the wall, causing a picture to drop to the floor. He gave Patrick a hard glare that spoke volumes. Patrick had crossed the line. Daniel turned around and stormed out of the shop.

"Dammit, Patrick," Maggie said as she came from behind the counter. "Honestly, why? Daniel has always defended you. He didn't deserve that."

"Maggie, you started it, again. This is why I don't need you or anyone else in my business."

Patrick sat down in his chair. The day was turning out to be fan-friggin-tastic.

***

Amber

The dinner rush was finally over. Amber couldn't be happier as she looked outside through the large front windows of the diner as the last customer pulled away. She had sent her mother home a little while ago, and Dylan was in the back helping with the dishes. It had been just a terribly long day, and she was more than ready to go home.

"Mom, what else do you need me to do?" She turned and saw Dylan stand behind the counter, wearing an apron that was too large for him, his cheeks red and his hair wet with sweat. He had been helping them out the last couple of days. It was fun working with him and reminded Amber of the times she spent with her dad at the diner.

"You did all those dishes?"

"Yep, I even mopped the back and everything," Dylan added proudly.

Amber smiled. "That's great, then let's get ready to head home."

They did a couple more tasks before they pulled their bikes through the door and mounted them. The cool evening breeze felt amazing after sweating all day. The sky had traces of orange, red, and pink as the sun started to set behind the mountains. Amber relished the quiet sound of the bicycle tires spinning against the asphalt. She looked over at Dylan, who looked relieved to be out of the diner.

"You did great today, Dylan. I'm really proud of you."

He smiled, and she saw his cheeks grow pink from blushing. "Thanks, Mom. You were right, you know?"

"Oh really, about what?" They coasted on a slight down grade and let the natural force of momentum carry them.

"About working at the diner. I can see now how you did enjoy it as a teenager. It's not so bad, I guess."

"Well, I love you being there." Amber pedaled as the approached a slight incline, and they rounded the corner to their street.

"Hey, Mom, when do you think we will get to go over to the O'Brien house again?" Dylan asked as they stored their bikes in the garage.

"I'm not sure, sweetie." Amber wasn't quite sure how to answer her son. Things were a little strained between Patrick and her. He wasn't acting himself when she was over at his family's house, though she did appreciate his kindness to Dylan. Amber enjoyed visiting; she was quite fond of Mary and found they both shared a passion for baking and cooking. Amber spent the evening getting to know Maggie, Rachel, and her family, and really found herself liking the O'Brien family. What Amber couldn't understand was why Patrick didn't want her around them; they were great.

"I hope we can see Patrick and his brothers again. They're pretty cool."

Amber hoped so too, but after last night she went

233

home with a lot of uncertainty.

***

"Oh good, you two are back. Your father was starting to worry," Lynn said as Amber and Dylan walked through the door.

"Sorry, we enjoyed a little bit of a longer ride home."

"Don't listen to your mother. I know my girl can handle herself, plus she had that guy with her." Her father was sitting on his recliner, the news blaring from the small TV in the living room. Dylan went up and gave his grandfather a hug. "How's things at the diner, Amber? You burn it down yet?" he teased as Amber plopped down on the couch next to her mother.

"Well, if you'd hurry up and get better, you wouldn't have to worry. But as of today, no structure fires," Amber joked back. Lately her father had seemed better. He was eating again and had more energy; even the color was returning to his face. They had met with the oncology doctor a week ago and would be doing further scans to see if the chemo was working.

"I know you got everything under control there, hon. I appreciate more than you'll ever know."

"Dad, I know. It's funny because just today Dylan mentioned he actually liked helping out," Amber added proudly. Dylan, who was seated next to her, rolled his eyes and groaned.

"The boy should be out fishing and riding his bike with his friends."

"Oh, but he's been a great help," her mother countered. "We've needed a strong guy around the place to fill in while you were away. He's just keeping your post warm for you, dear."

Amber felt her body grow restless in the noisy living room. Her parents loved watching TV, they had their favorite shows, some of which Amber couldn't get into, but she tried when they would beg her to watch with them.

"Hey, I'm going to shower and then I have some blog stuff I need to work on," Amber explained as she headed toward her room. Dylan got up and grabbed his laptop, setting it up on the dining room table. Amber considered joining him but thought better of it. She would need to be able to concentrate on her blog, to give it some undivided attention that it had been lacking. Then she planned to journal; she needed to try and work through some of the conflicting feelings she was having, all of which were about Patrick.

***

Amber was pouring a cup of coffee for a customer when she saw Maggie come into the diner. Their eyes connected, Maggie giving her a broad smile as she weaved her way to the counter.

"Hey, Amber," Maggie greeted her and tried to take a seat at the counter. Amber was surprised at how much more Maggie's belly was protruding and saw what a difficult time she was having trying to get on the stool. "I think I'll take a table instead. This darn belly is starting to cause some issues. If I have to push my seat back in my car any further, I won't be able to reach the pedals." They both laughed, because it was the awful truth.

"Well, you look great. You're honestly glowing."

"Aww, thanks, I really appreciate that. Because I'm starting to get to the point where I can't see my feet anymore."

"Been there. So what can I get for you and the baby?" Amber asked sweetly. She really liked Maggie and hoped they could become closer, not even for the sake of Patrick, but because Amber craved some female interaction.

"I actually came in to see you. Do you have a couple minutes to sit and chat?" Maggie looked up at her hopefully.

The breakfast rush was dying off, and Lynn was in the back prepping food with Dylan for the next wave of customers. "Sure, I got a little time. You want some tea or anything to eat?" Amber offered as she fluttered toward the counter near the coffee station. She needed caffeine; coffee sounded great right now.

"Tea would be wonderful," Maggie answered politely.

"You take any sugar, cream, or honey?" Amber called out. She quickly poured hot water into one of the standard, boring, beige mugs that they'd always had. Her parents never thought to order anything different, she had suggested in the past, and their response had been simple, "It's what's on the inside that counts." They did have a valid point there.

"Just sugar, please."

Amber carried their drinks and all their fixings,

along with two scones on a tray.

"That looks good." Maggie eyed the homemade huckleberry scone. Huckleberries only came in around a certain season, and you had to know where to find them. Pickers kept their locations secret, and the precious, sweet, little, red-looking berries were worth their weight in gold.

Amber sat down, enjoying the feeling of actually sitting and resting. When she was working she found herself in constant motion. There was never a dull moment or time to get bored, especially with her father being ill; her mother and she were carrying the weight of the diner.

"So what's up?" Amber asked, adding some creamer and sugar in her coffee. She watched the brown turn milky and appealing, and she could hardly wait to start sipping. She grabbed hold of the warm mug and inhaled its rich aroma. Yes, she loved coffee, especially that first cup of the morning, but now, this was her third, but who was counting?

Maggie took a small bite of the scone, closed her eyes, and moaned in delight. "This is delicious. Dare I say that it's better than my mom's?"

"I won't tell her." Amber giggled at the compliment. Mary O'Brien was well known in the community for being a fabulous cook and baker. Amber had enjoyed her cooking on Sunday, though it was a simple BBQ, mainly because she had so many guests, but from what Amber tasted, it was all fantastic.

"Did you make these?" Maggie held up the scone before she sunk her mouth on it.

Amber nodded and felt herself blush. "Yeah."

"No wonder my mom likes you. You guys are like two culinary peas in a pod." They both laughed and then sipped on their drinks.

Maggie released a content sigh. "So I might as well just come out with it. What's going on with you and Patrick?"

Amber took her time responding, as things were complicated. She hadn't spoken to Patrick since Sunday, granted it was only mid-week, but they had been chatting every day before that. So she knew all was not well.

Cautiously, she answered as honestly as possible, "You know, I'm not too sure. I sort of thought that maybe there was something, but right now he just seems like he might need a little room."

Maggie rolled her eyes and gave her a lopsided grin. "Well, he's been needing space for over four years. Probably longer, even." Maggie took another sip of her tea and continued. "He really loved Beth, and he's been through hell and back trying to cope. But he just shuts us all out."

Amber nodded again. "I see that." Without selling Patrick out, she kept her responses vague.

"So you can probably imagine my surprise, when I see you two at the grocery store together. Now, Amber, please don't think I mean this in a bad way. I don't. In fact, I'd be thrilled if he was dating you. I just don't like him lying about it or feeling like he needs to hide things."

"I completely agree with you." Amber scanned the room in case she was needed, but luckily today was proving to be a slow one. "I think Patrick's a good guy, he's sweet, and even my son adores him.

Actually, Dylan is like, over the moon with all your brothers. He just thinks they are the coolest group of guys. But I just don't know what Patrick and I are doing."

"They thought the world of Dylan. It was all they talked about after you guys left. As for Patrick, well, be patient with him, if you can. He's getting better, believe it or not, well, until recently. I think the wedding brought back a lot of feelings, and then with me and Rachel both having babies. It's a lot to take in. There hasn't been any births since the twins, and well, you know that whole story."

Amber frowned; her heart broke for Patrick. She understood that kind of trauma, that hole that you get sucked into during the grieving process. "I totally know where he's coming from. When Peter was killed, it was the most awful, terrifying thing that I had ever been through. I wasn't prepared for anything like that."

Maggie reached for Amber's hand. She didn't realize that she was starting to shake and that tears were falling down her cheeks. Two years had passed, but she still had a difficult time talking about his death. Patrick had double that time to process everything, and he still struggled; it was something that many people didn't quite understand themselves, let alone knew how to counsel others who were going through it. Death and grief were not easy; whether it was expected or sudden, moving on and coping proved to be almost more challenging.

"It's a hard thing, Maggie," she was finally able to say as she tried to sip her coffee, the warm liquid hitting the emotional lump that was forming in her throat.

Maggie gave her a sympathetic look. "Just don't allow Patrick to push you away. He'll try, trust me. He does it to everyone he cares about."

Chapter Eighteen

Patrick

"Just how long are you going to keep this up?" Patrick asked. Daniel glared at him and continued hammering. It had been several days of no speaking, no jokes, or relentless teasing, nothing. It was actually starting to bother Patrick. He figured after their fight, if you would even call it that, and that Daniel would cool down and act normal. Not the case, no, Daniel was completely ignoring Patrick to the best of his ability. They had been out at another job site, and the ride there had been filled with uncomfortable silence.

Daniel refused to answer Patrick. "This is ridiculous." Patrick started to storm away. He didn't have time for this nonsense.

"Maybe if you would actually apologize, people would want to talk to you," Daniel called after him, causing Patrick to stop in his tracks. *Apologize?* What did he do?

"What?" Patrick turned around fast.

"You know, say you're sorry." Daniel moved forward.

"Why do I have to? What did I do?"

Daniel rolled his eyes. "It's the way you treat everyone, like they haven't got a clue in their damn heads how it is for you. You treat everyone like crap the second they want to help you or if they are concerned."

"Oh, come on, I only ask that people leave me alone," Patrick argued.

"People? Is that all we are to you then?" Daniel challenged him. "Because it's funny, I thought we were your family. Would you want your sons treating you like this?"

Patrick considered this, he tried to reason that he would want to give them their space and privacy, but in his heart he knew differently. Of course he would want to know what was happening in Finn or Connor's life; he would want to give advice and help them. That's when it started clicking together, and Patrick saw that it was more than his family pestering him for information and trying to make him talk. They wanted to help him. He knew that they cared, but he just didn't see how they could help him. How could they offer advice when not one of them had been through what he had? Except for one.

"I would want my sons to come to me. You're right, Daniel." Patrick lowered his eyes and stared at the ground, focusing on some stray pebbles and bits of weeds trying to grow through the cracked concrete.

"Really?" Daniel seemed surprised.

"I'm sorry, especially to you. You have always tried to not get in my way. You and Liam have been good brothers to me. Far better than I have been to you guys," Patrick admitted.

"You know what?" Daniel started as he put his hand on Patrick's shoulder. He darted his attention up toward the brilliant blue sky.

"What?" Patrick asked, a little confused.

"We need to go fishing. Fishing fixes everything."

***

Amber

Amber was busy grilling up some onions to put on a burger when she heard someone come into the kitchen. She turned and saw her father.

"Dad, what are you doing here?"

"I wanted to make sure everything was still standing." He laughed as he stretched his arm across her shoulders.

"You feeling okay?" Amber was concerned he was pushing himself too hard. It was wonderful seeing him, but she just wanted him to rest and get better.

"Today, yes, I feel good. Good enough to check on you ladies." He winked as her mother entered the kitchen.

"Dean, you should be home resting," Lynn scolded, but her eyes glowed with happiness.

"Yeah, you two just want to run this show by yourselves. Too bad, this is my kitchen," he teased.

243

That was true. He had always been the cook; he had a passion for food. That's where Amber got her talent for creating amazing dishes with ease. Her mother was the smile behind the service; her sweetness is what kept the customers happy, while her father's great food kept them coming back.

"How's it been today?" her father asked as he stared at the grill. Amber moved the caramelized onions onto a patty waiting on a plate.

"Well, with it being Moose Days, it's been a little quiet. No surprise," Lynn answered. Moose Days was a fun carnival type of festival that happened every July. Vendors from the surrounding area would set up booths to sell their wares, and there were food trucks galore. Even the Saucy Gents, the famous BBQ sauce and BBQ truck, came all the way up to Birch Valley to partake in the event. There were rides and games, and musicians would perform on the giant stage in the park; it was really a wonderful thing for the community. It was best treat to celebrate the summer, and Amber remembered eating cotton candy with her friends, riding the Ferris wheel, splashing in the small river that ran through the park, running in the lush grass with bare feet. She was excited to take Dylan that evening after they closed the diner.

"You guys going to go tonight?" Amber asked as she handed off the fully dressed burger to her mother.

"We might, huh, Dean?"

He eagerly nodded. It was great seeing him looking more like her dad, the guy who wasn't trying to fight cancer.

"I'm going to take Dylan. I think he'll enjoy it." Dylan was in the lobby wiping a couple tables and assisting his grandmother.

"Oh, I bet he will. You loved it every year." Amber could see her father was itching to cook.

"Dad, do you mind making this next order? I need to take a quick break," Amber asked as she went to untie her apron. She didn't need a break, but she could tell her father wanted to be in front of his grill, doing what he did best.

He smiled at her, winked, and quickly grabbed a nearby hanging apron. She sent a silent prayer to God, thanking him for healing her father. She knew it wouldn't be long before he was back at the diner.

"Where are you going?" her mother asked as Amber walked past the counter.

"On a little break."

"What about the order I just gave you?" Lynn's face twisted in confusion.

"Mom, he's got it." Amber tried to assure her mother. This was good for her dad, to feel like he was normal again. It was a terrible thing to be ruled by a sickness, having the threat of death hanging over you, and this gave him even more of a reason to fight and get well. He loved being in the diner. He was needed, and sometimes that reason alone was enough to push a person to pull through.

***

The air was permeated with the smells of fried fair food and sweet kettle corn that was being cooked in an open copper vat. The sun was low in the sky, allowing the brilliantly colorful lights of all the rides to illuminate the park. Laughter and screams echoed loudly, and music played from the center stage, which sounded like some type of bluegrass country, but it was perfect for the event. People were out dancing, eating, and just enjoying themselves. Children were weaving in and out of the crowds, faces painted, clutching balloons with sticky hands. Amber soaked it all in. This was one of her favorite things about Birch Valley.

"Isn't this awesome, Dylan?" Amber asked as they sat at the bank of the river, watching the swarm of people amid the flurry of activity and listening to the happy sounds of Birch Valley. Their feet soaked in the cool running water. She sipped her huckleberry lemonade she had treated herself to, savoring the sweet flavor. This was what summer was all about.

"It's pretty cool, Mom," he replied as he chewed on a foot-long corn dog.

"So you want to go on anymore rides or do you want to get ice cream later?" Amber offered. She wanted her son to get the full experience.

"Yeah, let's go on some more rides and maybe hit up some of the games."

"You're on." Amber was giddy to be sharing this fun time with her son. She hadn't felt this happy in such a long time, and it was great seeing Dylan's face light up at everything he saw. This was good for them; they'd needed this. It was wonderful just for the two of them to spend this much-needed time together. They ran into her parents earlier, but they hadn't stayed too long, as her father looked exhausted but claimed he was fine. She worried he was using up all the energy he was finally getting back and begged him not to overdo it. He simply hugged her and told her to have a good time. Now that he was back home resting, her mind was at ease, and she was savoring every last morsel of fun she could squeeze out of the evening.

***

Maggie

"We need to see if they have any baby blankets," Maggie told Rachel as they walked through the grassy aisle lined with vendors. "Mom said she came earlier with Dad and Grandpa Paddy, and she mentioned the Belsky family had a booth set up."

"I wish I knew what we were having. I have wait until next month for my ultrasound," Rachel complained as she sipped on her lemonade.

They all were at Moose Days at the large park in the center of town. Michael and her brothers had taken off with the kids and were visiting the carnival side of the fair. This suited Maggie just fine; this allowed her and Rachel to browse the booths and spend some quality pregnant girl time together.

"You don't want to be surprised?"

Rachel shook her head. "God, I have no patience. I was like this at Christmas. I always wanted to know. This is like way worse." They both laughed as they stopped at a booth to browse a table that displayed homemade jewelry.

"It's like the ultimate surprise, and it was so

exciting to find out on that day. It totally beats Christmas."

"See, I figure I'm going to be in so much pain that I won't enjoy the surprise. Plus, you know me, I like to plan things. I want to know how to decorate the nursery. Besides, I have two I have to plan for now," Rachel commented as she lifted up a silver pair of dangly earrings. "How much for these?" she asked the woman seated across from the table under the white tent. After hearing the price, she fished out her cash and purchased them. Turning to Maggie, she said, "Aren't these pretty?"

"Very. I like these." Maggie held up green beaded hoops. "I'll take these, please," she told the woman.

They continued to walk along the aisle, pointing out things that caught their eye. "Oh there's the Belsky booth," Maggie said. She saw Hannah smoothing some quilts that were hung on a rack. "Hi, Hannah."

"Oh, hello. How are you ladies today?" Hannah asked both Rachel and Maggie as they stood looking at the quilts.

"We're great. I have been telling Rachel all about the beautiful quilts you make."

Hannah blushed. "Are you looking for ones for a nursery?"

Both Rachel and Maggie nodded in agreement. "Yes, I love this one." Maggie held up a pastel yellow quilt with delicate blue flowers. The attention to detail was impeccable. "This is gorgeous."

"I really wish I knew what Liam and I were

having. These are really lovely," Rachel commented as she examined several quilts. One was a rose pink, the other a cornflower blue.

"Hi," Hannah's sister, Nina, said as she walked up to the tent with Daniel in tow. "Look who I found, Hannah."

Maggie watched as Hannah blushed again and darted her eyes away. Nina was wearing shorts that were indeed dangerously short, revealing long, thin, tan legs. She had a rainbow-striped halter top that left little to the imagination. Her long, almost bleached blonde hair was hanging loosely on her petite shoulders.

Daniel smiled at Maggie and Rachel, then turned toward Hannah. "Hi, Hannah, how's it going?"

"Good," she replied nervously.

Daniel moved next to Maggie and looked at the quilt she was admiring. He met Hannah's eyes and asked. "Did you make these?"

Nina slithered over to him and gently pried his hand away from the homespun material. "All she does is sew these stupid things."

"I think they're pretty nice, actually," Daniel shot back lightly.

Nina flipped her hair, annoyed at the lack of attention, and looped her arm through Daniel's. "You should go get ice cream with me."

"Um, sure, I guess," Daniel replied as he shrugged his shoulders.

Hannah stood there, frozen and quiet as she watched her sister. Maggie looked at Daniel, who seemed completely unaware of the obvious flirtation from Nina and the ill effect it had on

Hannah.

Nina practically dragged Daniel away. He gave a wave to Rachel and Maggie and told them he would see them later. Maggie rolled her eyes with annoyance. She despised girls like that; she knew that Nina wasn't really interested in her brother, but it was apparent that she just wanted to rub it in her sister's face that she could scoop up any guy and have him do anything she wanted. Maggie had seen the envy in Nina's eyes when Daniel was complimenting Hannah's work.

"Is she always like that?" Rachel asked. Maggie covered her hand over her mouth, trying to stifle the laughter. She was surprised that Rachel didn't mince words and called out the obvious.

Hannah sighed and her eyes seem to follow Nina and Daniel. "Well, she's use to getting whatever she wants, even if she doesn't really want it."

"I'm sorry, that was so rude of me. It wasn't my place," Rachel apologized.

Maggie patted her back. "You just said what we were all thinking."

Hannah offered her a half smile. "She's right, but it's nothing new. So were you interested in a quilt today, or maybe you would like me to make one special?" Hannah diverted the topic of conversation.

"I want this yellow one. It's beautiful and will work if this little one is a boy or a girl." Maggie rubbed her belly.

Hannah carefully removed the quilt from the rack, gingerly folding it and placing it in a large bag. "What about you?" she asked Rachel.

"You know, I find out the gender next month.

Would you be willing to make me two when I find out?"

"Two?" Hannah cocked her head to the side.

"She's having twins," Maggie proudly announced.

"Really? Oh, that's wonderful news." Hannah's face lit up with surprise. "You just tell me when you know what you're having, and I will make something special for you."

"Aww, that's so sweet, thank you, Hannah," Rachel said.

"Well, I'd better go find Michael and the rest of the gang. Thanks again, Hannah. I can't wait to put this in the nursery."

"I'm so glad, and please, if you need anything else made, don't hesitate to ask." Hannah gave Maggie a quick hug and then hugged Rachel.

"Hannah, I will be letting you know when I find out. Now, I'm jealous that Maggie has one."

"Yeah, but you get two," Maggie reminded her.

"Good point."

"Uh oh, I see Mel." Maggie started laughing as her daughter ran up to her, who was practically dragging an enormous plush moose.

"Mommy, look what Daddy won for me," Melanie squealed excitedly. Michael shrugged and gave Maggie a lopsided grin.

"Now how are we going to fit that in the car?" Maggie asked, waving goodbye to Hannah, who was shaking her head at the ridiculously large prize.

***

Patrick

After he carried each of his boys into the house, completely exhausted and tuckered out from the long and happy day at the park festival, Patrick found he was more than ready to retire to bed. The day had been fun; he would admit that. He enjoyed the time he'd spent with his brothers, it'd reminded him so much of his childhood, and he knew his sons loved every second at the carnival. As he yawned and stretched, a lingering thought that had been pestering him most of the day cropped up again—Amber. He still hadn't talked to her in almost a week. Patrick wasn't quite sure what to do, he'd avoided the diner, and the nagging guilt was starting to get to him.

"It's okay, Patrick...you need to move on. You promised me." He shot straight up in his bed, his eyes searching through the blackness of his room. Beth's voice, he heard it, he was sure of it. Patrick hadn't been dreaming about her, but he heard her voice. There were no nightmares accompanying her voice, no sharp or blurry images of her, but he'd heard her, hadn't he?

She wanted him to move on, to remember his promise to her. Patrick lay back down, staring up through the darkness at his bedroom ceiling. Maybe it was the thoughts he had before bed, perhaps it was from missing Amber, because it was starting to kill him to not hear her voice or see her smile, or touch her. He needed to touch her. He hated this empty feeling of longing, and that was why he couldn't be in a relationship. He had protected his heart from feeling anything for over four years, and to have someone penetrate through that thick, calloused wall so quickly scared him. What if something happened to her? Could he handle going through another cycle of soul shattering grief? No, there was no way he could do this all over again. No, Amber was getting too close, making him feel too much.

Promise or no promise, Beth was asking for too much. How could she honestly expect him to move on, to find a mother for their boys? She was their mother. How was she able to lay there, literally dying and have enough sense to implore him to not shut his heart out, to love again? What if the tables had been turned, what if it were him, lying there, broken and uttering his final pleas, would he have been able to ask her to go out and find a replacement? He didn't honestly know. Patrick only knew that he was the one left behind. He had been asked to promise her, and the moment he did, Beth closed her eyes and the machines started to hum a distinct sound he would never forget. She was gone.

Somehow sleep finally took hold of Patrick. It must have, because all of a sudden daylight flooded his room. He threw his comforter off of him and swung his legs over the bed. Patrick felt as tired as did as when he'd gone to bed. Today was going to be rough; it was the start of the weekend, which meant entertaining the true loves of his life, Finn and Connor. He'd better start breakfast and fuel up with strong coffee, extra strong.

***

Amber

She was just starting a new pot of coffee when she heard the ever-constant bell on that old weathered string chime. Amber looked toward the large door and saw Mary O'Brien making a beeline for her.

"Good morning, Mary," Amber said as she casually braced herself against the counter.

"Just the lady I came to see." Mary had a mischievous twinkle in her eyes.

Amber faked a worried expression. "Uh oh."

"Oh, you stop." Mary patted her hand as she took a place at the counter. "My church has asked me to bake for our summer event we hold every July, and I need to call in some reinforcements."

"Ah, okay, what are you needing to have baked?" Amber asked.

"Well, I don't need to have someone bake it for me. I need help baking at my house."

Amber nodded. She figured Mary was seeing about buying pies or baked goods from the diner. People were always ordering desserts to take to special events or even just for home.

"I need you to come over this afternoon, if you'd be so kind. Maggie and Rachel are lending their support, but God love them, neither have the culinary skills that you have. So will you help?"

How could she tell this positively sweet woman no?

"Of course. I'd be happy to help."

"Fantastic, I knew I could count on you. I truly appreciate it. You're welcome to bring that sweet boy of yours over too."

"I'm sure Dylan would like that very much. Thanks for inviting him." Amber smiled. It was a kind gesture, and she knew that her son would love a chance to go over.

Mary told her when to come by the house and thanked her again, swiftly leaving the diner. Amber stood and was instantly hit with regret about accepting Mary's request. Her first thought was that Dylan might get his hopes up about Patrick, who he was incredibly fond of. She doubted Patrick would even be there, and that suited her just fine, but she felt bad for her son. They hadn't talked in almost a week; she could safely assume whatever romance they had going on was probably over now. Amber had spent a lot of her evenings journaling, trying desperately to sort out her emotions. She missed Patrick terribly, his laughter, witty comments, and his touch; she craved that above all. Amber's body had never been given that kind of attention ever before, and it had responded to the way he could orchestrate her pleasure. Patrick was loving and tender, but there was a sexy and erotic streak that left her spellbound. Then there was the conversation she'd had with Maggie, who begged Amber to be patient with her brother. The balance of wanting him and wanting nothing to do with him was starting to kill her. She wasn't sure she was ready for this kind of emotional turmoil in her life, especially now that life was starting to fall back into some kind of normalcy. She looked over and saw her father, dressed in his apron, wearing a satisfied smirk. Things were getting better each day. If nothing else, seeing her father's health starting to return proved that even in the bleakest of times, sometimes things just worked out.

Chapter Nineteen

Amber

"Do you think Patrick or his brothers will be there, Mom?" Dylan asked as they pedaled their way to Mary's home.

"I'm not too sure, I guess we'll find out when we get there. But please don't be disappointed if they aren't, okay?"

"That's why I brought my laptop." Dylan wore his trusty backpack filled with his laptop and some games in the event he did get bored. He was thrilled when Amber told him that Mary had invited them over, but now Amber herself was filled with dread. What if Patrick was there? She wasn't entirely sure she wanted to see him. Her goal today was to bake, to enjoy whatever cooking needed to be done, that was it.

They rode through the tree-lined streets. Very few cars were out driving on that sunny afternoon. Most people were probably out at one of the many surrounding lakes, frolicking in the cool comfort of

257

the water in summer and basking on the sandy shores had always been something she loved doing. People in Birch Valley took advantage of the gorgeous weather during these precious months. Fall, winter, and spring could be brutal, but summer made up for it. Amber could smell the distinct and delicious scent of BBQ in the air. To her, that meant families were outside enjoying themselves, and that summer was in full swing.

As they turned the corner, Amber spied the O'Brien house ahead. Dylan noticed too and started to pedal faster. They parked their bikes to the side of the home near the garage. Amber rang the doorbell and waited.

Mary came to the door, already wearing an apron. This one had large sunflowers all over it. The apron was cheery and happy, just like Mary. "Well hello, dears. Come on in."

Once inside the home, Amber inhaled the spicy scent of cinnamon. Instantly she knew there was an apple pie being prepared. Mary motioned for them to follow her back.

"It smells amazing in here, Mary," Amber commented as Dylan trailed behind her. She saw Rachel and Maggie, both in aprons, working in the kitchen.

"Oh good, reinforcements," Maggie said, a smudge of flour on her forehead.

"Hi guys, it smells great." Amber walked all the way into the kitchen. Dylan stood nervously next to her. "Mary, where can Dylan hang out? He brought his computer to keep himself entertained," Amber explained.

"Well, Dylan, would you like to go into the living room? You might be more comfortable in there. Besides you won't have to listen to us ladies," Mary offered and then ushered him back toward the hallway.

"I'm glad you came. It's too hot to be baking," Maggie complained and wiped her forehead with her arm. That's how the flour found its way on her, Amber guessed. It was a little warm in the kitchen. The windows were open, and it still wasn't quite enough to cool the room down.

"So where can I help?" Amber asked as she saw Rachel peeling apples. Maggie was measuring flour and other dry ingredients into a large pastel green mixing bowl.

"Not sure, I'm sure my mom will find something for you to do. She had no problem finding us jobs." Maggie laughed as she stirred the contents in the bowl.

"Well, I'm happy to help."

"I'm glad to hear that, dear," Mary commented as she entered the kitchen and handed Amber an apron. This one was covered in large colorful flowers. How could one woman seemingly own so many different styles of aprons? Whatever the reason, Amber was fully amused.

"Where do you need me?" Amber smiled at Mary, who led her to an open spot at the counter. She explained what she needed done in order to make her signature crust. In all honesty, Amber wasn't needed there at all. This was just an excuse to get her here, and the sweet thoughtfulness of the gesture warmed her heart.

The women chatted and discussed everything from babies to married life. That topic was a little difficult for Amber, so she concentrated more on her task as Rachel explained how happy she was. Amber was delighted for Rachel. The beginning days of marriage are beautiful with the new appreciation and wonderment of actually being someone's wife. Amber knew that feeling, and she missed it terribly.

As Amber was setting a hot pie from the over on a rack to cool, she heard a door close. Moments later, Patrick was filling the archway to the entry of the kitchen. She glanced up and almost burned herself when she noticed him. His eyes were filled with a quiet panic; he obviously hadn't expected to find her there.

"Hey, Patrick," Maggie said as she placed a dirty dish into the sink.

"Hey," he answered quietly, his eyes never leaving Amber.

She swallowed; he looked good, too good. "Hi, Patrick," she was finally able to squeak out.

He nodded and gave her a tight-lipped smile. Sadness washed over her. What had happened between them? She felt her stomach go sour. She couldn't look at him anymore.

"Amber was kind enough to help your poor mother out. Isn't she a dear?" Mary asked as she hugged him. "She even brought Dylan."

"That is nice, Mom. I didn't see him. Where is he?"

"Living room. Might be nice if you say hello." Mary patted him and practically pushed him out of the kitchen. Daniel entered as Patrick vanished.

"Hello, ladies," Daniel said as he tried to sneak a cookie that was cooling on a tray. In addition to baking several pies, they had made cookies and even some muffins. Amber was just about spent from all the stirring, kneading, measuring, and overall baking.

"Hey, Amber, Mom mentioned that Dylan was here. We are actually on our way out to go fishing at Liam's. Would you mind if we brought him with us? We're taking the twins and Melanie," Daniel explained as he nibbled on a warm chocolate chip cookie.

"I guess that would be okay. I don't mind, but are you sure it's not too much trouble?" Amber asked. She wasn't sure she wanted Dylan to go. He might get the wrong idea, and after the way Patrick seemed just a minute ago, she knew things were now uncomfortable.

"Well, yeah, that's why I'm asking you. I think it'll be fun for him. All of us figured a little evening fishing would be great, and we wanted to include him."

"Okay then. Do you mind dropping him off back at our place?"

Daniel nodded. "Of course, probably be sometimes after eight I'm thinking, maybe even closer to nine. The fish bite a little better once the sun starts setting."

"That's fine. Thanks for inviting him."

"No problem, he's a great kid. Well, I'd better go tell him. I wanted to check with you first."

Amber smiled. She appreciated the consideration

but still felt a little uneasy about the idea.

Daniel went to find Dylan.

"Well, that was nice of the guys to take Dylan," Rachel added as she plopped down in a seat at the table.

"Yeah, it was." Amber looked down, suddenly feeling overcome by sadness and regret.

"You okay?" Maggie asked.

Amber tried to look away, but she felt tears starting to develop. "I don't know. It's just hard, I guess."

Rachel came over to where they were huddled by the kitchen sink. "Am I missing something here? What's wrong?"

"Well, Patrick and I were…" Amber started but felt her voice give out.

Maggie sighed. "They were seeing each other and Patrick is being Patrick. Rachel, you know how he gets."

Rachel frowned and gathered in to hug Amber. "Aww, Amber, I'm sorry. I didn't realize you had been dating him. He's so damn secretive."

She wiped her tears and said, "I know, it just sort of happened, and it was going pretty good, or so I thought. I don't know what happened."

"Patrick is what happened. It's like I told you, he gets all weird and withdrawn. He loves shutting us all out. He just got into it pretty badly with Daniel. I'm glad they worked it out, but it was a nasty argument."

Amber knew that Patrick had his issues, but it was so hard for things to have been left open ended. There was no closure, no breaking up, but had they even really ever been officially together?

***

Patrick

"Thanks so much for inviting me to go fishing with you guys," Dylan said as he sat in the front seat next to Patrick as they drove to Liam's house. Finn and Connor were napping in their car seats, and Patrick was enjoying his visit with Dylan. The kid was intelligent and actually pretty darn funny. But it was his manners and genuinely polite nature that grabbed Patrick's attention.

"Hey, this is one of the best fishing spots, and it just happens to be at my brother's lake."

"That's so cool."

Patrick kept his eyes on the road and asked, "Have you been fishing before?"

Dylan shook his head and explained. "No, not really. Mom talks about how she used to go. I think I may have went once with my dad, but I don't really remember."

"Well, you'll have fun, I promise."

"Will we catch any fish? Do we eat them?"

Patrick laughed. Dylan was full of questions; he reminded him a lot of himself. Always searching for answers, wanting to know everything, and not afraid to ask. Patrick really liked this kid. But his feelings for Amber were muted; he was putting those to rest. It had been difficult seeing her in the kitchen with his family. Again, she just fit in too easily, and somehow that bothered him.

They made the tight, narrow turn onto the road that led them to Liam's property. Daniel was driving behind him in his own truck, kicking up a wild cloud of dust.

"Wow, this is your brother's house?" Dylan's eyes grew wide, his mouth slightly open.

"Yep, he owns several acres, and that lake is his." Patrick pointed to the shimmering body of water. He parked the SUV. "Do you mind helping me wake up Finn and Connor?"

"No, it's no problem. They're real cute kids."

"Thanks, they really like you too."

Dylan blushed and went to gently wake one of the boys. After rousing them from their nap, they all walked to Liam's door, where he was waiting for them.

"Hey, guys, you made it." Liam was carrying a small tackle box. "I just got done getting a pole ready for you, Dylan. I'm glad you were able to come out here with us."

"Thanks for inviting me. This place is so cool." Dylan's eyes were still filled with wonder as he took in the scope of how large the property was and how different it was from living in the heart of town.

"Glad you like it." Liam looked at Patrick. "You guys ready to head down to the water? Michael's already down at the dock with Melanie."

Liam was planning on taking them out in the small fishing boat. Patrick helped carry a couple more poles before they made the trek to the lake. He was going to hand one to Dylan but noticed that he had grabbed the hands of Finn and Connor. This simple gentle act touched Patrick. Again, he saw more of himself in Dylan, the big brother, always looking out for his younger siblings, but Finn and Connor weren't his siblings. A quick thought whipped through his mind, *Dylan could be.*

There were camp chairs set up along the shore, more fishing gear strewn out, a couple of ice chests planted on the water's edge.

"Uncle Patrick and Uncle Daniel." Melanie squealed as soon as she saw them marching down the small hill. She ran up to them full speed and plowed into Patrick. He bent down and kissed her on top of her rust-colored hair.

"How's my favorite niece?"

She giggled and looked at Dylan."Hi."

Dylan smiled at her and slowly released Finn and Connor, who ran toward the water.

Patrick called out for them to be careful. They understood the rules and were wearing little life jackets as an extra precaution.

"Do you wanna play?" Melanie asked. Dylan looked up at Patrick, unsure of what he was to do.

Patrick said, "Why don't you guys play until we get the gear all figured out? Dylan, there are tons of frogs here. Melanie is the best at catching them."

"Really? That's so neat." Dylan set off with Melanie, looking every inch like a country kid. *This would be good for him.*

Daniel caught up to Patrick and commented, "Boy, he's a nice kid."

"I know, I really like him. This will be a good time for him."

"Has he ever been fishing?" Daniel asked as they continued down to the shore.

"He says he thinks his dad took him a long time ago, but he doesn't really remember."

Daniel frowned. "Well, that's sad. Poor guy."

"Yeah, I know."

"So, how are things going with Amber?" Daniel sank into one of the camp chairs once they made it to the shore. Michael was already sitting, and Liam took his place in an empty seat. Patrick joined them, and they all stared out at the calm water. The boat was tied to the small weathered dock.

"I don't know. There's not a whole lot to say," Patrick finally answered Daniel.

"Too bad, she's hot and her kid's cool." Daniel opened the bright red ice chest next to his chair. "Anyone want anything to drink?"

Michael reached out and said, "I'll take a soda." Daniel handed a can of cola over to him. "Thanks, Daniel."

Liam accepted one from Daniel, and Patrick did as well. The fizzy carbonation tickled his throat as he swallowed big, hearty gulps. The chilled soda was refreshing. The air was still hot, the sun was almost sitting behind the mountains, and soon the temp would start to cool down.

"So you aren't seeing her anymore?" Liam asked. "I thought things were going pretty well there for a while."

This was exactly why he didn't want to be in any kind of relationship. He couldn't stand the questions that his loving family pestered him with.

Patrick just shook his head, and Liam continued, "That's too bad. She's a real sweetheart. Rachel really likes her."

"Maggie too. Too bad, sounds like she would have been a good one for you," Michael finally chimed in. Michael didn't usually voice his opinion when it concerned Patrick. They didn't quite have that type of relationship.

"Yeah, well, I'm not interested." The second the words were said, he almost regretted them. He knew it was a lie. If only they were true and he could make himself believe them. He just had to force himself, but that was hard when a twelve-year-old boy ran up to you with a bright and childlike smile, carrying a bucket of frogs.

"Patrick, check these frogs out." Dylan's voice was filled with excitement. Melanie stood next to him, her proud and confident smile sitting on her dirt-smudged face. Finn and Connor scurried up to Dylan, begging to have a look inside the bright red plastic bucket.

He peered into the bucket. At least a dozen small frogs were swimming in some lake water the kids had collected. "Wow, you guys got a lot of those little guys."

Dylan's eyes, which were the same blue-green lagoons as Amber's, shot up at Patrick. "Thank you so much for bringing me here. This has been the coolest day."

Patrick's heart thudded hard in his chest, against that calloused wall he had worked so hard to build, and he thought he was in trouble when he met Amber. Now, he found himself instinctively wanting to be this boy's father figure. When the hell did that happen?

***

Amber

"Well, this has been so much fun. Thank you for inviting me," Amber said as she was removing her apron and getting ready to leave.

"We need to hang out more," Rachel stated from where she was sitting. They had all been drinking tea and finally resting after all that baking—ten pies, dozens of cookies, and muffins. They were exhausted.

Maggie nodded in agreement after sipping from the elegant tea cup she was holding. "For sure, we should plan a girls' day or something."

"That would be fun," Amber said.

"I think we should plan another cooking project together," Mary suggested. She held up a perfectly baked cookie and took a bite.

"I'm good on baking. Thanks, Mom," Maggie teased, and everyone laughed.

"Well, I'd better head home. You ladies have a good night. Thanks again." Amber waved as she left the house. Even though she was tired, there was a happy pep in her step as she bounded off the steps of the porch. She mounted her bicycle and started for home. The street lights had already come on, even though it still wasn't quite dusk, but a couple stars had already popped through the violet sky, signaling that night was near. As she pedaled past Mary's street, she hoped Dylan was having fun. She was thankful that the O'Brien men had included her boy into their small pack. He needed that strong

268

male presence; she just wished things were better between her and Patrick. After talking more to Mary and Maggie, she learned a lot about Patrick. It helped her understand that he never really got help for his grief, and that he had coped entirely on his own. That's not what Amber did; she'd met with a counselor and she attended support groups, after she felt like she wasn't being the mother she needed to be for her son. But journaling was what finally saved her. From what the O'Brien ladies were telling her, Patrick hadn't done a darn thing since Beth died. He refused to talk to anyone, even them. He had completely shut down and shut everyone out; his focus was only to try and raise his sons. It broke her heart hearing Mary retell the stories of the past four years, all the times she just wanted to help her son and to make everything better for him. Amber understood exactly where Mary was coming from. She knew the tears that Mary cried; they poured from her eyes too. She had a son who was grieving, and all she wanted to do was make things better for him, to ease his heartache and suffering somehow. To make it all go away. Wasn't that their job as mothers, to shelter their children from pain and to protect them from life's dreadful blows? It sometimes felt like an impossible battle, and now, Amber felt a stronger bond and closeness with Mary, knowing that they'd both endured that war.

She cruised along, enjoying the feeling of air gently raking her face as she zipped down the quiet neighborhoods. She scanned the road for any cars and enjoyed seeing the cute homes that all had festive-looking flags hanging from their front porches, neatly trimmed grass and hedges, just perfect little slices of America. Amber was glad to be here; it was actually starting to feel like this is where she belonged. Spending that afternoon and the early evening with women, who she now considered friends, made her heart feel glad. It wasn't until that very moment that it sunk in, that this was her new life, Dylan's new life, and that this was home now. She felt light and positive, even with how things were with Patrick. She felt confident that even that situation might get better.

Amber was almost to the main street when she noticed out of the corner of her eye something bright blue. Then she felt a sudden thud and heard the distant sound of brakes screeching. Her brain grew foggy as she strained to focus her thoughts. She could see her green bicycle on the faded and warm pavement, but she wasn't on it. As she saw the metal tweaked and twisted and her back tire spinning in a wobbly manner. She couldn't wrap her mind around why this was happening. She was confused. Amber could hear voices, and then ringing sang loudly in her ears. A sharp pain that splintered through her body, her eyes grew heavy, and darkness was closing in fast. She tried to outrun it in her mind, but it chased her down and finally pinned her. Everything went black.

Chapter Twenty

Patrick

"Okay, wait, what, Mom?" Patrick watched as Liam squinted, trying to understand the call he'd just answered. "Here, let me have you talk to him, okay?"

Patrick was confused as Liam handed him the phone. "Here, it's Mom."

"Hey, Mom, everything okay?" Patrick asked into the gray, cordless phone.

"I tried calling your cell phone." His mother's voice was filled with panic.

The cell service was terrible there, so it was no real surprise she hadn't been able to reach him. "That's okay, what's wrong?" Patrick was firm. He knew something was not right.

Mary paused and asked, "Is Dylan with you?"

"Yes, why?" His patience was growing thin; he sensed her reluctance.

"Okay, I just got a call from Amber's parents. They were trying to find Dylan. I told them that he was probably still with you guys."

"Why, Mom? What happened?"

"Amber's in the hospital. She was struck by a car on the way home from here, Patrick." She spoke slowly. He now knew why his mother was dreading having to tell him. They knew what happened the last time a call like this was made; they knew what the outcome had been.

"Mom, how bad was the accident?" Patrick started to pace. He lowered his voice as he asked his mother; he didn't want Dylan to overhear him.

She started sobbing. "I don't know, Patrick. I don't know."

"Okay, I'm coming now. Should I bring Dylan? Or leave him here with Liam?"

"You might want to bring him to the hospital, Patrick, just in case, dear." She started to cry again.

They hung up, and Daniel, Liam, and Michael were gathered around in a semi circle a few feet away. "What's going on?" Daniel asked, his face scrunched in worry.

Patrick looked to see where Dylan was. The boy was sitting near the shore, holding a fishing pole and laughing with the other kids. "Amber's been in an accident. She's in the hospital."

"What? When?" Daniel probed. He didn't handle stress well and was starting to freak out a little, which scared Patrick. Had he been like this when they got the call about Beth? He hadn't really thought about it until right now.

"I don't know anything. Mom was pretty shook up, though."

Liam put his hand on Patrick's shoulder,

squeezing it gently. "You want me to watch Dylan or go with you?"

"Yeah, you need us to help do something?" Daniel offered, shoving his hands inside his pockets.

Patrick saw the concern on all of their faces; they all were reliving it too. Something clicked. The notion had always sort of been there, but Patrick now knew that he hadn't been the only one truly grieving as he watched Daniel start to tear up and Liam and Michael stare at the ground. Patrick knew Beth's death had hurt all of them, not just him. He could see that now, that it wasn't just her death, but knowing what their brother was going through, the pain that he was feeling. They had grieved for him. Guilt bottomed out in his sick stomach. There would be time for apologizing later. Right now he needed to go to Amber.

"Dylan," Patrick yelled. Dylan perked up, smiling wide, and waved. He was just a boy. Patrick sent a silent prayer. He even asked Beth to please help as he watched Dylan jog up the small hill.

The smile faded as he neared Patrick and the rest of the men. "What's wrong?" Dylan asked.

Patrick inhaled deeply, borrowing strength from somewhere deep inside. "We need to go to the hospital. Your mom has been in an accident."

Tears instantly shot down Dylan's face. "Is she okay?" He had been through this before too. He knew what it could mean.

"I'm not sure, but we need to go find out. I'm here with you, okay?" Patrick wrapped his arm around Dylan's shoulders and ushered him to the car. He looked back at his brothers. They had all been through this kind of hell before.

***

"Is my mom going to die?" Dylan's eyes were red and his voice was cracking as he spoke.

The ride to the only hospital in Birch Valley seemed to be taking forever. It was normally a ten minute drive from Liam's house back into town, but he felt like his tires were stuck in tar and he just wasn't moving fast enough. He peeked down at his speedometer, which confirmed that he was actually going well over the speed limit. Patrick needed to get it together. He suddenly realized he was in the position of being a protector and needed to be the strong one, the one in control, and looking back at it now, it was his parents that were his rock when Beth was dying.

As they pulled into the parking lot of the hospital, they quickly unbuckled their seatbelts, almost running into the ER.

Patrick was hit with a torrent of images; the smells locked into his memory all came flooding back, crashing into his brain, waves of remembrance drowning him. He feared what Amber looked like. Would she be like Beth, hooked up to machines, marred, broken, and dying? His heart was breaking. He couldn't bear the thought. This was not the hospital Beth died in; she had been airlifted to Spokane. So walking inside and seeing the beige walls and white floors didn't spur on any additional memories.

They found the front desk and asked for Amber's

room or if they had any information. Patrick was in mid sentence when he heard some call Dylan's name. Out of a corner in the vacant waiting room, there were her parents, Lynn and Dean Herrick.

"Dylan, oh thank goodness. I was so worried about you." Lynn's eyes were red and swollen. She wrapped her arms tightly around Dylan; she wasn't about to let him go anytime soon. Dean looked awful, his eyes were wet from crying, and both parents looked distraught. He nodded at Patrick.

"Dean, any word on her condition or what happened?" Patrick asked. He felt his frustration and anxiety rising out of control.

"They said that the driver of the car called the ambulance, and she was taken right in. The nurse over there says that a doctor is coming out to talk with us soon." Dean started tearing up again. He balled up his fist and bit his hand, his bottom lip quivering. Amber's father was hanging on by a mere thread. Patrick wasted no time; he didn't hesitate as he pulled Dean in for a hug. He didn't recall Dean being so thin and almost frail. Then again he hadn't seen him at the diner in over a month. It wasn't a subject that Amber really brought up after he met her that first day on that country road. She was more like him than he'd realized. She kept some worries shelved away, not wanting to discuss everything that was happening in their lives.

A man in blue scrubs came out into the waiting room, and he went straight to them. His face wore no expression; he was trained to have no emotion or give anything away, and this man had years of practice.

"Amber's family, I presume?"

"Yes," her parents said unison. The doctor asked for them to follow him. He led them through two enormous doors that swung open automatically after he swiped his badge. Patrick stood there, left behind to wait with Dylan.

"How come he doesn't want us to go back?" Dylan asked, the fear apparent in his eyes.

Patrick could handle this. He would be able to navigate through this. He kept telling himself that Dylan needed someone and that someone was going to have to be him.

"Let's go sit." He took Dylan to the corner where his grandparents had been. It had an excellent view of the large doors they had just gone through. "They usually can only take two at a time. The rooms are very small here," Patrick explained. He didn't want to be honest, not for one damn minute. He didn't want to tell Dylan that his grandparents might be being told the most unbearable news.

"We didn't go to a hospital when my dad died," Dylan was telling Patrick as they both stared at the doors.

"Really?"

"No, two guys from his work came and told Mom. I was doing homework, and they knocked on the door." Dylan started to cry again, and Patrick grabbed the boy and pulled him tight to his side. Dylan muttered against Patrick's ribs, "I never got to say goodbye to my dad. Now, I won't get to say goodbye to my mom. It's so unfair."

He was right; it was unfair. Patrick heard loud

voices and saw Liam, Daniel, Mary, and Maggie entering the ER waiting room. They turned and saw Patrick, all of their eyes searching for answers as they stared at him.

"A doctor just took her parents back." He wanted to scream that he wanted to go and find out, that he wanted answers, and that he needed to see for himself how she was.

They all took seats that were close to each other. "Anyone need coffee?" Maggie offered. Patrick shook his head and kept rubbing Dylan's back, trying to soothe him.

Mary nodded. "I could use something warm. Dylan, would you like to come with me and see if they have any hot cocoa?" Mary stood and reached for Dylan's hand. He didn't rise up quickly; he didn't seem to want to leave Patrick. "It's okay, love. We'll be right back."

Dylan looked at Patrick, in which he nodded encouragingly to follow his mother to the cafeteria. After they left the waiting area, his siblings gathered closer around. Daniel and Liam moved several chairs closer; Maggie sat next to Patrick.

"How are Finn and Connor?" Patrick asked. He already knew they were okay and in the reliable hands of someone in the family.

"They're at my place with Rachel," Liam answered. "You doing okay, Patrick?"

"It's so hard sitting here, not knowing."

Maggie rubbed his arm. "She's going to be okay. Are you sure I can't get you anything?"

Patrick shook his head. "I'm good, thanks."

They all sat there, uncomfortably waiting, and

that was why his mother had taken Dylan in search of hot chocolate. She knew that this would be torture, and again, it was like another break through, he realized that his family had sat in a waiting room, their hands tied as they waited for answers. God, that had to have been hard. There was so much more at stake; there were two babies in limbo and Beth. He now fully understood it all; he saw that life was precious and that you are never prepared. He lifted his head out of his hands. "Guys…"

"Yes?" Maggie whispered. Daniel and Liam's attention was completely on him.

"I guess what I'm trying to say is, is that I get it."

"Get what?" Daniel furrowed his brow in confusion.

"I get that you guys also suffered, that it wasn't just me."

Liam looked down for a moment. "Patrick, we loved Beth. But you lost her, she was your heart and soul, we know that. Hell, I totally understand, now that I found Rachel. We just wanted to be allowed to help comfort you."

"Yeah, it wasn't like we were saying that our grief was nearly the same or that you didn't get the worse end of it," Daniel added.

"Grief is grief, guys. We all lost her. You guys lost a piece of me too. I'm sorry I shut you all out." Patrick didn't realize that the tears in all of their eyes were mirroring his. He felt his cheeks grow wet.

"No matter what happens, we're here. We always will be. We're O'Briens, and we stick together," Maggie said.

"You're right." Patrick saw the same doctor headed straight toward the double doors.

"Patrick?" the man asked. "Amber would like you to come back. She said everyone could, if you'd like."

Patrick leaped out of the chair, and he turned to his siblings. "You guys want to go see her?" The siblings all looked at each other, unsure of what to do, but decided they would go with him. If he was willing to let them be apart of something where he may need support, they wanted to be there for their older brother.

The doctor led them through the doors after swiping his badge again. The halls were spotless, and their shoes squeaked on the waxed, heavy duty white linoleum. They passed several rooms. Some had their doors partially opened. They couldn't see anything, but Patrick couldn't help but feel slightly curious and then guilty. They reached a room at the end of the hall, where the doctor moved to the side allowing Patrick to enter first, his siblings trailing behind. Maggie had her hand on his back and could be heard whispering, "It'll be okay."

Patrick saw her, sitting up in the bed. This wasn't what he expected at all. He smiled and felt his heart explode with joy and thanks as he noticed few scratches and her arm in a sling. He went to the side of her bed. Amber's eyes were glowing with happiness as soon as she'd seen him. She smiled at each of his siblings but returned her gaze to Patrick.

He reached for her. He needed to touch her, to see if this wasn't just imagination. Was she okay? How badly was she hurt? His mouth opened to ask, but without him realizing or taking a second to fight himself, he kissed her. His hands gently cradling the sides of her face, he spotted a few bruises and minor cuts, but she looked amazing. There were no tubes, wires, or machines keeping her alive. Patrick sent a silent thank you to God and to Beth.

"When I heard…" Patrick kissed her again. Amber pulled back, staring back at him in confusion.

"You do realize our whole family is like right here, right?" Amber whispered in his ear.

He nodded, but he didn't care. He was elated that she was okay; he knew now how much she meant to him, how much Dylan meant to him. Patrick felt the hardened wall around his heart break away. He was more than ready to love again; he just didn't expect to find it his first try. He was ready to live up to his promise to Beth and knew that she would approve.

Patrick bent down and kissed Amber again, right as Dylan burst into the room, almost yelling, "Mom." He ran to Amber's bedside, and Patrick stepped to the side. Dylan reached for his hand, giving him permission. "It's okay, you can kiss my mom."

***

Amber

Everyone laughed, even Patrick. The family all continued to visit. Amber tried to tell the story of what happened, though bits and pieces seemed to confuse her. Her body ached, but she was going to be okay. As she felt Patrick's hand holding hers, she realized he hadn't stopped touching her since he walked in. Amber couldn't get over it; she prayed that this wasn't a dream, that she wouldn't wake up and find that they still weren't talking.

He rubbed his thumb on the top of her hand, which was gentle and sweet. Amber realized how scared Patrick must have been when he'd heard about her, and she knew that it took a lot for him to face those fears, to be strong for her son. Dylan kept telling her how Patrick was reassuring him and how he comforted him. He was a hero in Dylan's eyes.

Maggie, Daniel, and Liam stood at the foot of her bed. They all told her how happy they were that she was okay. They offered their help with anything she might need. Patrick instantly said whatever she needed, he would take care of. Maggie was quick to remind her brother that he needed to accept help, and he laughed. Things were different now, changed in some way. Amber could see it in all their eyes, like a terrible dark cloud that had lifted, allowing the sun to shine again.

Mary took her turn next to say goodbye, and she offered to help in any way she could. She promised to visit the next day. She gave Patrick a kiss on the cheek. "I'm proud of you," Mary whispered to him but loud enough so Amber could make it out.

Once Mary left, her parents stood at her side. She noticed how exhausted they looked, but it was nothing compared to the light snoring of Dylan, who was lying in the bed next to her.

"Do you want me to take him?" Lynn asked in a hushed tone.

Patrick looked over and smiled. "I can drop him off at home later."

"Thanks, Patrick. We appreciate it," Dean answered, extending his hand to Patrick, who rose from his seat that was next to Amber's bed. He walked over and enveloped her father in a hug. This caused Amber's heart to squeeze and made her question just how long she had been passed out. It felt very *Wizard of Oz*; nothing made sense, this wasn't how things were before the accident. What had changed so drastically, that Patrick O'Brien, of all people, was hugging her parents and even kissing her in front of everyone? She could still taste his lips on hers.

"Sweetie, you make sure to rest," Lynn harped gently.

"Yes, Mom. Thanks again, you guys." Amber was given another side hug and kiss by both her parents. Patrick embraced them together; the three of them huddled together confused Amber. She had so many questions, and much like Dorothy had felt, it didn't make any sense. They waved goodbye and quietly left her room.

Patrick went back to his seat, and he reached for her hand again. His palms were warm as they molded against her skin, and this simple act of affection caused Amber to experience so many sensations. The trauma of what she had been through, or what she remembered of it anyway, and to have Patrick next her, it was all so overwhelming.

"So wow, huh?" Amber started, her eyes burning as she felt all her emotions bubbling to the surface.

Patrick nodded. "I was so scared, Amber." He

gently used his thumb to wipe away the tears that were escaping her eyes.

"I can imagine, but I don't understand all this." She pulled her hand away and instantly felt the loss of connection. She used her arms to emphasize what she meant by 'all of this,' because it was all encompassing, and she just couldn't wrap her head around all the changes.

"Babe, I don't want you to think about things right now. Your mom's right, you need to rest."

"I just need you to explain to me what has changed, like, between us, Patrick? None of this makes sense. Just earlier today, you wanted nothing to do with me." She felt her head starting to throb; her arm was beginning to ache. Whatever pain meds they had given her were wearing off. She had been told by the doctor that they were keeping her overnight to watch out for concussion and if there is any other issues. For being run into by a car, she was doing okay; it was this nonsense with Patrick that had her feeling upset and emotional.

"Amber, stop." He kissed her forehead. "We can discuss this when you've recovered a little. It's been a long day. You got hit by a car. You realize that, right?"

"Well, yes, of course, I know that," she argued. "I just want some answers."

"There is time for answers. Right now, you need to go to sleep. I'm going to take Dylan home."

The mention of her son's name off Patrick's lips made her heart sing. Was it too much to hope for? She didn't want to risk the disappointment.

"Patrick, thank you for looking after him,"

Amber said quietly.

"I was happy to. We needed each other to get through this." He stroked her hand and looked at her with his green eyes. She'd missed the way he looked at her. But his stare was different, something had definitely changed, and she intended to find out what it was, exactly. But for now, her eyes were growing tired and she was starting to feel the pain buzz through her body.

He kissed her again and then started to gently wake Dylan. "Hey, buddy, it's time to wake up. I'm going to take you home, okay?"

Dylan slowly moved. His eyes were sleepy, his voice groggy. "Can I go to your house, Patrick?"

Amber hadn't expected that, and apparently neither did Patrick. "Well, I think your grandparents are waiting for you back at home." The pleading look in Dylan's eyes broke her heart. It obviously had an affect on Patrick. "You know what? Let me call them and ask."

"Thank you," Amber mouthed to him, when he caught her eyes on him. He smiled and kissed her again. She saw Dylan smile, for a brief moment. She almost felt like they were a family.

***

Patrick

He had just dropped off Dylan back home so he could shower and change his clothes before returning to the hospital. Patrick had cooked him a simple breakfast of eggs and bacon. It was surreal sitting and eating with him. Yesterday, he had all the makings of a boy. Today, he looked older, a little more grown up.

As Patrick drove, he found himself headed in a direction to a destination he hadn't been to in a very long time. But he needed to go there; he needed to talk to her. As he parked along the curb, he realized the grass was still wet, the sun shone brightly, and as Patrick walked, it blinded his eyes. He could feel the warm rays touching him. It was soothing and banished the chill that was settling deep inside him. Row after row, he trekked to the spot. He knew exactly how many paces; even after four years, he still remembered. Then he found it. Her name, masterfully carved into the large stone, polished and gleaming in the morning sun. The grass was neatly trimmed; semi-wilted flowers stood limp in a copper vase. Someone had come to visit and talk with her, but it wasn't him. But he was here today, and he needed to tell her that he was finally ready to accept the promise she had asked him to make. The promise he had buried along with her for over four years.

"Hi, Beth…" Patrick started. How does one really talk to someone that's gone? He didn't really know, but something inside him told him this was the only way and that this had to be done.

"I'm sure you already know why I'm here. You always knew everything." This was proving to be far harder than he'd imagined. He felt his throat tighten, his stomach tighten into sick knots, but he continued on. "You always knew the right answers. You knew even as you spent your last moments here what our boys needed. What I would need."

He reached for the gravestone. The sun was already heating the rock up. He ran his fingers along the beveled edge. The words stood out bold against the soft gray color, the words in black:

Loving Daughter, Wife, and Mother.
Gone, but never forgotten.

The words couldn't be truer. She was gone, and he'd never been able to forget her. She had been a loving daughter, wife, and mother; though she never got to meet her boys, she knew exactly what they needed. As she clung onto the last breaths of life in her body, she'd selflessly begged for Patrick to keep his heart open. She wanted her boys to have the opportunity to have a mother and for Patrick to find love again.

Patrick started to weep. Maybe he couldn't do this. Maybe he'd misunderstood her request. A slight breeze lifted the low hanging, whimsical branches of a nearby weeping willow. Did he dare take that as a sign? He didn't know anymore as he wiped his eyes. He could almost hear her voice floating on the gentle breeze, reassuring him that this is what she meant and what she wanted for him.

"I'm sorry, I never could listen. You know that. I'm stubborn," Patrick began. It was starting to get easier, telling Beth everything he had sheltered inside of him. "I took out all my pain and anger on my family. I now see how wrong I was, how my hurt and losing you messed me up. When you died, Beth, a part of me went with you." He felt like he was purging the last four years of vile, diseased, anger, and was now beginning to heal.

"I'm ready now to have that part back." Patrick looked around. He then noticed a figure in the distance—a man. The person was headed in his direction, his back slightly bent, and upon closer observation, the man became more clear, dressed in a finely tailored gray suit, carrying a matching gray hat. The shock of white hair gave his identity way.

"Grandpa Paddy?" Patrick called out to him. He jogged toward his grandfather. He noticed the red, raw eyes. They were his eyes, a remarkable green that everyone commented on, the same eyes that he shared with his father and all three of his siblings. They were all because of this man, his namesake, Patrick O'Brien.

"Good morning, lad. I see you're visiting." Grandpa Paddy's voice was weak. He had a difficult time walking and was using his cane today. Patrick spotted a bench close by and guided them to it.

"I was here to see Beth," Patrick finally said once they sat. Their view was of the long field of neatly mowed grass, in the finest shade of green, but headstones littered this perfect patch of land. It was quiet and peaceful, just as it was intended to be. They were the only two people there in the small cemetery.

"That's good of you. It does good to talk to the Mrs. They still know what to say, and they let you do a lot more of the talking."

Patrick gave him a smile. "How do you ever move on? Does it ever become easier?"

"My boy, you are still a young man. I'm old. I was old when your grandmother died. I knew I would never find another. There was no one that could ever fill her place."

"I know, but…"

Grandpa Paddy lifted a wrinkled and spotted hand and stopped Patrick. "You won't be replacing Beth. You are simply doing as she told you. She had good sense, that lass." His eyes started to water, before he continued, "You chose a good woman. She loved you with all of her heart. You will chose another one when the time is right, son. There's so many years left for you to be happy, for those precious lads to have another woman like their mother to help raise them and care for them. You aren't replacing her, Patrick, you are just doing what she wanted." His grandfather took hold of his hand and squeezed it firmly. He had made his point.

"But I felt so guilty. When I met Amber, I didn't expect to feel again, especially not like this."

"Then it seems to me you have already found the right one again. The time we get in our lives is precious. The people in our lives don't always stick around for the entire show. It's important that you live life while you can, even if others are gone, because someday you will be gone too."

Patrick nodded. His grandfather was right. Beth already knew that when she'd begged for Patrick to promise her that he would be open to finding love again and to give their sons another mother, someone to care for them. She wasn't asking him to replace her but to simply try to find another to love. She knew that they were young and that she didn't want Patrick to grow old alone, that he still had a lot of time left. Looking back at it now, if the tables were turned, he would have made her promise him the same damn thing.

He looked over at his grandfather, who had grown quiet, reflecting on his own grief. Patrick no longer saw himself. He saw only his grandfather. A man who understood the perils that life can play on the heart, he had loved and lost and was now biding his time.

Patrick was ready now to start living, to start moving forward. He would never forget Beth. How could he? She'd given him two of the most precious things in his life. She would always live on in their sons, but she was gone, and he accepted that.

***

He taped the last box shut. Using a black marker, he wrote that it was to be saved for Finn and Connor. Patrick looked at the empty space. It felt weird, but it was part of the process. Patrick had several large boxes ready to donate to a women's shelter in Spokane. As he finished and closed the now empty closet door, he heard his doorbell ring.

Patrick opened the door and there stood Amber, her arm in a sling and Dylan standing next to her, balancing several boxes of pizza.

"Dylan," Finn and Connor squealed together as they pushed past Patrick and tugged on the older boy's shirt. "Come on, we want to play with you before we start the movie."

It was Friday. Their tradition continued, except

now two more people were included.

Amber came inside and instructed Dylan where to set the boxes. On her way to the kitchen, Patrick stopped her. He gently scooped her into his arms and kissed her delicately on the lips.

"Movie and pizza okay?"

"It's Friday, that's why I brought the pizza, and I held up my end of the bargain. Now I'm expecting you to honor yours. So, what movie are we watching?" Amber replied playfully.

"True. I have something I want to show you." Patrick reached for her hand and led her through his kitchen and out to the patio, where Finn, Connor, and Dylan all stood, giggling.

"What's going on?" Amber asked suspiciously. Then she saw it. Her eyes grew wide, and her hand covered her mouth. A bright green bicycle was parked there, a brown basket attached between the handle bars.

"Surprise," the kids all shouted.

Amber's eyes were filled with tears. Patrick brought her to him, and Dylan walked up carrying a bicycle helmet and handed it to him.

"Next time you go riding, wear this, please."

Amber laughed, and Patrick brushed his lips across her forehead. "Do you like it?"

"I love it. Thank you so much." Amber looped her good arm around his neck and stood on the tips of her toes to reach his sweet lips that smiled as she kissed him.

July was now gone, and so many things had changed. Patrick felt like his whole life, which had been derailed four years ago, was now finally back on track. Summer was not quite over, and they planned to enjoy every last minute of it, together.

Epilogue

Daniel

Antlers was hopping tonight, music blaring from the aging jukebox, with laughter and drunken chatter filling the room. Daniel was sitting at the bar, alone, and working on his third drink. He swirled the amber liquid, watching the partially melted ice cubes bang against the sides of the glass. His eyes stared ahead, the walls of the darkly lit bar had countless horns, or *racks,* as they were known as in Birch Valley. Most were the products of successful hunts and mounted by the owner himself. It made the place legendary.

He didn't come to that Antlers often, but when he did, it was either to shoot some pool with a couple of his buddies or to hang out with his brothers, to share a pitcher of beer and some rattlesnake skins, which were delicious pieces of onion coated in spicy batter and deep fried; they were a favorite treat for everyone in town. His brothers, that's why he was here. He hadn't spent much time with them the last couple of weeks. Liam was now a newlywed, and Patrick had finally overcome the grief of being widowed for more than four years by meeting a woman that Daniel was sure would probably end up becoming the next Mrs. O'Brien. Not that he didn't want his brothers to find love and live happily ever after, but what about him? Why wasn't he able to meet "the one"? It was as though these women that his brothers met just fell into their lives. They didn't have to go on some hunt to find their perfect match; it just came easily to them. Daniel, for some reason, struggled when it came to finding love. He considered the reasons behind his struggle. For starters, he didn't really look like Patrick, who had been known as the most attractive guy in all of Birch Valley their entire lives. Liam was the boy next door; he played up on this, flashing the stupid grin that all the women found extremely sexy, and it had obviously worked on Rachel too. No, what did Daniel have? Sure, he had the almost starry, famed O'Brien emerald green eyes, but he wasn't tall like his brothers, he didn't have their strong jaw, or their athletic, lean muscular build. No, he was shorter, stockier, and his jaw was rounded. He always looked almost jolly; he wasn't traditionally handsome like his brothers. Deep down he wished he looked more like them. It had always bothered him, but he never shared this desire with them. He didn't disclose that he felt almost ugly at times, that his over-exaggerated confidence was just a facade, hiding his low self-esteem and great deal of self-doubt.

It was his self-doubt that kept him from pursuing

girls. He feared rejection above all, usually relying on jokes as a half-hearted attempt to make it look like nothing. He hadn't really been in a serious relationship ever, he was nearing thirty in a couple of years, and it bothered him. He was lonely it was as simple as that.

Daniel put the glass to his lips, when he heard a familiar female voice call out to him. "Hey Daniel." Nina Belsky, in all her tan and blonde glory, sidled up next to him. "You should buy me a drink."

He poured that last remaining contents in his glass down his throat. It burned. The sensation caused a blinding effect; his brain was becoming a tad fuzzy as he looked at the gorgeous Nina. Her hand was on her jean-clad hip; the jeans were almost molded to her long legs like a second skin. She wore a sparkly white top, which was almost sheer, the material flimsy and thin, and the spaghetti straps bright against her golden skin. Nina's blonde hair was swept up in a careless knot, loose strands curled around her neck. Her pouty lips were stained the deep color of a rich, red wine, the kind he remembered having to drink for communion. Nina batted her thick, black lashes at him and placed one delicate hand with painted nails on his arm. This was a girl who was used to getting what she wanted. And right now, she wanted a drink.

Daniel tapped the ancient wooden counter to get the attention of the bartender and signaled for him to make two drinks. Maybe she was "the one"?

About the Author

I was born and raised in southern California and relocated to beautiful eastern Washington state. The rural small towns that speckle this vast area have inspired my ideal setting for most of the stories I write. The pine and tamarack trees covering the towering mountains, the shimmering lakes and rivers, the abundant wildlife and a feeling of a time forgotten, stirs so many of my creative juices. I can't thank my parents enough for dragging this city kid on long roadtrips up to this rugged foreign area, because now it is my home and I truly love my life here.

Reading was something that spurred me to begin writing at a young age. I enjoyed creating characters, different settings, and describing anything and everything. Storytelling, I have found is something I have inherited from both of my parents. I love attention to detail, using words to fully bring the picture alive, that is something I got from my dad. Creating characters and figuring out their story and how to achieve their happy ending comes from my mom. Then there is the smell of a book, new or old, the weight of it in your hands as you balance it open, seeing all those beautifully typed words spun and woven into sentences, this was created by a writer. I knew that was what I wanted to be when I grew up.

Over the years I fiddled with a story here and there, but it wasn't until 2015 that I realized it was time. Time to get those dreams down on paper (or my laptop) and so The Cloverleaf Series was born.

Coming from a family that is focused on being involved in each other's lives as much as possible created a great deal of inspiration and ideas for The Cloverleaf Series. My family is one that has weathered several terrible storms and still somehow keeps propelling forward. During those sunny times we can be seen gathered around, eating good food, sharing memories, and laughing until we can't catch our breath. We fight hard and love hard.

Romance, I simply love it, that's why I write it. I remember my mom giving me my very first paperback romance novel. It was a pretty exciting one filled with suspense and an overall excellent storyline, she had just read it and she felt it was suitable for my teenage eyes. That was it, I was hooked. I began to devour these romance stories that varied over the years from sweet to sultry, I consumed thousands of books and stories over the years. Each time I finished reading a novel, the desire to write my own grew stronger. As ideas for books swirled in my mind, it always had a romantic element to it, and I suppose it always will. What is there not to love about falling in love and finding that special person to share your life with? Who doesn't wish for passion, butterflies in your stomach, and that happily ever after?

As a reader, I can't even begin to thank all of the writers that have created so many emotions for me, falling in love with characters, mourning their loss, sighing as I close the final chapter or smiling when everyone lives happily ever after. As a writer, I just want to do the same.

Facebook:
http://facebook.com/authorgloriaherrmann

Twitter:
http://www.twitter.com/@gloriaiswriting

Website:
http://www.gloriaherrmann.com/

Goodreads:
https://www.goodreads.com/authorgloriaherrmann

Instagram:
http://www.instagram.com/authorgloriaherrmann